A TISKET
A TASKET
NOT ANOTHER
CASKET

A TISKET A TASKET NOT ANOTHER CASKET

A MERMAID BAY CHRISTMAS SHOPPE MYSTERY

HEATHER WEIDNER

First published by Level Best Books 2025

This novel is entirely a work of fiction. The names, characters and incidents portrayed in it are the work of the author's imagination. Any resemblance to actual persons, living or dead, events or localities is entirely coincidental.

Heather Weidner asserts the moral right to be identified as the author of this work.

Author Photo Credit: FBJ Studios

First edition

ISBN: 978-1-68512-856-2

Cover art by Level Best Designs

This book was professionally typeset on Reedsy.
Find out more at reedsy.com

Stan, thanks for all the love and support.
Dawn, thanks for all the encouragement and support. I miss you.

Praise for the Mermaid Bay Christmas Shoppe Mysteries

Selected as one of the best Cozy Debut Novels of 2023

The Book Decoder

Sticks and Stones and A Bag of Bones

"Another fun and interesting installment in an already popular cozy mystery series. Mystery and scandal rule this charmer. With main characters you feel like you know, twists and turns keep you reading."—Heather Douglass, NetGalley Reviewer

"Heather Weidner has everything I like in a cozy mystery. Good characters, charming town, and a bag of bones washing up on shore. Plus, a local murder. Jade Hicks the owner of a Christmas shop, and Christmas shops are always popular in beach towns, looks into the crime and hopes to save the town's Christmas in July festival. This is a terrific start to the Mermaid Bay Christmas Shoppe Mystery series."—Jackie Layton, Author of the Low Country Dog Walker Mysteries

"I enjoyed this light and fresh whodunit that kept me on my game. The author did a great job in presenting this well-written and fast-paced drama where mischief and mayhem was afoot where scattered notes and bits of voodoo seemed to plague the residents of Mermaid Bay. Who wanted the bookstore owner dead? There's a town full of potential suspects and I had a great time following along with Jade as each clue gathered took us closer to the killer's identity. What drove this tale was the visually descriptive narrative, the engaging dialogue, the small-neighborly atmosphere and the likeable cast of characters that includes Jade, Nick and Chloe. Overall, this was a great read and I look forward for more exciting times in Mermaid Bay with Jade and her friends."—DruAnn Love, Dru's Book Musing

"*Sticks and Stones and a Bag of Bones* by Heather Weidner is the first book in the Mermaid Bay Christmas Shoppe Mystery series. This is a good beginning to what looks to be a fun series. I really like amateur sleuth Jade Hicks, who owns the Christmas Shoppe, "Tis the Season in Mermaid Bay. She is very personable and intelligent. The secondary characters are quite likable too. I especially like Sheriff Nick Driscoll and Jade's new friend Amy. This was a fun read and I look forward to the next book in the series."—Margey Hager, NetGalley Reviewer

"Very entertaining cozy mystery with a bunch of fun characters. I knew I would like it from the title and cover, and the story was a smooth read start to finish. The motive was obvious to me almost from the start, so I was surprised that the investigation did not move along more logically and quickly. The spark between Jade and Nick is sweet, and the two seem well suited to each other. Nick may be the cop, but Jade is a bona fide sleuth in her own right. And the recipes at the end are quite a bonus!! Fun read!"—
Autumn Danner, Goodreads Reviewer

"What a pleasant surprise. This is a new to me author. I came across this book on a New Release page and added it to my TBR list. Because of the series name and cover, I was just going to add it to my Christmas TBR list (because I never read the synopsis). Then, this showed up in the Recently Added list at my library, so I figured what the heck. I'm so glad I borrowed it.

"This book starts off like a traditional Cozy Mystery but it really doesn't follow the typical footprint, which was fun.

"No spoilers; however, the murder happens early but it's almost an afterthought throughout the rest of the book. Yes, it's mentioned but there are other mysteries to be solved that may or may not be connected (you'll have to find out for yourself).

"I really enjoyed the cast of characters and beachside small town they live in. I'm really looking forward to more books in this series."—Debra Jo Burnette, Room of Required Reading Bookstagrammer

"On a cold and dreary January weekend I took a virtual vacation to sunny, summer-y Mermaid Bay, thanks to the wonderful writing of Heather Weidner. *Sticks and Stones and a Bag of Bones* celebrates Christmas in July in a fictional beach town, which not only brought a favorite holiday into play, but was accompanied by peaceful and relaxing strolls on the beach. Oh, and did I mention murder? Yes, the main character Jade Hicks is in a perfect position to help solve the untimely death of a local store owner, along with the unfunny pranks that plague this small town. From the get-go when a suitcase of bones washes up on the beach, until the exciting ending when the mysteries (plural) are solved, well, what's not love about this well written, character-drive, fast-paced cozy mystery? Only downfall is that it will be a YEAR before I can make another visit to Mermaid Bay!"—Jayne Ormerod, Author of *Goin' Coastal*

"Good start to a new cozy series! I was approved for this one after it was already released and I listened to the audiobook. The narrator was delightful—entertaining, different voices for each character and emotions thought out. I loved getting to know these easy to like characters and look forward to reading the next one in their series!"—Anne Edester, NetGalley Reviewer

"This was a really good start to a new series! The characters were so much fun and I can't wait for more of them in the future books! The mystery itself was also entertaining and interesting and kept me reading. Definitely a quick read too!"—Tiffany Newton, NetGalley Reviewer

"I loved the range of characters, some quirky, others annoying, and some I'd like as friends. The relationships between the friends were warm, and I wondered if or when the sheriff would move into the love interest column."—Cynthia Smith, NetGalley Reviewer

"This is a really good mystery very well written with great characters I highly recommend for all mystery lovers."—Shelly Meyer, NetGalley Reviewer

"First in a new series. I found it highly enjoyable. Mermaid Bay sounds like a fun town. With Christmas in July comes a bunch of trouble ensues ending up in murder. Jade, the owner of the Christmas shop sets out to find the murderer. A good solid mystery with characters that are wonderful."—Renee Winter, NetGalley Reviewer

"The first book in the Mermaid Bay Christmas Shoppe Mystery series is *Sticks and Stones and a Bag of Bones* by Heather Weidner. This is a strong start to what appears to be an entertaining series. I liked the small-town seaside location, the Christmas store, and the cat and dog's role in the narrative."—Jody Joy, NetGalley Reviewer

"If you love starting cozy mystery series with book one, read this! *Sticks and Stones and a Bag of Bones* has so many of the elements that make a cozy mystery enjoyable: a diverse batch of characters, an adorable small town, a dog and a cat, and a perplexing mystery. I highly recommend that you read this charming cozy mystery!"—Christy's Cozy Corners, Book Blogger

"If small-town mysteries are what you enjoy, *Sticks and Stones and a Bag of Bones* won't disappoint."—Lori Van Buren, Novels Alive

"This is a "feel good " story, great for a beach visit or travel. Don't expect page-turning action. Do expect likable characters in an adorable village by the sea. I would definitely visit Mermaid Bay myself."—Beth Youngblood, NetGalley Reviewer

"I am not new to Heather Weidner's writing so I will say this: I knew this was going to be a brilliant series debut. I enjoyed reading every bit of this book. There were plenty of red herrings, an interesting set of characters and side stories, a couple of furry babies—a dog and cats, and, not to forget, a dash of romance.

"The mystery kept me guessing till the end. I loved the characters and their side stories. Apart from Jade, the one other character that I liked the most is that of Amy. She's so energetic, enthusiastic, and full of ideas—I would love to see a cozy series featuring Amy as main character.

"If you are looking for a new cozy series, love year-round Christmas shoppes and furry babies, and excellent storytelling, you might want to give Sticks and Stones and a Bag of Bones by Heather Weidner a try."—Rekha Rao, NetGalley Reviewer

"She pens an intriguing tale of the lengths a shady character might go to. It is engrossing."—Amary Chapman, NetGalley Reviewer

"*Sticks and Stones and a Bag of Bones* combines Christmas and beach living in an enjoyable start to a new series."—Cozy up with Kathy, Book Blogger

"Great book by Heather Weidner. I'm really liking this series, and its characters. This was a fun cozy. I liked trying to figure out who done what. I'll definitely be reading more from this author."—Valerie Blankenship, NetGalley Reviewer

"I enjoyed this first in the series book. Lovely characters, fun to read and a great mystery. I can't wait for the next book."—Stacey Bradley, NetGallley Reviewer

"An entertaining and compelling cozy mystery I thoroughly enjoyed. Well plotted, likeable and fleshed out characters, a lovely setting. The mystery is solid and kept me guessing. It's the first I read in this series and won't surely be the last. Highly recommended."—Anna Maria Giacomasso, NetGalley

Reviewer

"Quick, easy, entertaining and a year-round Christmas shop. What's not to like about that?— A good cozy mystery that takes you one a ride, entertains you and as it isn't too long you can read it quickly and easily. I love a book like that. Great characters, a bit of fun and of course a good old bag of bones! I enjoyed this one and recommend as a fun, easy reading book."—Donna Robinson, NetGalley Reviewer

"I enjoyed the characters and the realistic problems of any town dependent on tourist dollars and the ever present problem in beach town areas of development vs. keeping a smaller town feel. There were plenty of twists and turns in this mystery to keep you guessing until the end. Of course, I loved the furry friends and the touch of romance. A good read when you are looking for a light cozy or longing for a beach getaway."—Juliane Silver, NetGalley Reviewer

"I enjoy my visits to Mermaid Bay. I like the characters and enjoy the dialog between Jade and Nick."—Dawn Tarrant, NetGalley Reviewer

"The quiet beachside community was thrown into disbelief by the murder of one of their own. Jade couldn't help being curious about the strangeness happening in their community, so she put on her sleuthing cap and began searching for answers. She was a businesswoman with a penchant for investigating crimes. This cozy was an intriguing and entertaining one."—Cherry-Ann London, NetGalley Reviewer

"Fine start to a brand-new cozy mystery series! Mermaid Bay is a tourist town in coastal Virginia and has a bunch of small shops with Christmas themes. The first sign of trouble is a suitcase found on the beach with a collection of bones in it. Then there are the threatening notes, voodoo dolls, and finally a murdered (unpleasant) bookseller. Jade does her part to help solve the crime even though no all of her efforts are appreciated by her good friend Sheriff Nick."—Jan Tangen, NetGalley Reviewer

"This was a fun start to a new cozy mystery series, and I would definitely pick up the second! I enjoyed the cast of characters and the beach town setting. The story is as much about the relationships of the town residents as the mystery, making it a very enjoyable read."—Amanda Waggoner, NetGalley Reviewer

"I recently discovered Heather Weidner and was really intrigued to read this book, the first in the series. I might be a little biased as I live in Virginia, but I enjoyed this book and hope to see more in the series. There's never a dull moment in this town…a suitcase of washed up bones, voo doo dolls, threatening letters and smashed windows…oh my!"—Kim Schade, NetGalley Reviewer

"I really loved this book in a new to my series and author. I can't wait to read the next one. The characters and location really add to the plot. This book keeps you guessing until the end."—Lori Ruth, NetGalley Reviewer

"This was a light, fun cozy with some great characters. I love Chloe."—Lisa Garrett, NetGalley Reviewer

Twinkle Twinkle Au Revoir

"This was such a wonderful and enjoyable read!!!! I loved this book and highly recommend it to anyone who enjoys this genre."—Sophie L., NetGalley Reviewer

"Cute cozy mystery."—Kaye Temanson, NetGalley Reviewer

"*Twinkle Twinkle Au Revoir* by Heather Weidner is a candy-cane sweet and totally engrossing mystery. Highly recommended!"—Rekha Rao, The Book Decoder

"Just loved this cozy mystery. Loved the plot and characters. Couldn't stop reading. Love the fact that the recipes for the cookies mentioned in the book is given at the back of the book. Will definitely try making them."—Jacqueline Van Der Merwe, NetGalley Reviewer

"This is a fun, entertaining, cozy read. The various characters are quirky, entertaining, intriguing and fun. I found the amateur sleuth Jade relatable, and I enjoyed spending my time with her."—Laura Lagace, NetGalley Reviewer

"A nice and solid cozy mystery that kept me guessing. Well plotted and fast paced, well rounded and likeable characters."—Anna Maria Giacomasso, Librarian

"The perfect who done it! The story is easy to get into and I would recommend this book. I will be looking out for this author in the future."—The Little Book Corner

"The mystery, while light in keeping with typical cozy style, was well plotted, and made you wonder if the incidents were related to one another."—Melanie Steward, NetGalley Reviewer

"*Twinkle Twinkle Au Revoir* by Heather Weidner is the second book in the charming Mermaid Bay Christmas Shoppe Mystery series."—Christy's Cozy Corners

"*Twinkle Twinkle Au Revoir* is a lighthearted breezy mystery that combines Christmas decor and Valentine's Day dreams showing that there's no business quite like show business."—Cozy up with Kathy, Book Reviewer

"This was a very enjoyable story where Hollywood comes to Mermaid Bay. It had great characters and a plot that kept you trying to figure out who dunnit. I would recommend it to everyone!"—Helen Scaglione, NetGalley

Reviewer

"Loved reading this book. I missed the 1st book in the series. But I will definitely be reading it. I couldn't put this 1 down. I highly recommend this series!"—Chris Gerst, NetGalley Reviewer

"I love holiday themed movies and cozies, so this one was marriage made in Heaven. the characters are great and I love how they all made this even better with quirks and all. I will definitely keep this author on my reading list for further books."—Cindi Austin, NetGalley Reviewer

"I highly recommend the highly entertaining cozy mystery, *Twinkle Twinkle Au Revoir* for its charming setting, true to life characters, and captivating mystery!"—Christy Maurer, NetGalley Reviewer

The Fireworks Competitors

Zanetti Fireworks

- Aldo Zanetti, the patriarch of the family
- Marco Zanetti, father of Elio and Lorenzo
- Elio Zanetti
- Lorenzo Zanetti
- Francesco Zanetti, father of Remo and Paolo
- Remo Zanetti
- Paolo Zanetti

The Pefferly Fireworks Company

- Ephron Pefferly, the patriarch of the family
- Daniel Pefferly, father of Brianna and Zeke
- Brianna Pefferly
- Zeke Pefferly
- Ellen Pefferly Jennings, Goose's mother
- Walter "Goose" Jennings
- Abner "Tank" Edwards, employee and family friend

Crack, Boom, Bang

- Trey Adkins, co-owner and brother to Will
- Will Adkins, co-owner and brother to Trey and pal of Roscoe, the border collie

Chapter One

"Stop him. Stop that guy!" One of the workers yelled as he chased a guy in a black hoodie toward the end of Suggs Pier. Jade Hicks, owner of 'Tis the Season Christmas Shoppe, pulled her clipboard closer to her as the pair thundered past inches away from where she was watching the setup. Their feet pounded and shook the wooden decking.

Three more workers from Zanetti's Fireworks joined the chase, and Jade pulled out her phone from the pocket of her puffy coat and strained to see where they went. The wind off Mermaid Bay caused tendrils of her long, red hair to escape from her ponytail. Pushing the stray locks out of her eyes, she leaned over the railing for a better view of what was happening in the sand below the pier.

The hoodie guy poured on the speed and leapt over the top of the sand dune, headed for Neptune Road and town. When the Zanettis finally reached the sand dune where the hoodie guy was last seen, they paused and looked up and down the beach. Jade bobbed up and down, pointing frantically toward the street, hoping someone saw her. She yelled, but her voice was lost in the wind.

Then, out of nowhere, the hoodie guy hurtled over another set of dunes near the brick building that housed Mermaid Books and the Busy Bean Café. He doubled back across the sand, and the Zanetti team followed in hot pursuit.

The hoodie guy zigzagged in the sand and disappeared under the pier. Jade and her part-time maintenance guy and store Santa Claus, Bernie Nash, edged closer to the wooden railing on the other side. None of the men dashed out. They waited several heartbeats, and still no one appeared.

Bernie waved his arms and yelled, "They're under the pier. Down there! Hurry!"

Jade and a gaggle of locals followed Bernie down the ramp and under the wooden structure that had been a fixture in Mermaid Bay for as long as anyone could remember. The breeze whipped around the wooden pylons, and Jade tucked her hands in her pockets. A briny, damp smell from low tide tickled her nose. By now, four Zanetti guys, who all had a strong family resemblance with dark wavy hair and squared jawlines, stood around the hoodie guy like it was a game of Farmer in the Dell.

As the circle of men constricted around the guy, Vivian Turner, president of the Mermaid Bay business council, waded into the mix. "Enough. This is not how we expect our contestants to behave. I said enough. This is unprofessional." She twisted the fingers of her glove into a pretzel.

Ignoring her shrill spiel, Paolo Zanetti, the youngest member of the fireworks family, yelled, "We saw you, Zeke Pefferly. You were creeping around trying to steal our trade secrets. And we caught you messing with our setup. You're trespassing, and then you ran like a chicken."

Paolo's taller brother Remo chimed in. "Pretty low, Pefferly. I'm sure we'll be underwhelmed next weekend with the stuff your company's got. I mean, if ya gotta cheat and steal to win…come on, man."

Paolo jabbed his finger at Zeke. "Your stuff is crap, so you have to go around sabotaging the competition. Does that make you feel powerful? Maybe it's the only way you can win."

Zeke squared his shoulders, and the hood slipped back. The thirty-something's face scrunched into an evil sneer, and he lunged toward Paolo, head-butting him in the stomach.

The brawl was on. Paolo and Zeke wrestled around in the damp sand as the other Zanettis and a growing crowd egged them on.

Before Jade could tap in her password, Vivian whipped out her phone and jabbed 911 with her index finger. "There's a fight in progress under Suggs Pier. Send the police. I'm afraid it'll get out of hand. Need help pronto. Please send more than one officer. Yes, we're under the pier. And the crowd is growing."

Jade tapped a text to Sheriff Nick Driscoll for good measure. A slight smile crossed her face. Nick had been her friend and her rock for a long time, ever since she had moved in with her grandparents after her parents' tragic deaths upended her world. She felt her face flush when she thought about them as a couple. *It seemed like everyone in town, except Nick and I, knew we'd end up together.* She always got a little tingle in the pit of her stomach when she thought of him.

Vivian flapped her arms around in a weird, bird-like dance behind the men who were rolling around in the sand. "Stop it! Right now. This is not acceptable." The wind off the bay muffled most of her words.

No one intervened in the fight as the two men pushed, clawed, and punched each other. Sometimes Paolo was on top, and then Zeke dominated the tussle. It looked like a jumble of elbows, knees, and flying sand. If it weren't real, it would have looked like one of those old cartoon fights.

Sirens broke through the wind and crowd noise. Everyone but Paolo and Zeke paused to watch the sheriff and Deputy Sebastian Sanchez trudge over the dunes. A guy in a red hoodie and board shorts stopped playing Frisbee with his border collie and joined the swelling crowd on both sides of the pier.

Sebastian waded in and pulled Paolo off of the prone Zeke.

"What is going on here?" Nick bellowed.

Zeke rubbed his temples and rose sluggishly from the sand.

Everyone yelled a version of the events at once.

Vivian, the town's librarian, when she wasn't running business council events, stuck two fingers in her mouth and let loose with an eardrum-splitting whistle. "Y'all be quiet and let the sheriff sort this out."

"Thanks, Vivian." Nick tilted his head toward Paolo and Zeke. "Now, one at a time. What is all this about?"

Paolo, bleeding from his mouth and nose, waved his arms and lunged at Zeke again. Sebastian stepped between the combatants and forced Paolo to step back a few feet.

"Enough," Nick roared, pulling out a pair of handcuffs from his utility belt that rivaled Batman's. He dangled them in front of Paolo, who wiped the blood from his lip on his jacket sleeve. He let out a long puff of air like a beachball with a slow leak and stared at Zeke Pefferly.

Another Zanetti stepped forward. "We were staging the pyrotechnics for our show on Saturday. You know, for the competition. And Paolo and I noticed this guy." He jabbed a beefy finger in Zeke's direction. "He was skulking around taking pictures. Then my brother saw him touch one of our switches, and he pocketed something."

"And you are?" Nick asked.

"Elio Zanetti. His cousin." He pointed at Paolo, who tried to staunch the blood with the corner of his shirt.

Sebastian turned his head and clicked his shoulder mic. "This is Deputy Sanchez under Suggs Pier. Please send rescue by to assist. We have someone with a severe nosebleed and bloody lip."

"I'll be okay." Paolo wiped away blood and pinched the bridge of his nose to slow the bleeding.

The deputy released the microphone, and the dispatcher responded, "We have a wagon en route." The police radio squealed, and Paolo plugged one ear with a finger.

Turning toward Paolo, Sebastian said, "We'll have someone here in a minute to take care of you."

"I'll be fine. He's the problem. Check his pockets," Paolo insisted, pointing at Zeke.

"Yeah, he took something," a third Zanetti, who looked like he could pass for Paolo's twin, said. "I saw him. He thought he was being slick."

"And you are?" Nick asked, stepping forward to help Sebastian keep a distance between Paolo and Zeke.

"I'm Lorenzo, their cousin." He pointed first at Paolo and then Remo and Elio." Turning toward Zeke Pefferly, he said, "I saw him put something in his pocket while he was taking pictures of our equipment. I think he pulled off a couple of our electric matches."

"Do you have something of theirs?" Nick asked Zeke.

Zeke jammed his hands in his front hoodie pocket and turned it inside out. A candy wrapper, an e-cigarette, and a handful of small wires drifted down and landed in the sand.

Lorenzo lunged forward and grabbed at the collection of stuff. "See. Our electric matches. My grandfather created those red and black ones, especially for our shows. They make the displays go off in synchronization. See. See. Our logo. Right here." He moved his palmful of proof under Nick's nose. "These belong to us."

Sebastian pulled a bag out of his utility belt and held it open for Lorenzo to drop them inside. Then he leaned down and bagged the other items.

Nick cut his eyes at Zeke, who defiantly stared at the Zanettis. "Turn around," Nick ordered as he cuffed his hands behind him and read him his rights.

After the pat down, Zeke cleared his throat and jerked his head to move his longish bangs out of his eyes. "And I want to press charges against him. He assaulted me, and everyone here was a witness. Someone has to have a video of it. I was attacked."

"Because you're a thief," Lorenzo yelled, jabbing his finger in the air at Zeke.

"Silence!" Sebastian ordered.

Before he continued, a breathless Nell Jones, Mermaid Bay's intrepid puff reporter, pushed her way through the crowd. "I have it all recorded. I got it right here. This is my lead in Tuesday's edition about the firework competition and the scandal."

Vivian made a harrumphing noise.

"Please send me a copy," Nick said as two EMTs with a plastic box that looked like it could hold fishing tackle trudged toward the group.

"I want one, too," Zeke yelled over his shoulder.

"The rest of you can see it on the *Beach Comber* website this afternoon," Nell said, tapping something on her phone's screen. The reporter's round cheeks flushed with excitement at the scoop.

Paolo plopped down in the sand as the EMTs checked his nose and mouth and dabbed away the blood. They opened wipes and gauze and pressed gently on his face. Then they checked his eyes and head. After poking and prodding, they checked his mouth and teeth.

A female EMT broke the silence when she said, "You'll be okay. It doesn't look like you need stitches. Nothing's broken. And no chipped teeth. If you experience dizziness or nausea later, seek medical attention right away. There will be some swelling for a couple days."

"He's fine," Lorenzo said, stepping toward his cousin. "We did worse to each other roughhousing around my grandparents' yard as kids. Can't tell you how many concussions and broken bones we racked up through the years. He'll be fine by tonight."

Sebastian waved Lorenzo back and handcuffed Paolo. "We're taking you both to the station where we can get this sorted out."

"That's not fair. He started this," Paolo whined and tilted his head in Zeke's direction.

Zeke kicked sand toward Paolo, who grimaced and yelled, "Pefferly, you'll be sorry you ever messed with us. I hope you don't wash up on a beach somewhere."

Nick grabbed his arm and half-drug him across the sand. Sebastian followed suit and guided Zeke toward the SUV.

Lorenzo opened his mouth to retort but closed it quickly when one of the older family members glared at him. The crowd dissipated like the morning fog as the EMTs, police, and their charges made their way toward town. The only noise was the occasional caw from the gulls that swooped in and out of the surf, looking for breakfast.

Vivian sighed loudly as the rest of the Zanettis returned to the pier. "That's not how I pictured kicking off our holiday fireworks spectacular. The Mermaid Bay Business Council prides itself on fair play. Cheaters never win," she said, gritting her teeth. "This was supposed to be three weekends of fun. Not the scene of corporate espionage and fist fights." Vivian turned and shuffled in her UGG boots toward the parking lot.

Jade looked at Bernie, who shrugged his shoulder. "I'm headed to the pier to see if the Zanettis need anything. There's got to be more to their story." Bernie patted down his fluffy beard when the wind whipped off the water and caused it to flutter. "Sounds like we need a guard to watch all the fireworks and electronic doodads. I'll be over at your store after lunch in plenty of time to do the Santa visits. Hope nothing else explosive happens here. That was enough excitement to last us for a long time."

Chapter Two

Jade hustled past the bookstore, coffee shop, and hot dog stand in the small beach town that prided itself on preserving its past, located near Virginia's historic triangle of Jamestown, Williamsburg, and Yorktown. No all-night drugstores or big box establishments here. Mermaid Bay reminded her of the 1950s beach with its cozy cottages and quaint neighborhoods that her grandmother had talked about when Jade was younger.

She jogged across the street in front of a single-story building, home to the town's real estate office, antique store, and pizzeria that stood next to the empty lot beside her store. From the sidewalk, she glanced at 'Tis the Season, a converted beach cottage with a long front porch full of rocking chairs waiting for spring. Her pillows and country holiday decorations added to the charm. A chilly breeze whistled around the building, and she double-timed her steps.

When she opened the store's back door, her white French bulldog greeted her with yips. "Hey there, Chloe," she said, picking up the roly-poly dog.

"We're up here," echoed from the store's front lobby.

Jade hugged Chloe and set the wiggly dog down in the workroom that doubled as the store's office and kitchenette. She pulled the Dutch door that separated the public and private spaces behind her and greeted her aunt Lorelei, who leaned on the front counter near the cash register. Two tall Christmas trees stood sentry on either side of the door and twinkled a welcome to visitors. The glass ornaments sparkled and created rainbows all around the small room.

"Hey, there. What's shaking? We've had a steady stream through here today already. And the fireworks show isn't until tomorrow. Wonder if we'll get any tour buses?" Lorelei mused, filing her pearly pink nails that matched her Angora sweater and cream-colored slacks. Her honey-colored hair, cut in a stylish bob, made her look more youthful than her mid-fifties.

Neville the Devil Cat pranced by and hopped up on the ledge of the dividing door. He sported a candy-cane striped bowtie with a silver jingle bell. A low growl emanated from the workroom. Neville, a stray that Jade's grandmother had adopted as the store's mouser, had a love/hate relationship with Chloe. The cat still viewed Chloe and Jade as interlopers, even though they had moved in over three years ago after Jade's grandmother's death.

"Chloe, you should see how festive Neville looks in his fancy collar," Jade said, patting the cat on the head.

The black and white tuxedo cat, oblivious to what Chloe thought, licked his front paw as growls that sounded like muttering came from the back room.

Lorelei laughed. "They really like each other. They don't want anyone to know."

"Chloe still looks for him on mornings that y'all aren't here." Jade smiled. She was thrilled when her aunt asked to take Neville home on nights and weekends. She had tried having him in her house, but it didn't quite work out with the rambunctious dog. Her bungalow wasn't big enough for the pair's rough-housing. Neville took his stint as the store mouser seriously and claimed ownership of the place when he was there.

"I think that's their act. Chasing through the displays is their favorite part of the day." Lorelei dropped the emery board into her pale pink Michael Kors handbag.

Jade's phone buzzed, and she fished it out of her back pocket. "Hi, Bernie. How are you?"

"Just wanted to let you know I was running a bit late. The Zanettis noticed some damage after this morning's dustup, and I had to call Nick back over. I think he got everything squared away this time. I hope this isn't a sign of trouble." Bernie let out a long sigh.

"No problem. See you when you get here. I have plenty of cookies and goodies waiting. I even brought you some of your favorite hot cocoa Christmas cookies."

"What's up?" Lorelei asked when Jade disconnected the call.

"There was an altercation at the pier this morning. Zeke Pefferly, one of the firework competitors, was caught taking pictures of the Zanetti's equipment. He messed with some of their stuff, too. He took something called electric matches. Bernie said something else happened after I left, and he had to call Nick back."

"I'm sure the sheriff was thrilled about that." Lorelei's perfectly manicured eyebrows scrunched together. "So, two of the three companies competing for the big Memorial Day and Fourth of July fireworks contracts got in a fight. I'm sure Vivian's having heart palpitations. This doesn't match her vision of order and fair play. She has high expectations and gets a little judgy when things don't meet her standards," Lorelei said with a laugh. "Who knew fun fireworks were really a specialized business rife for corporate espionage and shenanigans."

Jade nodded. "The Zanettis gave chase, and there was a fight under the pier. Nell said she got a recording of it. She said next week's edition of the *Beach Comber* will feature the altercation."

"Vivian will be overjoyed. Her fireworks festival will be the center of Nell's gossip column." Lorelei jotted something on a sticky note. "I'll have to remember to check it out." Her voice trailed off.

"Nick and Sebastian took away both brawlers, Paolo Zanetti and Zeke Pefferly," Jade said as her aunt scribbled a note with all the flourish of John Hancock.

Her aunt's mouth formed a small "o," but she didn't respond until she stuck the note on her phone's screen and slipped it in her purse behind the counter.

"You okay?" Jade asked. "You seem a little distracted."

"Sorry. I was thinking about something I need to do after work before Steve picks me up. We're having sushi in Williamsburg. There's a lot going on with the holidays fast approaching." Her aunt spun the large emerald ring on her right hand and stared out the store's front windows.

Stomping on the wooden porch distracted both of them and sent Chloe into a barking jag. Bernie stepped inside and set his maroon velvet toy sack on the floor. "Wheweee, it's cold out there. I never thought I'd get away from the pier this morning. Nothing but trouble. Those guys are definitely on my naughty list." He shut the door, and the tiny bells attached to the knob jingled. "I had to wait until after Nick was done a second time before I could skedaddle over here. More of the Zanetti's stuff was missing. Vivian will be on a tear when she finds out two of her contestants are still trying to ruin each other."

Lorelei leaned forward over the counter. "Do tell…"

Bernie adjusted the velvet sleeves, trimmed in imitation ermine, on his classic Victorian costume. "Just some crazy antics this morning. It seems the Pefferly kid took some gear and messed with some kind of grid setup that took the Zanettis a long time to configure. I tuned them out when they fussed about the details. It's for some fancy-schmancy timed firecrackers or explosives or whatever. It's all high-tech now. Just like everything else. What happened to bottle rockets and cherry bombs?"

Bernie patted down his fluffy white beard and made a beeline for the goodie table filled with a variety of Christmas cookies and fudge. "Yum. Don't mind if old Santa grabs a couple. This'll tide me over until lunch." He picked up a handful and wandered to what had been the beach cottage's living room. His red velvet and gold throne sat next to the large, white fireplace. Jade had converted it to an artificial fireplace, and the cozy glow could be flipped on year-round in an instant with a remote. All the trees, with their blinking white lights, cast a festive mood on the walls as the shadows danced and Christmas music floated from room to room.

"Want any coffee, Bernie?" Lorelei yelled into the first showroom filled with about twenty themed Christmas trees in what Jade had dubbed the "Toy Room."

"Just some iced water would be nice. Even if the fire isn't real, this suit is hot," drifted in from the next room. "Hey, did you hear the latest that's got the good folks of Mermaid Bay all in a lather?"

Jade stepped through the doorway and handed him two bottles of water as

Bernie settled in his fancy chair. "There's more besides today's altercations?" she asked.

Lorelei popped in and almost skidded to a stop in her designer heels. "No, what's going on?"

Bernie took a swig of water and wiped crumbs off his beard. "There's a new post on that gossip site called Mermaid Whispers, and no one knows who's behind it. And it's all about our sweet 'lil town. There's a blog or website thingy, too. The writer's got some juicy stuff and some snappy comebacks to the comments. I followed it, so I didn't miss any of the chatter. Can't wait to see who gets roasted next. It's always important to stay tuned into what's going on around town."

Lorelei pulled out her phone and tapped on the screen. "Interesting. I'm sure Nell is loving the competition." Her eyes widened as she scrolled through the posts.

Jade tried not to grimace. "I'll have to check it out. But for now, I'll be in the back if you all need me. Let's see how many orders came in overnight." Jade, reaping the benefits of the hefty investment she put into the store's online store, was pleased that she could reach a bigger audience than the visitors to the little beach community. It was hard enough to keep a brick-and-mortar store going in a seasonal beach town, but the online orders saved her business during the pandemic. A slight smile crossed her face. The online shopping and the taping of the Love Channel movie in and around Mermaid Bay last fall helped introduce her business to an even larger, worldwide audience.

"Time for a little break and clear my head. I'll help you in a minute." Lorelei ducked into the lobby. The bells on the door jangled, and all Jade could hear was the heat blowing through the vents and her piped in Christmas music. Jade smiled to herself. Her Aunt Lorelei had always kept a watchful eye over her, and her willingness to help out at the store when she didn't have to work, provided a resource that Jade knew she could always depend on.

Jade busied herself with printing five sheets of orders and gathering the requests from under the Christmas trees, which always reminded her of an Easter Egg hunt. At last count, her store had over three hundred and twenty festive trees, all with different themes and peach baskets below filled with the for-sale decorations on display.

As Jade put the packaged orders in the crate for the afternoon pickup, a loud "Whoa, Doggie" emanated from the living room.

Jade set the crate behind the cash register and hurried over to where Bernie waved at a toddler who wasn't too sure about visiting the large man in the red chair. The little guy waved from the safety of his mother's arms. He wasn't keen on getting any closer to the big, bearded guy.

"What's up?" Jade asked in a low tone after the family moved into the Rainbow Room.

"Sorry. Probably got too excited there. It seems that this Mermaid Whisperer or whatever it is scooped Nell. She won't be happy when she sees this." He waggled his phone in her direction.

Jade touched his sleeve to steady the view. "Hmm. Interesting. There's a bunch of information about the two fireworks families and what happened this morning. Who had time to gather all that information so quickly? You think it's Nell?"

"Nah. She was all excited about getting her video up on the *Beach Comber* site, and she fancies herself a journalist. She'd look down her pointy nose at this. And BTW. That's young-people talk for 'by the way.' There's no Nell video yet. She is gonna be madder than a wet hen."

"It has to be somebody who knows what happened this morning," Jade added.

Bernie's lips formed a straight line. "Maybe. With a fancy cell phone and a police scanner, it wouldn't be that hard." He waved his phone around again and flopped back in his chair. "The Mermaid Whispers thing didn't have any video, but there were plenty of links to the Pefferly and the Zanetti's websites. I've got to see what the guys at the pier are saying about all this. I'll see if I can find out who the source is. This town can't keep a secret for long."

Chapter Three

The next day sped by. After two tour buses and seven pages of online orders, Jade rested her head on her arms on the desk.

"Whoooeeeeee! What a Saturday!" Patti Hall, Jade's other part-timer known to everyone as Peppermint Patti, bustled in the back and plopped down at the empty desk. "I think that's it for today. What a workout. I hope the fireworks draw a presence tonight. Brrrr. It's chilly. Oh, I was talking to Myra with one of the tour companies that came through here today, and she said they were visiting sites in town before the show. I'm so excited. What a fun idea to celebrate the holiday season."

"So far, it looks like a boost for the local businesses if Vivian can keep the two companies from fighting with each other. Chloe and I plan to head over at sundown to get a primo spot for viewing."

A slight frown crossed Patti's face. "I guess you've seen the new gossip page?" Patti whispered.

"Why are we whispering?"

Patti's contagious laugh rang out. "I don't know. It seemed like a juicy little secret. What is this Mermaid Whispers thing? It's driving everyone crazy. And he or she knows so much, so it has to be a local. There was a teaser in today's post about a Romeo and Juliet thing that was going on with a feud. Now I'm dying to see the next post. Who could it be? And what are they feuding about? It makes Mermaid Bay sound like a soap opera."

Jade shrugged a shoulder and picked up her phone. "Swell. Just what we need around here."

"You know everybody knows everybody's business. It's part of the town's

DNA. News has spread around here like wildfire for decades. Social media has nothing on our gossip grapevine." Patti rose and put a folder and stack of receipts on Jade's desk. "I closed out and did a quick inventory check. There's a spreadsheet with the decorations we're low on. If you don't need me, I need to get ready tonight. My mom and sister are coming over to watch the boom-booms with me."

"Have fun. See you next week." Jade flipped through the folder. Great numbers to end the year on.

Reaching down to pet the dog, she said, "Come on, Chloe, let's do our closing rounds and head out." The chubby dog's ears shot up, and she trotted after Jade through the store, sniffing around for Neville the Devil Cat.

"Neville's not here today. He's hanging out with Lorelei."

The pudgy dog didn't believe her and tore through the store looking for her archenemy.

After making sure all doors and windows were locked, she left all the twinkle lights on to make it festive for tonight with folks driving through town for the holiday lights tour.

Grabbing her purse and Chloe's leash, she zipped her winter coat and stepped out the back door. Pizza D'Action, the town's pizza parlor, and Hot Diggity Dogs, across the street, had crowds that rivaled those in the summer. Changing her mind about grabbing a quick dinner, she nudged Chloe toward the sidewalk and home. The little dog had other plans, and she sniffed every blade of grass and pebble on their walk.

When they finally made it to the bungalow, Jade filled Chloe's bowls and rummaged through the refrigerator for dinner. Settling on leftover spaghetti and some grapes, she scanned through her phone and read the latest posts on the Mermaid Whispers site. What kind of feud could be going on in Mermaid Bay during the off-season? Jade would have surely heard something about it.

"That's enough gossip. Chloe, we need to get a move on. It's time to get decked out for tonight's festivities. Time to sparkle and shine."

After finding her warmest sweater, leggings, and holiday scarf, Jade pulled out her Christmas necklace and elf hat. She found a lighted collar and a fuzzy red and green Christmas sweater for Chloe. "Let's hit the sand and find a spot." Jade picked up a blanket, and Chloe yipped and waddled toward the door.

The pair moseyed down the pearly white oyster shell path that led to the beach. Chloe sniffed the air and darted toward the people noises. The breeze ruffled Jade's hair, and she took a deep breath. Even chilly, the salty air smelled like home. The beach would always be her happy place.

As they approached the crowd, Jade scooped up the pudgy dog to keep her from being underfoot. It did look like a summer crowd, except for all the coats and mittens. The icy breeze off the water sent a shiver down her back. "Let's get a move on," she said, slogging through the dry sand. Chloe looked up at her with her big chocolate-colored eyes.

A waving figure on the deck of Hot Diggity Dogs caught her attention. Jade climbed the weather-scarred wooden steps and headed to one of the picnic tables that had been there since she was a kid.

"Hey, I saved you a seat," Amy Pemberton yelled, still waving both arms. "Hey, Chloe. You guys come up here and get away from that crowd."

"It's good to see you." Jade hugged her friend and bookstore owner, and Chloe squeaked when she didn't like being the cheese in the middle of a hug sandwich.

"Sorry, Chloe," Amy said. "Todd's inside still helping with the surge. He's thrilled about lots of business this late in the season. Not sure if he'll make it out here in time to watch the spectacular, but we can still have fun. I've claimed this table for us." Amy pointed to the wooden picnic table with lots of names, hearts, and dates carved into the scarred top with several layers of paint colors peeking through.

Amy, who took over the bookstore after a family tragedy, had started dating hot dog stand owner and surfer extraordinaire, Todd Brickman. The shy, local surfer and the boisterous bookseller from Massachusetts made quite the pair.

Amy interrupted her thoughts with, "Have you seen the newest place in town for chatter? I heard everyone's in a tizzy and can't wait to see what gets posted next." Amy paused and stared out across the water. "What the heck is that?" She pointed toward the darkening sky.

A small airplane cruised up the shoreline, pulling a sign behind it.

"They usually do advertising like that in the summer," Jade said. "It's a little late in the day for that."

"Come back next week. Tonight's amateur hour," Amy read aloud. "That's kinda rude."

"Sounds like the competitors are stirring up stuff," Jade said, settling on the wooden bench and draping the blanket around Chloe and herself. *Wait until Vivian finds out about this. It won't meet her standards of excellent sportsmanship.*

Before the sun set behind the trees across the street, the plane and its message flew overhead two more times in case anyone missed it earlier.

"Wow," Amy said. "First, the new sassy blog, and now this. This isn't what the business council envisioned for this event. Wonder if Vivian will schedule another emergency meeting to put an end to this nonsense." She wagged her finger and did her best Vivian impression.

"Probably. Especially after the fight yesterday." Jade scanned the shoulder-to-shoulder people near the pier. Barely any sand showed with all the beach chairs and blankets.

Amy nodded. "Todd's staff overheard some of the hunky Zanettis talking over dinner. It seems the other team stole some valuable, super-secret fireworks thingy and tried to mess up their show. The two teams have declared war, and they aren't taking hostages. And we get to watch the fallout. Crazy."

"The EMTs had to treat one of the Zanettis after the fight," Jade added.

"I was inside Hot Diggity Dogs when Sebastian and another deputy came in. He said both guys had been released and were awaiting their court dates. Sounds serious," Amy said.

Jade's eyebrows shot up under her bangs. Nick had been so busy this weekend. She hadn't heard from him. She pulled out her phone and sent him a text. **Super busy? I hope all's well in MB.** She followed that with a string of heart emojis.

Where are you? he responded almost immediately.

On Todd's deck with Amy, she replied.

Doing traffic and crowd control. It's gonna be a long night. Call you tomorrow.

She sent a smiley and another heart.

"Hey, ask him if he wants to go on the tacky lights tour. Todd wanted me to see if you guys can go. He got the hearse all cleaned up for the occasion," Amy said.

Jade tapped the question into her phone. Todd said that the hearse, his latest purchase, was to transport his surfboards to competitions, but Amy looked for every opportunity she could find to cruise around in the creepy vehicle. She used it to collect books for a Halloween book drive at her store, and she's talking about planning some kind of haunted tour.

Jade's phone dinged, pulling her away from her thoughts. She laughed out loud and held up her phone for Amy to see. **Wow. A hearse for the holidays.** He followed that with a smiley and a skull and crossbones. "We're in," Jade said. "What time?"

"Let's say six if that works. That way, we can have dinner first. What do you think?"

Jade sent a string of Christmas emojis, and **6 tomorrow work for you? See ya then.**

"This will be so much fun," Amy squealed. "Let us know where you want to go to dinner. Then we'll cruise around town in style. It'll be a holiday tour that you'll never forget. I'll bring snacks. I wonder if I can get Todd to decorate it with lights and those little Rudolph antlers I bought for him."

Before Jade could comment, the tri-county high school marching band blasted Christmas tunes near the pier. She, Chloe, and Amy climbed up and sat on top of the table for a better view. So far, the noise and the people didn't seem to bother the Frenchie, who curled up in Jade's lap under the blanket.

After a medley of holiday favorites, Bernie's "Ho, ho, ho" boomed from speakers on the pier. "Merry Christmas, Mermaid Bay. Tonight, we bring you the first of three fireworks extravaganzas. We are proud to feature Zanetti Fireworks. Each weekend, you'll be treated to a different show, and at the end, you can vote for your favorite. The winner will get the big

Mermaid Bay contract for next year's Memorial Day and Fourth of July shows. Oh, I almost forgot. If anyone would like to stop by and see this jolly old elf, Santa will be at the end of the pier until nine-thirty. Come by and visit. And now, without further ado, I present the Zanettis."

Music blasted from the speakers, and the inky sky over the bay lit up, followed by ooohs and ahhhs from the crowd. The show was back-to-back explosions and synchronized vignettes. The noise echoed off the water and the buildings. Chloe snoozed quietly in Jade's lap.

About forty-five minutes later, the noise stopped, and the quiet echoed in Jade's ears as the smoke drifted out over the bay. The crowd gathered their things and headed to vehicles parked anywhere they could find a spot. Nick and his team would be busy for a while, directing traffic and tracking down lost kids.

"That was impressive," Amy said. "Even though my ears will be ringing all night. I need to go check on my sweetie. See you guys tomorrow. Can't wait." She waved and disappeared through the hot dog stand's wooden screen door.

Jade put Chloe on the deck and picked up her blanket. "It looks like it's thinning out, Chloe. Most people are going in the other direction. Ready to head home?" She folded her blanket and tucked it under her arm.

Dots of lights from cottage windows and strings of Christmas lights outlining decks provided a small amount of light for their walk home. Jade switched on her phone's flashlight app, and they picked their way over the sand.

The ringing in her ears had died away, and all she could hear as they approached the turn to their cut-thru path was the rumble of the waves and Chloe's occasional snort.

She turned the corner and jumped when she spotted a couple leaning up against the wooden fencing. Jade swung her light, and the guy moved his hand from the gal's lower back to shade his eyes. "Hey, watch it," he grumbled.

"Sorry. I didn't know someone was back here." Not moving her light, Jade paused and stared at the pair. "Paolo? Is that you? Hey, the show was really good."

The girl, overdressed for a walk on the beach in winter, turned on her four-inch heels to face Jade with a mind-your-business look. The rail-thin woman with long, platinum hair looked slightly familiar. Jade did a mental scroll to try to place her.

"I'm fine. No thanks to her dumb brother," Paolo said. "My lip still hurts, but I'll recover. It still functions."

The girl opened her mouth to say something, but Paolo planted a wet kiss on her.

His lips couldn't hurt that bad if he was sucking face like that. Glad they couldn't see her non-poker-playing face that gave away her true reaction, Jade said, "See you all around. Be careful. It gets cold out here this time of year."

"Ha, we're from New Jersey and Pennsylvania. This is nothing. Plus, I'm all she needs to keep warm." Paolo pulled the young woman closer to him.

Chloe let out a yip on her way past the pair who had resumed their liplock.

Chapter Four

The soft winter sun streamed through her bedroom curtains, and Jade rolled over and glanced at her clock. "Chloe, we need to get a move on if we want a Sunday morning walk before work." The butterball of a dog rolled over and continued to snore.

After a steamy shower, Jade grabbed a coffee and an energy bar. Chloe made an entrance when she heard kibble hit her bowl.

Jade poured a second coffee in her to-go cup and leashed up the Frenchie. On their way to the store, Chloe wanted to sniff every scent she encountered. "Lots of interesting smells from the crowd last night, huh?" Jade picked up a discarded hamburger wrapper and dumped it in her neighbor's trash can at the curb.

The dog dawdled, and the normal five-minute walk took almost twenty. As Jade turned toward the store's back door, something caught her eye in the empty lot next door. Near the fence, it looked like someone had dumped three or four black trash bags. "For Pete's sake. How lazy are people? Just because it's an empty lot doesn't mean you can leave your junk there," Jade grumbled. "This is not a dumping ground."

As she moved closer to the oleander hedge and privacy fence at the back of the property, Jade stopped and let out a gasp. She picked up Chloe and hugged her tightly against her chest.

Taking a couple of steps closer, Jade's stomach dropped to her feet, and an icy chill, not from the crisp morning, streaked down her spine.

After a few hesitant steps, she leaned in to see if the person lying there was okay. No breaths. Fear rocketed through Jade and settled in the pit of her stomach.

Breathing in and out through her nose, she tapped 911 into her phone. When the dispatcher answered, she said, "Hi, this is Jade Hicks at 'Tis the Season. My dog and I found a body in the field next to the store. Could you send the police?"

"Again? Oh, sorry. That slipped out. Hi, Jade. This is Kate from high school. I'll send a deputy right over. Does the person need an ambulance?"

"I don't think so. I can't find a pulse." Jade recoiled after touching the body's cold skin.

"Are you okay?" Kate asked.

"Just a little freaked out. I wasn't expecting to see this." Jade glanced over her shoulder to see if anyone else was around.

"The deputy will be there in a couple of minutes. Do you want to hang on the line with me?"

"I think I hear a siren. I'll go wave them over. Talk to you later." Jade disconnected and tapped a quick text to Nick. She let out a heavy breath and squeezed Chloe again as Sebastian slammed his SUV door and hitched up his gun belt.

"Morning, Jade. What happened?"

"I have no idea. I haven't had a chance to see if the security cameras caught anything. He's not breathing, and I couldn't find a pulse." She shivered again and squeezed Chloe closer.

"Recognize him?" Sebastian asked, pulling on a pair of black gloves.

An olive-skinned guy with dark hair lay in a fetal curl near two trash bags.

"I thought he was Paolo Zanetti at first, but he doesn't have any of the bruises from the fight. He's definitely one of the Zanettis, but I don't know his name."

Sebastian wrote something in a small notebook and nodded. Jade pulled Chloe closer to her as Sebastian checked the deceased's pockets. The dog made a series of grunting noises that made Sebastian crack a slight smile. "ID says it's Lorenzo Zanetti from Atlantic City."

Jade let out a breath she didn't realize she was holding as a crew of EMTs and two deputies arrived. She stepped back as one of them encircled her lot with yellow police tape.

Chloe yipped as Nick approached. He gave them both a quick one-arm hug. "Morning. You okay?"

Jade nodded and smiled. "Hey. Sorry to drag you all out so early after a long night. I'm going inside to check the cameras. I'll send you what I find." A sinking feeling descended as she carried Chloe toward the store. Not another body in Mermaid Bay, especially this close to Christmas.

"Okay. We'll be in to talk to you later." Nick turned to face the nearby deputies and was swallowed up in their conversation.

Jade paused. "Uh, Nick. Not to be crass or anything, but I have Bernie and a bunch of kids scheduled today for Santa visits. Should I cancel? Should I even open today?" She took a deep breath to keep her voice from trembling.

"The forensic guys will tent this area off. They'll probably be done sometime this afternoon. It should be okay to open. I'll let you know if anything changes."

Jade smiled faintly. She suddenly felt her energy waning. She had to shake the dark feelings before the doors opened. Her guests expected the magic of Christmas, not a scene from a horror flick.

Inside, Jade dropped her things on the extra desk in the workroom. The warm air suddenly seemed stifling, and she tried to swallow the wave of panic that she could feel building in her stomach. Shaking off the morbid thoughts, she double-timed her opening routine. By the time the coffee maker chugged and spewed steam, her laptop had booted.

She settled on her couch to scan through hours of dark security-cam footage. Trying to keep her mind from wandering, she stared at the screen. "What was that?" Chloe rustled in her bed. "I think something's out there." Jade backed up the recording and slowed it down. Around two-thirty in the morning, two, maybe three figures, darted past the backdoor camera on the far side of the field and disappeared in the jet-black darkness of the vacant lot. On the porch camera, she caught three dark figures running across the parking lot. One of them carried what looked like a trash bag. The timestamp was a few seconds earlier than the other camera's view.

What were those men doing? Her cameras didn't catch any other movement.

She copied the clips and emailed them to Nick as footsteps echoed at the back door. Chloe switched into Terminator mode and zoomed toward the door when she heard a series of taps.

Nick stomped to knock the sand off his boots and stepped inside.

"I sent you the camera feed…" she said as he kissed her.

"First things first. Good morning. Missed seeing you."

"I missed you, too. Want some coffee?"

"Yup. But nothing frou-frou. Thanks," he said, lowering himself into her guest chair.

"Should I make one for Sebastian?"

"Nah, he's on a health kick," Nick said. "He said he's giving up caffeine. We'll see how long that lasts."

After she handed him a to-go cup of steaming dark roast, he asked, "So, what do you know about Lorenzo Zanetti?"

"Not much. Only that he looks a lot like his cousin who was involved in that fight."

"When did you see the Zanettis last?" Nick watched her stack files on her desk.

"I guess at the fight. Under the pier. I don't remember seeing him at the show. But I really wasn't looking for him either."

"Anything else about the Zanettis that was odd?" He looked at her over the edge of his cup.

Jade pursed her lips as she rewound yesterday's events in her head. "Amy said that Todd's staff overheard the Zanettis talking at Hot Diggity Dogs the day of the fight. They were complaining about the other team and their underhanded ways of stealing proprietary secrets. Oh wait, I did spot Paolo making out with a blond after the fireworks."

"Where?"

"Down near the cottages near where the cut-thru to my house is. They kinda surprised me when I rounded the corner. He didn't say her name, but he did mention that she was kin to the Pefferlys. And she looked like she was dressed for a night of club-hopping – not a walk on the beach in the winter."

Nick's mouth twitched slightly. "Anything else?"

Jade shook her head. "Uh, did you see the sign that plane was trailing? That was kind of a surprise."

Nick nodded. "Everybody saw it. Multiple times. So much for friendly competition."

Jade pursed her lips. "It seemed a little over the top for a Christmas fireworks festival."

Nick shrugged. "Competitive industry, I guess. My guys will tent off the crime scene out there. Hopefully, they'll be done before most of Mermaid Bay wakes up and goes outside. You should be able to carry on as normal."

"Do you want to take coffee out to the EMTs? Maybe water for Sebastian?"

"Thanks, but Sebastian is on a smoothie kick. And the forensic people can't have anything that could contaminate the crime scene." Nick rose, and his utility belt made snapping noises. "Not sure if I can still do the tacky lights tour tonight. I'll text you later to let you know how the day is going. But it doesn't look good."

"I understand. I'll let Amy and Todd know. We can reschedule," Jade said.

"If you think of anything else, call me." He plopped his Smokey Bear hat on his head and strode out the door.

She usually opened the store at noon on Sundays to accommodate the church and brunch crowds, so that gave her the rest of the morning to fill online orders and do some internet research on the Zanettis and Pefferlys.

Grabbing a notebook, she jotted down everything she could find on the two firework families. She learned more than she ever wanted to know about pyrotechnics, but the science and technology behind the displays were cool and very expensive. Jade didn't realize that different substances made specific colors. It was a flashback to eleventh-grade chemistry. She had to keep reminding herself that she was looking for info on the people when she got lost in videos of spectacular displays.

Not having any a-ha moments, she closed her laptop and rested her head on her arms. She'd have to switch to social media if she wanted to find out anything about the two families, especially the younger members. She started drawing a rough family tree in her notes to keep all the names in order. Was Lorenzo's murder some part of a long-standing feud or a tragic coincidence with really bad timing?

She and her business were thrust into another murder, and she had to figure out how all the pieces fit together before it ruined the Christmas festival and possibly the whole holiday season.

Chapter Five

A "whoooo-hoooo" and a knock on the back door caused Jade and Chloe to startle. Jade opened the door and peeked out behind Patti at the white tent near the fence. Police and forensic technicians milled around in the grass and sand. Several police cars, an ambulance, and a couple of black vans dotted the perimeter of her empty lot. She let out a long breath through her nose. *They're here longer than Nick thought they would be. Thankfully, no crowd had gathered to gawk.*

"I was not expecting all that commotion out there this morning." Patti bustled in and handed Jade a tray of homemade goodies.

"Thanks. You outdid yourself." Jade slipped a cookie with red and white crystals from under the cellophane.

Before Jade could offer any details, Patti continued with, "I was baking for a cookie exchange with my book club, and I brought over some extras for you and Bernie. What happened out there?" Patti asked, dumping her purse, coat, and scarf in the office chair across from Jade.

More knocking and Chloe's yipping interrupted their conversation. Jade opened the door again, and Bernie strode in, dressed in his Victorian St. Nicholas regalia, with a duffle bag and a velvet toy sack.

"I wanted to get a closer look at the action over there," he mumbled. "But your Nick seems to have it all walled off. Okay, Jade, what's the scoop? All the guys want to know what happened." Bernie's eyes lit up when he spotted the cookies. "Don't mind if I do."

"Chloe and I found one of the Zanettis out there this morning by the fence," Jade said.

"Was he…" Patti's sweet smile turned into a grimace, and her eyes widened to saucer size.

Jade nodded, and Patti continued, "Oh, my stars." Patti's hand flew to her mouth. "Another murder in Mermaid Bay. What is going on around here? Do they know what happened? And it's soooo close to Christmas. People are going to think Mermaid Bay's a dangerous place."

"No. I got a flash on the cameras of two or three guys going around the edge of the property, but nothing else. Nick and Sebastian said the victim is Lorenzo Zanetti."

"I don't remember what he looked like. There are a bunch of brothers and cousins in that family, and they're all about the same age," Bernie said.

"That is such a shame, and their show was good. So tragic." Patti popped a hot chocolate pod in the coffee maker and turned to stare at Jade. "I know you. What have you found out about it?" After a couple of beats, she continued. "Come on. I know you can't resist. You helped Nick solve Emory's murder and the one for that reporter at Ruby's B and B last fall when the Love Channel was here. You're doing research. I can tell, and I see that little gleam in your eye. Tell us what you know. Spill it."

"I learned way more than I ever wanted to know about fireworks. There are some cool videos out there. It's not just lighting a fuse. I got lost in all the razzle-dazzle, but it was time to take a break and see if there were any new online orders. I'll look for the Zanettis on social media later if it gets quiet here."

"Let me know what you find. Hopefully, Nick and his boys can wrap this one up quickly before the holidays. If you all need me, you know where I'll be." Bernie tilted his head toward the Toy Room.

"See ya, Bernie," Jade said. "Holler if you need anything."

"I knew our Nancy Drew was on the case. Speaking of that, did you see Mermaid Whispers this morning? There were some teasers about a romantic tryst that will get everyone jazzed about. I'm dying to find out who this Mermaid is. He or she is driving Nell crazy by posting all the juicy stuff before her column in the weekly comes out." Patti's mischievous giggle filled the back room.

"Interesting. The Mermaid is giving Nell a run for her money. At first, I thought the gossip writer might be Nell, expanding her possibilities with a new blog," Jade said.

"No, I don't think so. I saw her in the Busy Bean getting coffee yesterday, and she was on a rant about irresponsible journalism and gossip rags. She said this was the last thing the community needed," Patti added.

Jade stifled a laugh. "She would definitely know about sensationalized stories."

"No comment. Here, give me the order printouts, and I'll gather the stuff. You spend your time figuring out who did this awful thing. Plus, I love visiting with all the ornaments. I do miss Neville jumping out of the trees and giving me a heart attack, but I'm glad he's living his best life at Lorelei's condo."

Jade handed her the report, and Patti rolled a cart through the store to gather the items. She whistled Christmas tunes as she strolled through the showrooms.

About twenty minutes later, Patti danced into the office with a full cart. "I'm back. Did you miss me?"

"Always. I need to go visit the bookstore for a minute. Call me if you get a rush," Jade said.

"No problemo. Chloe, Bernie, and I will have a staff meeting while you're gone." She laughed. "We've got this. Have fun. I'll have all this boxed and labeled by the time you get back."

Jade slid into her winter coat and picked up her phone. "Be back in a few. Do you need anything while I'm out?"

Patti shook her head and started packing the orders for shipping.

Jade's stride slowed as she walked down the sidewalk. Onlookers stood near the yellow police tape and watched the technicians come and go from under the tent. Not recognizing anyone except the guy in the red hoodie and his border collie, Jade picked up her pace and crossed the street.

The bookstore looked deserted while a steady stream of brunchers zipped in and out of the Busy Bean next door. Jade climbed the wooden steps to the front porch of Mermaid Books and peered in the front window. She pulled on the door and stepped inside. Amy had transformed the shop into a cozy place to hang out with lots of beach reads and bookish events. A gray, fuzzy flash caused Jade to jump. Mr. Darcy, Amy's cat, zipped by again, leapt on the counter, and licked his paw.

"Hey, there. Where's Amy?" Jade asked, letting the Persian with the bright green eyes sniff her hand before she petted him.

"I'm back here," Amy yelled. "Putting the kids' section in order. We had a youth scavenger hunt in here yesterday, and the place is a mess. But we had fun, so it was worth it. Be right there."

Seconds later, Amy appeared around the corner and dusted her hands off on her jeans. "It's good to see you. I didn't know a handful of YAs could turn a store upside down. But they did. What's up? You look tired. Can I get you some coffee or tea? I have chai."

"No thanks. See all the activity this morning?" Jade pointed toward the front window.

"Lots of lights and sirens near your place. That can't be good. I was going to call you, but I got sidetracked with a big delivery. What's up?"

"Chloe and I found one of the Zanettis in the empty lot. Nick and his team are investigating."

Amy flattened her lips. "Was he..."

Jade nodded haltingly.

Amy grimaced. "So we probably should reschedule our date night and tacky lights tour. Not a problem. Let me know when you all are free. People keep their lights on through the holidays, right?"

Jade nodded. "Sorry about that. Nick's schedule doesn't lend itself well to planning too far in advance."

"Or even planning. Oh, the exciting life of the town sheriff. So, what happened? Any deets?" Amy leaned forward. "You had a front-row seat. I know somebody died, but it's like we're right in the middle of some true crime drama."

"I wish I wasn't smack dab in the middle of it. When we arrived this morning, I thought someone had dumped trash in my lot, and I was fit to be tied. It was a shock to find that it was really a body."

"Who? Who? I need details." Amy leaned over the counter toward Jade.

Jade snickered. "You sound like Woodsy Owl." She paused and plastered on a somber look. "It's Lorenzo Zanetti."

"I don't know him. So far, none of the fireworks people have come by my store, that I know of. On a side note, did you see the latest posts from the Mermaid?" Amy whipped out her phone and started tapping.

Jade pulled hers out, too, and refreshed the window for Mermaid Whispers.

"Oooooeeeee," Amy said. "I'm going to call her 'she' because I feel it's a woman writer. Plus, mermaids are female. And I'm dying to know who it is. I can so relate to her stuff. So from now on, she's M.W., or maybe I'll call her the Mermaid. Anyway, she teased us with a possible tête-à-tête. And now she's focusing on a Mermaid Bay feud. I'm dying to know who she is really talking about. Hey, here's a thought. Let's start a rumor that it's us. We're in a heated disagreement between our stores. We could milk this for some advertising exposure. We could be the talk of the beach for at least a week until something else comes along."

Jade chewed on her bottom lip. "I try to fly under the radar around here. There's enough drama without me adding to it."

"You know me, I'm a drama llama." Amy flipped her brown hair with purple-tinted ends behind her ear. "We could have some fun with this. Come on. I mean, we could really get the tongues a-wagging. It'll be a hoot to see what we can stir up."

"Speaking of causing a stir, any guesses on who's doing this blog? I heard that Nell was beside herself about the person scooping her."

Amy giggled. "I wish I knew. I'd be feeding her ideas for future shockers. Like did she know that the local bookseller was making out in a hearse with the hot dog king? Or what about our favorite Christmas store owner finally telling the world that she and our hunky sheriff are a thing? And don't get me started on all the stuff that Vivian frowns on. That would be fodder for a blog for months. It could be a special feature, ways to not be proper in a southern town."

"So, are you the Mermaid?" Jade asked, looking for any kind of tell on her friend's face.

"Ha! I'd love to give Nell and Vivian a fit. Too bad I didn't think of it first. It is perfect for this little gossipy, close-knit town. I hope she keeps them all guessing for months—or longer. Bless their little hearts," she said with her best put-on southern drawl.

Jade turned her head like Chloe did when she thought she heard something interesting.

"Don't get me wrong. I love it here. But you have to admit, everyone's nose is in everyone's business. But they're all as sweeeeeeeeeet as a pit-cha of grandma's ice teeeeee," Amy said, demonstrating more of her fake accent.

"Not bad for a chick from Massachusetts." Jade winked at her friend. "I'll see when Nick can extricate himself from this investigation. Maybe we can go on our tour later this week."

"Sounds like a plan. I can't wait to see all the decorations and lights. Double-date night!"

A large vehicle rumbled outside, and Jade spotted two tour buses rounding the corner, headed for her store. "That looks interesting," she said. "I'll send them your way to check out your cool stuff."

Amy smiled and held the door for Jade, who trotted out and yelled, "Local store owners suspend feud to drum up business. Love it."

Jade waved and smiled. *Despite her repeated denials, could Amy really be the secretive mermaid?* She zipped her coat and hustled toward the store as her phone alerted with rapid-fire texts from Patti.

SOS! Buses have invaded!

Hurry back!!!

Chloe's kissing everyone.

Hope I have enough cookies.

Jade had a minute to drop her things on the desk and slide behind the counter to help Patti answer hundreds of questions and hand out shopping baskets to the visitors.

Taking advantage of a lull in the crowd before the guests started checking out, Jade lowered herself down on the stool behind the register.

"Excuse me," a senior in an orange jogging suit said. She approached the counter with two friends in tow. "Ginnie here said this is where the Love

Channel filmed a show. Is that true?" She pointed to the taller woman in a purple, velour tracksuit with matching lavender hair.

"And did you get to meet Raphael Allard and Elle Valentine? I love all their movies," Ginnie gushed.

"Oooooh, yes," Patti squealed. "They filmed all over town, and when it airs be sure to look for the scenes they filmed right here in this store. We all got to be extras and hang out with the cast."

The third woman's eyes sparkled. "Right here?"

Patti nodded so vigorously that Jade was afraid that she would lose one of her Christmas tree earrings. "Raphael stood right about there." She pointed to the decorated tree near the door.

"Oh, my lands," the woman yelled. "Miriam, Ginnie, come take my picture. I never thought I'd stand where Raphael said his lines." She clutched her necklace and moved closer to the tree. "Where? Right here?"

Patti nodded. "I'll do it." She reached for the woman's phone. "So, all y'all can be in it. And yep, that's where he was. Elle was shopping in the scene they filmed here."

The three women oohed and ahhed while Patti snapped some photos.

After several shots, Miriam said, "You get in some with us. I can't wait for the Valentine's Day special. Gals, we've had our photo taken with extras from *My Coastal Valentine*. These are going on Facebook and Instagram and anywhere else I can think to put them."

"I'm sending them to my grandchildren and the mahjong club," Miriam said.

Jade stepped around from behind the counter and reached for the phone. Patti and the three seniors mugged for the camera in a series of shots.

"There," Jade said. "Tag us in your posts, and we'll be sure to share them."

"Thanks so much. This is so exciting. I think we have some time before we have to be back on the bus," Ginnie said. "Let's go explore this town. Where else did they film?"

"All over Mermaid Bay. The stars stayed at the B and B called the Pearl. They filmed at the hot dog stand, the coffee shop, and at the pier. The crew stayed in the lot next door. They had a big tent there and a bunch of trailers.

It was so cool," Patti said as she rang up the women's purchases.

"Oooooh, come on, gals. The bus will wait for us. Let's go get some pictures." Miriam shooed them toward the front door.

"And don't forget to check out the other businesses in town. There's a bookstore on the corner," Jade yelled as the trio headed for the front door.

"Uh, oh. Maybe I shouldn't have mentioned the lot." Patti chewed on her bottom lip. A flush of pink erupted on her cheeks. "I hope Nick's team has it cleared out. I'm sorry for that poor young man. And that our little beach seems to be ground zero for a lot of bad stuff lately."

"Last time I checked, the forensic team was still working out there. Nick and his guys are in for another long night."

"I hope they arrest someone soon. I feel like I'm always looking over my shoulder when I'm out. On a happier note, you know what we need? To plan events for the Love Channel's debut in February. There are so many fans out there. This could be a gold mine." Her mood shifted as quickly as the tide.

The pair spent the next hour checking out seniors and answering questions, mainly about the police activity in the field next door. When the last shopper hustled toward the bus with her purchases, Patti sunk down on the stool. "I'm pooped. That crowd wore me out. I got a rest up a bit. Tonight's trivia night, and I'll never make it through all the rounds at this rate. What about you? Any big plans?"

"Nope. It looks like Nick will be tied up with his investigation for a while. Chloe and I will hang out at home. We were going to look at all the Christmas lights, but we'll do it another time."

Patti made a pouty face. "But I know you will figure out who killed that poor young man. Go home and find out what evil lurks in Mermaid Bay. I've gotta get on the road. You okay here?"

"We're good. Thanks for everything. It doesn't look like there were any leftover cookies," Jade said, picking up the empty platter. When Patti reached for it, Jade continued, "Let me rinse that for you. If not, your car will be covered in crumbs and sprinkles."

"I've got it," Patti said with a dismissive wave. "My car is already covered in glitter from the wreathes I made at the craft and sip party the other night." Her melodic laugh echoed from the workroom as she packed up her gear. "Hey, you can't have too much sparkle this time of year." Patti flitted around the store, gathering her belongings. "Bernie had a poker game to get to, so he hightailed it out of here without changing into his civies."

Returning to the store's lobby, Patti said, "I think that's everything. Y'all have fun. Can't wait to see what pops up next on Mermaid Whispers. Ooooo. Sounds like one of those tell-all reality shows." The bells on the front door jingled when Patti pulled it closed behind her.

"Hey, Chloe. Wake up. It's time for us to head out." Jade heard the little dog's toenails skitter across the hardwood floor in the back. She opened the dividing door, and Chloe burst out like a firecracker.

"Let's do a walk-through and lock up here. Hopefully, there's something at home for dinner." Chloe zoomed off in search of crumbs or anything interesting left by all of today's shoppers.

When Jade locked the back door behind them, movement around the tent caught her eye. Two of the forensic guys were setting up outdoor lights. *Another long night for Nick's team. Way longer than any of them expected.*

Changing her mind about dinner, she said, "Let's go see what's going on at Hot Diggity Dogs." The pudgy dog's ears perked up, and she trotted toward the sidewalk with the hope of scoring a snack.

The wind pressed the glass door into Jade's calves as she entered the restaurant with a long counter and a handful of tables in front of large glass windows. She pulled the door shut behind her and said, "Whew. It's a bit chilly out there, and that wind is something else."

"Hey, Jade. The temperature's dropping. It wouldn't surprise me if we got some sleet or flurries tonight. It looks like Nick's guys are in for a long night. We've been watching them all afternoon. What can I get you?" Todd asked.

"Let's see." She stared at the menu that hadn't changed since his dad owned the place. "I'll have a regular with mustard and a side of onion rings."

"That it?" After she nodded, he continued, "What's shaking in your world?"

"It's been busy. We're headed home for a quiet night. Sorry, we couldn't do the lights tour with you know…." She tilted her head toward the front window at his hearse-mobile.

"We'll reschedule, and it'll still be fun. Amy's got all kinds of things planned," Todd said, handing Chloe a bite of a hot dog. "She won't let us out of it that easily."

"Sorry that you missed the fireworks last weekend. The show was pretty good. I can't wait to see what the other vendors do."

"Work calls. It's kinda nice to have a busy weekend in December. It puts us in the black for the yearend totals. I'll never pass up that opportunity," he said with a wink.

Jade nodded. Todd flipped her hot dog and wrapped it to go. He banged the wire basket to knock off the excess oil and tossed the onion rings under a heat lamp.

When he had wrapped her order, he said, "There you go. Maybe I'll get to see the show this weekend. Though it sounds like there's a lot of fireworks going on around town already." He grinned and handed her the paper bag.

"There's always something going on. Hopefully, next weekend will be as profitable." She waved and nudged Chloe toward the door.

The wind whipped off the bay, and Jade and Chloe double-timed their walk home. The pair made it to the bungalow in record time and settled in at the dining room table for dinner. Jade hopped up and put her onion rings in the air fryer for a warmup.

"Mmmm. That's better," she said when she returned to the table. She pinched off a little of the coating and handed it to the waiting dog. "Let's see what we can find on the Zanettis and the Pefferlys."

Chapter Six

Jade and Chloe extended their morning walk all the way to the other end of the block, where the Busy Bean and Mermaid Books guarded the entrance to Suggs Pier. Today called for a treat stop. Jade pushed open the glass door, and Chloe pranced toward the counter. The sun streamed in through the front windows and made the coffee shop's aqua and stainless-steel décor shine.

"Hello," James Fournier said. "What can I get you on this bright morning?"

"How are things? I'll have a white chocolate mocha to go." Jade swiped her card and slid it back into her wallet. "How's Sophie? I haven't seen her in a while." Jade looked around the hip restaurant and spotted some of the Zanettis at a corner table. Resisting the urge to rush to work, she decided to grab a seat and hang out in the welcoming restaurant owned by the Fournier brother and sister team.

"Business has been steady, and I like the holiday surge. Sophie's good, too. She's working days here and taking some online classes in marketing in the evenings."

"Cool, and yay for her," Jade said, reaching for the drink he offered.

"And here's a pup cup for your friend." James slid a Dixie cup across the counter, and Chloe danced on her hind legs. The soy milk and whipped cream didn't stand a chance against the Frenchie's tongue. She devoured the treat in seconds and looked around for a second one.

"I think she enjoyed it," Paolo Zanetti said. Jade turned to deposit the tiny cup in the trash can. The pyrotechnics guy and late-night lothario stood inches from her. *So much for personal space.*

He leaned down and petted Chloe, who rolled over and showed off for her new friend.

Jade smiled. "She is a hundred percent food-motivated."

"So is my brother and most of my cousins." He winked at Jade and continued to play with the dog.

"I am so sorry about your family's loss," Jade said, hoping to spark some conversation.

A sober expression crossed his face. "It's tough. Lorenzo was a good guy." The thin twenty-something ran his hand through his overly styled hair. He straightened to his full height, and Jade had to step back to see his face. "Even though we were cousins, we acted more like brothers. I'll miss him."

"It was tragic and so unexpected. Are you all staying in town?" Jade asked.

"We decided not to head back to New Jersey right away. We're at some place called the Pearl until your police say we can leave. Elio and I plan to check out the competition this weekend. We're here anyway. Might as well. Grandma and the rest of the family can't plan the funeral until they release his, uh, body. So we'll hang out here for a while."

"If there is anything I can do, please let me know," Jade said.

"It's a nice town, but not much action. What happened will always be a sad memory for us, but we're still hoping to land the summer contract." His expression perked up. "At least some restaurants are open here. Many of the places on the shore at home board up for the season."

"I guess this will give you time to spend with your friend from the other night," Jade said.

Paolo waved his hand for her to lower her voice. After peering over his shoulder, he replied with a grin, "Let's keep that on the down low for now. Nobody around here would approve. But yes, I'll get some more time to hang out with her. And that's always good," he said with a wink.

"Do you have any details about what happened to your cousin?" Jade asked, taking advantage of his chattiness.

"We were packing up to go back to the hotel after the show. Lorenzo's truck was filled first, so he took off. He never showed up at the hotel or whatever that place is. It looks like an old dollhouse. Anyway, we figured he stopped somewhere."

"Is that like him?" Jade asked.

"Not when we're working. He's pretty much all business. I mean, we all crash at other places at times, but his bae's back home. He wouldn't have gone out by himself. And it's doubtful he met anyone. His nose is always in a book. Plus, he had a truck full of our equipment. Grandpop is really adamant about protecting the equipment. He thinks spies are everywhere. We didn't realize he wasn't back until breakfast, when no one could find him. He and Elio were roommates, and he said Lorenzo's bed wasn't slept in. We all retraced our routes from the night before and found the truck in the parking lot by the pier. It was unlocked, but all the equipment was there. No Lorenzo. Someone had rifled through the console and the glovebox. But none of the firework crates were opened. And nothing valuable was missing."

Trying not to make it sound like an inquisition, Jade let out a sigh. "You don't think he went off with someone and left the equipment and the truck unlocked?" *That didn't sound like a robbery.*

"Nah, that's not like him. He's the responsible one. We were still at the truck when the police rolled up. And you know the rest."

Wracking her brain, trying to find a way to get more information about the blond she spotted him with, Jade paused. When he didn't say anything else, she added hastily, "I'm so sorry."

"No problem. I gotta get back. See ya around." Paolo patted Chloe again, and she draped herself over his shoes. He laughed as Jade picked up her dog. She carried Chloe to the front door and waved to James, who buzzed around behind the counter, filling drink orders.

Jade and Chloe stepped out into the bright sunlight, and the little dog let out a long growl as Jade fished around in her bag for her sunglasses. "What's up, puppy?" she asked as a guy and his border collie walked by. The dog ignored the Frenchie, who let out a series of snorts when they passed.

Down the street, they spotted Lorelei in her white Lexus tapping away on her phone. Neville lay sprawled out across the dashboard in the morning sun.

Jade waved, but her aunt didn't respond. "That's odd. Lorelei didn't even see us. She must be engrossed in something." Jade followed Chloe up the porch steps. By the time she had the lights on and her laptop booted, Lorelei and Neville sauntered in. Chloe growled and leapt forward before Jade could cut her off with the dividing door, and the chase started like the Indy 500. After two laps, Neville jumped up on the counter and posed beside the cash register, taunting his nemesis. Chloe, who got tired of waiting for the cat to return to her level, trotted to her bed in the office for a mid-morning nap.

"Well, that was fun," Lorelei said.

"You're up and at 'em really early." Jade winked at her aunt.

"I couldn't sleep. Neville and I did all the laundry, and after a nice breakfast, we decided to come in early to see what you and Chloe were doing. How are James and Sophie? What's going on at the Busy Bean?" She pointed to Jade's cup.

Jade shook her head. "James had a crowd this morning. I ran into some of the Zanettis at the Busy Bean." She reached over to pet Neville. "Not much going on here. Nick's knee-deep in that murder investigation. Chloe and I have been hanging out and hoping that he'll catch a break in the case."

Her aunt's eyebrows shot up under her platinum bangs. "The Zanettis are still in town?"

"They said Nick told them not to leave."

"Find out anything interesting about the young man who died?" Lorelei rummaged through her purse.

"Not really. Paolo said that Lorenzo had a girlfriend back in New Jersey, so it was unlikely that he went off with anyone that night. They found the truck unlocked the next morning at the pier."

"I thought all their equipment was expensive and super-secret," her aunt said.

Jade shrugged, and before she could comment, Lorelei continued, "But didn't you see one of them that night with one of the Pefferlys?"

Jade nodded. "Not the one who was killed. I saw Paolo, the one who got in the fight."

Her aunt nodded and tapped something into her phone.

"What are you up to? Taking notes? You aren't the mysterious blogger that everyone's obsessed with, are you?" Jade snickered.

Her aunt raised one perfectly manicured eyebrow and did a fake pearl clutch. "Do I look like a blogger to you? I thought they were all Gen Zs who stayed up all night and spent way too much time on their phones and drank kale smoothies."

"If you say so. But everyone I've talked to in town is on a quest to find out who the mystery person is." Jade disappeared into the office.

"You sure it's not you?" Her aunt yelled from the lobby. "You're in the right demographic."

"I'm not a fan of green smoothies," Jade yelled from the backroom. After grabbing a stack of orders, she stuck her head through the door. "Nope. No time for gossip blogging. I barely have time for a social life. This place keeps me busy enough."

"Hmmm. We need to work on that. I'm gonna have a talk with Nick. You both work too much. Okay, then I expect you to use your sleuthing talents and figure out who this person is. From the posts, I'm guessing they'd have to be a local." Lorelei's phone alerted, and she stared at her screen.

Chapter Seven

Knowing that there was a murderer on the loose in town caused Jade to toss and turn all night. When she couldn't go back to sleep, she padded down the hallway in her pajamas, did a load of laundry, and vacuumed the living room before dawn. Running out of household chores, she decided to jump in the shower and then catch up on paperwork and marketing tasks before the store opened.

"Come on, puppy," Jade said, juggling her bag, purse, travel mug, and leash. "Let's go for a ride today." She unlocked the door of her lime-green Jeep Wrangler and settled Chloe in the passenger seat for the short ride around the block.

When everything checked out during her opening routine at the store, Jade packed the overnight orders and dragged out items to make a gift basket for the Zanettis. Stuffing an oval, wicker basket with coffee, teas, specialty truffles, a magnet, and a calendar she had made of Chloe in all her seasonal outfits, she rearranged the green and red shredded paper in the bottom, so everything fit.

Jade whistled. "Let's go see if we can find some ornaments." She and Chloe stopped in what was one of the cottage's original bedrooms that now housed the holiday room. She checked out the Fourth of July tree and picked up a couple of firecracker ornaments. Not ready to return to her desk, the pair strolled through the display rooms to soak up the twinkle lights. The trees and decorations always brought back magical memories.

The bells on the front door jangled. "Hey, Jade. Jade, you here?" echoed through the store.

"I'm back here," Jade yelled as she wended her way through the showrooms.

"There you all are," her aunt said, almost bumping into Jade in the toy room. "What do you need me to start on today?"

"I'm working on a basket to take to the Zanettis. How about you cover the front while I finish that? I'll run over to the Pearl later to drop it off."

"Sounds like a plan." Lorelei patted Chloe. She turned on her red Versace heels and headed for the lobby. "Say hey to Ruby and Josie for me."

Back at the worktable, Jade added the ornaments and wrapped cellophane around the basket to hold everything in, topping it with a navy bow. Adding a sticker with the store's logo, she stood back and admired the gift. Needing a rest from the morning's activities, Chloe settled in her bed and found a comfy snoozing spot.

"Oh, how pretty," Patti said as she breezed in the office and made a beeline for the coffee maker. "What's the occasion?"

"Hey, wait. Did I schedule you and Lorelei on the same morning?" Jade asked, trying to remember.

"I thought you were expecting a crowd today." Patti added peppermint creamer to her coffee.

Jade twisted a loose strand of her hair that had worked free from her messy bun. *Did I really goof up the schedule? Have I been that distracted?* She hurried to the front counter and pulled out the folder of store information. Running her finger down the schedule, she checked the date. "Nope. Patti's scheduled this morning."

A look of surprise crossed Lorelei's face. "I didn't sleep well last night. See what lack of rest can do. Here, let me make a copy of that, so I can keep my dates straight for the rest of the year."

Returning with a copy, Lorelei handed Jade the schedule. She whistled, and Neville slinked over to the counter. "Come on, baby. Let's go home and take a nap. Obviously, I need one." She scooped up the black and white tuxedo cat and waved. "See you later, alligators." Jade made a mental note to call Lorelei later and check on her."

When the door closed behind Lorelei, Patti asked, "Anything I should know about? I see the new blog has been quiet. I can't wait to see what drops next."

Any word on who's behind it?" Jade asked, glancing at Patti, who tapped her foot as she flipped through an ornament catalog.

She shook her head, and her blond curls bounced back into place. "Nope. I don't even have any theories. Nell's all worked up about it. She's poking around to see if she can uncover the mystery blogger. She called me last night to see if I knew anything about it. And she even asked if it was me." Patti tee-heed at the thought. "Why would she ever think that?"

"Because you know everybody," Jade said. "And people tell you all kinds of stuff."

"I've lived here all my life," Patti said with a dismissive wave.

"My first thought was that it was Nell, but she's trying to make a name for herself with a wider audience. A blog that only the locals are interested in wouldn't help further that. Plus, it wouldn't make sense that her blog persona was competing with her reporter one. Nope. I don't have any theories, either. But it is the talk of the town." Jade gathered her things and tucked the basket under her arm. "I'm headed to the Pearl to drop this off. Be back in a bit."

"Okey-dokey. I'll work on the inventory if it stays quiet. Tell Ruby we missed her at book club."

Jade hopped in her Wrangler and drove through the tranquil neighborhood streets full of beach cottages and large Victorian homes. Ruby Ellis's three-story Victorian with its wrap-around porch and gingerbread trim looked like something out of a fairy tale. All the historic homes in the neighborhood, a few blocks from Neptune Road, reminded Jade of pastel-colored dollhouses.

Parking on the street, Jade trotted down the oyster shell path to the kitchen entrance. She knocked and looked around at Ruby's dormant garden. Her roses and flowers would explode into colorful bursts in time for the spring and summer weddings and teas.

"Hey, Jade. What brings you by on this brisk morning?" Ruby asked, almost pulling her into the B and B's industrial kitchen. "Can I get you some tea?"

"I'm fine. Thanks. I hope you all are doing well. This is for the Zanettis. I'm so sorry to hear about what happened."

"Some of them are up already. The younger ones usually sleep through the breakfast part of the deal. Go on back to the library. Aldo, the grandfather, was in there with his coffee and newspaper the last I checked."

Before Jade headed down the hallway, Ruby reached out, grabbed her arm, and whispered, "Hey, what do you know about that new Mermaid Whispers thing?" She made a sour face. "I'm hoping not to be featured on it."

Jade shook her head. "It's causing a stir."

"I'm glad the focus is off the Pearl. We had enough drama here with that film crew and that reporter's murder. Glad that's over. I don't need anything that scares away customers."

Jade wrinkled her nose, and Ruby continued, "Sorry. But I'm glad I'm not mixed up in this one. Last fall did a number on my nerves. I need a quiet holiday season to recover from that looniness." She paused and dusted her hands on her canvas apron. "I've got to get the second round of breakfast ready for the late risers. Sure I can't get you anything?" Ruby opened the stainless-steel refrigerator and pulled out eggs, cheese, and milk.

"No thanks. I plan to make a quick trip and head back to the store." Jade pushed the swinging door open.

In the library across from the dining room, Aldo and Remo sat in comfy wingback chairs in front of the roaring fireplace next to a towering Christmas tree covered in white and gold ornaments. "Hello. I'm Jade Hicks. I wanted to stop by and offer my condolences." She set the basket on the side table next to the family's patriarch.

Aldo cleared his throat and said, "Thank you. It has been a tough week for all of us."

"If I can help with anything, please let me know." Jade fidgeted on the plush oriental rug.

The older man nodded. When no one said anything else after a long pause that felt like an eternity, Jade waved and retreated to the kitchen. Not seeing Ruby or her daughter Josie anywhere, she let herself out the kitchen door.

Outside, a thundering voice caused her to freeze in her tracks. "I don't care what you think. We can't sit around and do nothing. We have to take care of this."

Jade tiptoed around the corner of the house and stuck her head out for a quick peek to see who the loud voice belonged to.

A tall man ranted and waved one arm around. "No. The police haven't said anything. I don't like being left in the dark. No. None of the equipment was stolen, but they couldn't find his phone. I don't care. We have to do something. We know it was them. They deserve a good beating. We can't not respond. I'm sick of all of 'em trying to steal our stuff." The man turned, and Jade closed her eyes for a moment to try to recall his name. *Elio. That's it. Paolo's cousin and Lorenzo's brother.*

Suddenly, Elio, who looked like he could have been a wrestler in school, whirled around and stared at her. Jade could feel the flush move across her face. She waved, trying to look casual and not like she was eavesdropping.

Elio glared at her as he walked to the other side of the yard to continue the conversation.

Not waiting for him to return, Jade hopped in the Jeep and navigated the warren of neighborhood streets. Her heart pounded in her ears. This conversation could have been nothing, but her first impression felt like it was more, almost something sinister.

As Jade pulled into the parking spot behind the store, her phone rang and interrupted her internal analysis of what she had overheard. "Hey, Amy. What's up?"

"Todd's leaving work early tomorrow. Before nine o'clock. He promised. Whoo hooo. Can you and Nick do the lights tour tomorrow?"

"I'll check and let you know. You doing okay?" Jade asked.

"Yep. But Tish might not be when she sees what the Mermaid posted this morning," Amy said in her sing-song voice. She let out a loud wolf-whistle, and Jade pulled the phone away from her ear.

"I haven't had time to look at it. What's up?" Jade asked.

"Well, it seems the blogger broke two Mermaid Bay secret romances this morning. Tish Taylor, our tough-as-nails beach Realtor and fashion plate, has had a not-so-secret fling going with that real estate developer, Jared Carswell. You know, the one who had that hoity-toity party at his condo in Seaport that I dragged you to. Remember, I had fun nosing around his place. Anyway, the Mermaid dishes that Tish, who wanted to keep the relationship secret, was expecting a ring from Jared for her milestone birthday this year. Well, it seems ol' Jared had other plans, and he dumped her for a newer model, a GenZ who he hired to manage his social media accounts. The blog reports that Tish isn't taking it well. You know, a woman scorned and all that. Anyway, Jared's new squeeze could pass for his daughter or granddaughter. Tish is not happy. If I were Jared, I'd watch my back."

Jade's eyebrows shot up. "And who was the other romance?" Jade felt a devilish grin creep across her face.

"Relax. It's not either of us. In fact, it's not anybody in town. Mermaid Whispers went on and on about the firework feud between the Zanettis and next week's group, but she said that even though they were hiding from their families, Paolo and Brianna had a Romeo and Juliet thing going on."

"Oh, them," Jade said.

"You don't sound shocked," Amy said with a hint of disappointment.

"I saw them together near my cottage the night of the murder, and they're a bit too old for the love-struck teens' analogy. And they only had lips for each other."

"Ooooh, insider information! Hmmm. Love is in the air. Well, it is the holiday season. Hey, I got customers. Gotta go. Let me know about our double-date."

"Bye," Jade said to dead air.

Miss you. Dinner tomorrow? she texted Nick.

Whatcha thinking? he replied.

Amy wants to do dinner and the tacky lights tour.

After a long pause, he responded, **Be at your place tomorrow after 6.**

She replied with a series of hearts and threw in some Christmas emojis.

Jade texted Amy Nick's response, and before she could put her phone away, it dinged with a string of smileys and Christmas trees from Amy. **Whoo hoo! Can't wait.**

Jade dropped her phone in her purse and headed inside the store. She and Patti puttered around the office the rest of the morning, and by the afternoon, the foot traffic had slowed down to next to nothing. The hands on her office Grinch clock inched forward, and still no new guests. The holiday shopping season shouldn't be that slow. Had the murder scared off business?

"Need me to do anything else?" Patti asked. "I'm excited about my new weaving class tonight. Whatcha planning to do?"

"I'm hoping to sneak in sometime to see the Christmas lights in town with Nick," Jade said.

"Sounds like fun, especially if it's date night." Patti wiggled her eyebrows. "Hubba hubba. Don't let the gossip blogger find out."

Jade felt a surge of heat in her cheeks. "Hopefully, it'll be a date, if he can get away from the office. He's been kinda busy lately. Thanks for getting the inventory straight and the trees dusted. The place looks great."

"My pleasure. I like to stay busy, plus it gives me a chance to look at all ornaments. Today, I spotted the frog and lizard ones you have in the animal room. They are so cute. I always see something new on my journeys through the store. Oh, I left a catalog that I doggie-eared on the counter. There are some cute pink piggy ornaments, and there's a company called Schylling that has a line of vintage toys. I think you need another display tree in the toy room." Patti winked and wiggled into her puffy coat.

"I love the nostalgia items," Jade said, flipping through the catalog. "Our customers do, too. They don't stay in stock long."

"I know. I had flashbacks to Christmases past when I was flipping through the catalog. See ya next weekend. I'm ready for more boom booms." Patti drifted out the front door, and the bells jangled when she pulled it closed behind her.

"Chloe, the sock monkey and pinball ornaments are cute." The Frenchie, more interested in her bed, opened one eye and then rolled over. Jade spent the next hour ordering ornaments and classic toys while the Frenchie drifted off to sleep and snored loudly near Jade's desk.

"Okay, orders are done. Let's do a quick walk-through and check on everything." Jade's voice echoed through the empty store, causing Chloe to jump up and do zoomies in the lobby.

"What's gotten into you? You're a ball of energy all of a sudden." Jade checked the doors and the timers for the twinkle lights.

After pulling the back door shut and wiggling the knob, Jade guided the Frenchie toward the Jeep. Chloe had other ideas as she pulled and darted toward the stores next door.

"You want pizza?"

Chloe yipped and pranced to the brick building next door and waited outside the glass door of Pizza D'Action until Jade opened it.

"Welcome," yelled Anthony Rossi, a meatball of a man with a ring of white hair surrounding the back of his head. "Grab a seat, and Delores will be right with you."

"Hi, Mr. Rossi. Could I get a small cheese pizza to go?"

"Call me Tony. It'll be up in two shakes of a lamb's tail. One cheese pie for you and your cute friend there."

"We're so glad to have a pizza place in town now." Jade moved toward the end of the counter covered in menus and cheese and pepper flake jars.

"Glad to be here. We retired and sold the place in New Jersey to my nephew and moved down here to be closer to my daughter and her kids. And thanks to you for having all those events at your store that drive the hungry customers over here. The bus tours are great! Though I see you did have a bit of unwanted action earlier."

Jade nodded. After looking over her shoulder, she lowered her voice. "The families of the two companies in the fireworks competition are feuding, and Chloe and I found something horrible in the lot."

Tony tsked tsked. "It's a shame. Fireworks, beaches, and Christmas are supposed to be fun."

Changing the subject, Jade said, "On a lighter topic, Santa will be back on Saturday if your little ones want to stop by."

Tony's wife, Delores, bustled to the front and leaned on the counter before Jade could continue. "That will be fun. We enjoyed the fireworks last weekend. There always seems to be something going on around here," Delores said.

"If my team or I can help you with anything, just holler. Hey, have you met Vivian from the business council yet?" Jade asked.

"The chatty one from the library?" Tony asked, smacking dough on a nearby counter.

Jade nodded, and he continued, "Yep. She told us all about what's going on and signed us up to volunteer with some Valentine's stuff next year. Delores is excited about it." He smiled a goofy grin and continued to pound the dough.

"She's got her finger on the pulse of everything that happens in Mermaid Bay. The business council has been really helpful with advice and networking when I took over my grandmother's store...."

"Hey, Delores, put some coupons in the bag for Jade, so she can give some to her customers." His wife nodded and added a stack of papers to Jade's order.

About fifteen minutes later, Tony pulled pizzas from the oven with a flat, wooden paddle. "Here's your pie. Enjoy!" he said, handing her a red and white square box and a plastic bag. "I put a couple Italian wedding cookies in the bag with the coupons. Let me know how you like them," he said with a wink.

"Thank you so much." Jade handed Delores her debit card.

When Delores returned the card with the receipt, Jade said, "Thanks. Chloe, it's almost dinner time." The Frenchie was all too happy to follow the cheesy scents in Jade's box.

When they pulled into her bungalow's driveway, her butterball of a dog didn't want to leave the pizza smells in the Wrangler. With some persuasion, Jade managed to coax the pudgy dog out and toward the front door. Once inside, Jade kicked off her boots and fed Chloe. After pouring a glass of peach tea, she settled in with her laptop and pizza at the dining room table. A couple of hours and three slices of New York-style pizza later, she had collected oodles of information about the Zanettis and the Pefferlys. She jotted what she knew on a stack of brightly colored stickies and stuck them to her dining room wall. Besides two lawsuits the companies had filed against each other over the last ten years for claims of corporate espionage and copying patented devices, Brianna and Paolo seemed to be the only human link between the families.

When she finished, Jade stepped back and surveyed her work. So far, she was unable to find anyone from town who was a suspect. Before she could ponder further about all the characters on her wall, a knock at the door sent Chloe into a barking jag.

The little dog turned into a big wiggle when she saw Nick at the door with a bag.

"Hey, I hope it's not too late," he said, stepping inside and handing Jade the bag. He kissed her before she could answer.

Jade felt a tingle of excitement spread through her. When Nick paused to cast off his jacket, she said, "Nope. Come on in, especially since you brought dessert. What is it?" She opened the bag and said, "Yum, cannoli. Mr. Rossi gave me some Italian cookie samples if you want a couple."

"Somebody else has been to Pizza D'Action," he said, pointing to the red and white box on the counter.

"It was Chloe's idea. You want coffee or something else to drink? Or pizza?"

"Coffee's fine. It's good to see you. Sorry, I've been the phantom boyfriend again," he said, standing in front of her murder wall. "Find anything interesting?" He stepped closer to read her notes.

"I was going to ask you the same thing. Any news on the killer?"

"Not much. We found a hoodie and a pair of jeans that were covered in blood in a dumpster in Seaport. And James and Sophie found a pair of bloody sneakers in their trash can at the Busy Bean. I'm waiting for the results to come back on all of it from forensics. I'm guessing it's all related, but you never know." Nick plopped down on her couch and turned the TV on to ESPN2. Chloe scored a spot next to him as he flipped through the sports channels and landed on a Wizards' game.

"I overheard Elio Zanetti talking at the Pearl, and he was having a heated conversation with someone. He said they haven't had an update from the police and that no one knows where Lorenzo's phone is," Jade said.

"Nope. We haven't found his phone or the truck keys. None of the valuables in the truck were stolen. It's a long process. Lab tests and the hundreds of interviews take time. Sebastian and some deputies are combing the area for camera feeds and witnesses. So far, nothing helpful. We'll run a spot on Crime Stoppers this week, hopefully to generate some fresh tips from the viewing public. Someone may have seen something."

When the coffee was done, Jade took two steaming mugs into the living room and settled on the couch beside Nick and Chloe. Nick had devoured his cannoli in seconds. "These crazy hours are killing me, but tomorrow we'll have dinner like real people."

"Are you still hungry? There's plenty of leftover pizza. It won't take but a minute to heat up."

"I'm good. Thanks," he said. "I need to head home and get some sleep."

"Sorry about the crazy hours. You should be having a quiet, off-season," she said.

"Not this year. Between the Love Channel's filming and all their drama and this, we can only hope for a cold winter where everyone stays home."

"And then it's beach season again," Jade said with a half-smile. "But first, we have the tacky lights tour in a hearse."

He snickered. "Because nothing says Christmas like a tour of the town in Todd's meat wagon," Nick said with a crooked smile.

They snuggled on the couch until Nick and Chloe's snores drowned out the basketball game. Jade pulled a soft blanket over everyone and switched the channel to an all-night marathon of true crime shows.

Chapter Eight

The next morning, Jade woke up on the couch to coffee gurgling in her kitchen. She blinked a couple of times to remember where she was and why someone was making coffee in her house.

"Morning, sunshine," Nick said, handing her a steaming mug. "I've got to head out. Gym and then back-to-back meetings. I promise I'll get out of there on time and be here at six for Amy's holiday extravaganza." Nick kissed her on the top of her head and patted Chloe.

When the door shut behind him, Jade folded the blanket and draped it over the back of the couch. She cringed at her reflection in the TV. "It's been a long time since I camped out on the couch. I need a shower. We might as well get this day started, too." Chloe didn't look too interested in seizing the day. Jade glanced at her dining room wall and noticed a new sticky note at the top of one column.

She moved into the next room for a better look. On a pink square, Nick had scribbled, "Pefferlys said the Zanetti boys were flirting with some girls with biker boyfriends in Seaport. We're looking into it." He drew a smiley face in the bottom corner. *Maybe there was a local connection after all. Or was he messing with her and her research?*

She cracked a smile and headed off for a hot shower.

About an hour later, Chloe and Jade pulled behind the store in the Wrangler.

With no part-timers today, Jade stayed busy with online orders and phone calls. The in-person visits tapered off after lunch, so she updated her newsletter and scheduled next week's social media posts.

Around four-thirty, she closed up shop, and she and Chloe headed home to find an outfit for tonight's double date. Three sweaters later, Jade landed on an oversized maroon tunic with black leggings and her thigh-high black boots. "Chloe, too bad I don't have a jaunty beret," she said, running a hot comb through her long red curls. Not a fan of hats, Chloe wandered off in search of a napping spot.

Jade touched up her makeup, fed Chloe, and checked Facebook while she waited for Nick, who pulled into the driveway at six on the dot. He had enough time to kiss her and step inside before "Dead or Alive" blared from Todd's horn outside. Jade sighed. She could almost hear her neighbors fussing about the hearse and all the noise in the neighborhood.

Jade grabbed her puffy coat and followed Nick to Todd's party machine. On the walk down the driveway, the curtains in the front window of the bungalow kitty-corner across the street fluttered. Then Mrs. Fairchild poked her head out the front door and scowled in their direction. Nick raised his hand and waved at the septuagenarian, who hurried back inside her house.

"I'm sure I'll have a message on my voicemail from her tomorrow," Nick said, holding the door for Jade.

The pair barely settled in the hearse's back seat before Todd sped down the driveway backwards. When he spotted Mrs. Swenson peeking out from her carport, he let loose with another round of the horn's song. Amy and Todd waved as another of Jade's neighbors stared daggers at the hearse's taillights.

"Hey, you guys. I'm so glad you could join us. I packed hot chocolate and Christmas cookies for our sparkly light tour. Do you all feel like getting dinner while we let full-on darkness approach?" Amy asked.

"Sounds good," Nick said. "Lunch was a stale doughnut and coffee."

"How about the Red Herring?" Amy asked. I want to try one of their po' boy sandwiches. Lisa said that they're to die for. I want to see how it ranks next to my favorite seafood restaurants from Boston. Maybe I'll do a blog post about it on the store's website."

"Bookseller and now food critic." Todd drove down Neptune Road, waving to everyone he spotted. "The catch of the day comes right off the boats at the Red Herring," Todd added.

"We'll see how it compares. I'll give my verdict after my taste test," Amy said.

Todd turned in his seat. "You sure the store's blog is the only one you're focused on?" he asked with a wink.

Amy scowled and then burst out laughing. "It's all I have time for. Who can keep up with all the gossip this town generates? I'm not the Mermaid. No matter how many times you ask." She pinched him lightly on the arm.

The foursome pulled into the gravel lot next to the weathered wooden building on the other side of Suggs Pier. "Looks like the next group is doing some setup for this week's fireworks." Todd pointed to the figures in black, moving boxes around on the fishing pier.

"It'll be interesting to see who the winner is," Amy said, hopping out and slamming the passenger door. "Maybe I'll add that to my blog, too."

Shedding coats and scarves, the two couples settled in a curved booth in the back corner of the seafood restaurant that has been a fixture on Mermaid Bay since as long as anyone could remember. Pine paneling covered all the walls, filled with mermaids, captain's wheels, shells, and framed posters from classic hardboiled mystery movies. Years of photos of famous guests and locals hung haphazardly in any open space among the other knickknacks.

After they perused the menu and ordered, Amy said, "So that confirms that you all have been checking out the new blog. So, who else is obsessed with whatever pops up next?" Her hand shot in the air, and she waved it around.

Nick raised one eyebrow.

"It's the center of a lot of conversations," Jade said. "And nobody's 'fessed up about who the author is. It definitely has to be a local."

Nick raised his eyebrow higher.

"See," Amy said, waving her phone at him. "The last big thing to cause tongues to wag was the revelation that Jared Carswell dumped Trish the Dish when she was expecting a rock of an engagement ring on her big b-day. She, I call the author a she because it sounds like one to me, and we all know it's a merrr-MAID. Anyway, she casually mentioned that the Pefferly girl was dating one of the Zanettis. I guess that's a big scandal in the fireworks world. Not sure who else cares about it or what all the hype's about. But I guess all will be revealed in due time. Can't wait to see what she drops next. Who knew so much was going on in a little place like Mermaid Bay?"

"I heard that Nell is beside herself and pulling out all the stops to find out who the blogger is. I saw her the other day, and all she did was fuss about the blogger and sloppy journalism," Todd said.

Amy opened her mouth but closed it again.

"So, we can probably mark Nell off the list since her journalistic integrity keeps her from stooping to a gossip blogger," Jade said.

Amy tried to stifle a laugh but gave up when a raucous belly laugh snuck out.

Nick gave Jade a side-eye, and the foursome dissolved into laughter.

"It'll be interesting to see what the Mermaid features next. Nell is going to be fuming if she gets scooped again. I hope the Mermaid writes something about me. You know you've arrived when you get roasted in the town's chatter blog." Amy's eyes sparkled with excitement.

The waitress interrupted with cheddar biscuits and drinks. "Your dinners will be out in a few minutes. "Sorry to butt in your conversation, but I heard you mention Mermaid Whispers. It's all our regulars can chat about lately. They've got a pool going about who's behind it."

"Who's in the running?" Nick asked.

"As of this morning, most money is on Nell, the collaborative team of Bernie and Cecil, and Josie Ellis."

Todd laughed. "I don't think Bernie and Cecil know what a blog is."

The waitress shrugged. "But Nell and Josie do. We're all waiting for the next installment." She retreated toward the bar.

"So, anything you can tell us about last weekend's unfortunate event?" Amy asked, lowering her voice and staring at Nick.

"We're waiting on some forensic reports and the autopsy. In the meantime, my guys are out hitting the pavement, chasing down every lead. It's a painstakingly slow process."

When he didn't continue, Todd added, "A bunch of the Zanetti guys were at my place after the murder. Their conversation, mostly about things they'd like to do to the killer and the Pefferlys, got a little loud. They didn't even try to hide their dislike for the other family. I had to glare at them a couple of times when it started bothering other guests. They weren't shy about speaking their minds. They said they were hanging around to see the Pefferly's show." Todd reached for a cheddar biscuit.

Before anyone could reply, the waitress and another waiter arrived with two large trays and passed heaping plates of food around the table. "If you need anything else, holler," the waitress said.

"Mmm. This is good," Amy said. "It rivals anything I had back home. I could get used to Southern cooking. Todd, how's your shrimp sandwich?"

"Just right," he said, stuffing French fries in his mouth.

"How's yours?" Jade asked Nick.

Nick nodded, dunking a biscuit in his clam chowder. "Those look stuffed full of seafood."

"You can never go wrong with shrimp tacos. Wanna bite?" Jade asked.

Nick shook his head, the four tucked into their dinners, and all conversation paused.

After passing on dessert and paying their tabs, the four headed to the hearse. Todd cruised through town and up and down the side streets to see all the creative decorations and light displays in the neighborhoods near the bay. Most of the decorations were lighted beach-themed displays with all kinds of colorful palm trees, mermaids, turtles, and dolphins. The town had gone all out on their decorations, many of which were synchronized to music.

Before Amy could serve snacks, Nick's phone rang, and everyone froze, hoping to catch a snippet of police business from his side of the call.

"Driscoll here. Yep. Got it. Be there as soon as I can." He disconnected and pocketed his phone. "Sorry to always be the wet blanket and to cut this short, but I need to get my truck and answer a call at the Pearl."

"Is everything okay with Ruby?" Jade asked, trying to push panicked, dark thoughts from her head.

"She's fine," Nick said.

Before he could elaborate, Todd interrupted with, "It's only two blocks from here. It'll be faster if we drop you off. You can get your truck later." Without waiting for an answer, he mashed the accelerator, and the hearse growled and leapt forward. Todd zipped through the neighborhood streets and took the corners faster than the neighborhood speed limit.

"Drive it like you stole it, baby," Amy said, adjusting the seatbelt that had locked in place across her chest. "Sheriff, you didn't hear that."

Todd turned the corner and screeched the back tires when he stopped in front of Ruby's. As Nick climbed out, he asked Jade, "You want my keys in case you need to move my truck?"

"Nah, I have a Jeep. Rarely do I get blocked in. I don't plan to go anywhere else tonight. It'll be fine where it is. Be careful." Jade looked out the side window. What's going on?"

"Ruby and some of the neighbors called in a fight. Thanks for dinner and the light tour." Nick kissed Jade. "I'll call you later." He slammed the car door and sauntered toward Sebastian and another deputy who were talking to a Zanetti and Pefferly in the soft glow of Ruby's porchlight. Everyone stopped and stared at the hearse at the end of the driveway. It didn't quite go with the Pearl's traditional white candles and holiday pineapple wreaths.

Todd moved the hearse in front of Mrs. Vanderbeek's house across the street. Within seconds, the parlor lights and the porch lights popped on. Jade thought she saw the front curtains move. She wondered if Todd's hearse would earn a mention in the next Mermaid Whispers.

"Roll down the windows. Let's see if we can hear anything. Hon, can you cut the engine?" Amy asked.

She leaned out the window and snapped some pictures. *Was she a concerned citizen, or could she be the blogger?* Jade waited to see if Amy would slip and reveal anything that would link her to the gossipy blog.

After almost forty-five minutes of no action, the trio started to squirm.

"It's more interesting on the crime stories on TV," Amy said with a huff. "I can only hear every third word from this distance, and my toes and fingers are freezing. Let's say we bag it. All they're doing is talking. I didn't even get to see a chase or a take-down. What a bust."

"Anybody want to see another street full of lights?" Todd asked.

"Nah, I'm over it for tonight," Amy said. "I need to go take a hot bath and put on my favorite slippers. I am half-frozen, and I'm from Massachusetts. That's saying something. Jade, you have to promise to tell us if Nick has anything exciting to report when he shows back up at your place. I can't believe these two families are still at it. What is so all fire important to cause this much trouble?"

Todd flipped his headlights on and revved the engine. Dodging some neighbors who had gathered around Ruby's front gate, Todd put the car in gear and rolled out of the neighborhood. "Anybody send Nell a tip?"

"Nah," Amy said. "It never crossed my mind."

"She's got a police scanner," Jade said. "See, her Fiat is parked over there."

Todd laughed as he mashed the accelerator, and the hearse leapt forward like Cruella's Coupe de Ville.

He pulled up next to Jade's mailbox. Jade said a silent thank you that he refrained from blasting his horn again. "Thanks, y'all for a fun evening. Sorry that Nick got called away." Jade picked up her purse.

"Again," Amy interrupted. "But at least our evenings end with all kinds of stories to tell. He's like a real-life superhero who's always called away to save someone or protect truth, justice, and the American way. It's good to see you guys. We'll try another night out after the holidays. Maybe something after New Year's?"

"Sounds like a plan. See ya," Jade said, shutting the door and hustling toward her bungalow. She could hear Chloe's barks from the porch. *I wonder which neighbor will comment first on Todd's hearse. I can see them peeping out their front windows.*

Not finding anything on TV and being too keyed up to sleep, Jade poured over her notes and updated them with the scraps of information she found out tonight. There was a whole lot of information that doesn't fit with anything else. Lots of puzzle pieces, but none of them reveal a clear picture of the killer.

About eleven-thirty, a knock on the door sent Chloe into full security mode. "Hey," Jade said after picking up the wiggly dog and letting Nick in.

"I hope I didn't wake you. I saw your light on. Sebastian dropped me off to get my truck. We've got to head to the station. Looks like another late night with a mountain of paperwork." He grinned, but Jade could see the fatigue in his eyes.

"Can I get you anything? I can pack you something to take with you," Jade said.

"Nah. I'm good. I'd like to get going, so I can get home before the sun comes up. That kid named Goose and his cousin Zeke went to Ruby's in search of the sister. The Zanettis denied that there were any Pefferlys there. It turned into a yelling-shouting match that ended up in Ruby's front yard. More excitement than that neighborhood has had since that battle down the road at Yorktown. Anyway, I suspect Zeke and company had reason to believe that Brianna was there."

"Ruby was beside herself. She likes things just so at the B and B," Jade said. "So, Brianna and Paolo were sneaking around under their families' collective noses."

"You the Mermaid Whisperer?" Nick cracked a smile.

"Nope. Just an interested bystander who had a dead body on her property. And I know Paolo and Brianna are a thing."

"Ruby and the Zanettis insisted that there was no Brianna there, but Josie told a different story. She said she saw her sneaking down the back stairs with a gym bag when the yelling started. She slipped out the back door, and Paolo left about fifteen minutes after she did. My guys are out looking for them. The Zanettis are sticking to their story that their guy wouldn't be with a Pefferly. Zeke said he was there to haul his sister back home and protect her honor."

Jade rolled her eyes. "Sounds like an interesting evening. You gotta love family dynamics."

"All in a day's work. Or night's work. I'll call you tomorrow. Love you." Nick kissed her and trotted toward his truck.

"Well, Chloe," Jade said, shutting the door behind him. "Our dates are never boring." *Short, but never boring.*

Chapter Nine

Jade settled in at her desk with a hot cup of tea to check the online orders. Light tapping on the front door interrupted her thoughts and sent Chloe on a tear through the store. The dog made her Frenchie whoooing noise as she galloped around in a circle.

Peeking out the window, Jade spotted a willowy blond on the porch. The ocean breeze blew the young woman's long hair as she stared at her phone.

Jade tried to hide her surprise at seeing Brianna Pefferly on her porch as she unlocked the door. "How may I help you?"

"Uh, hi. I heard about your store, and I thought I'd stop in since I had some time," the woman in the long coat and thigh-high stiletto boots said.

"Welcome. I'm Jade. This is 'Tis the Season, where it's Christmas all year. At last count, we had over three hundred trees. If you have any questions, please let me know."

"It's a neat little store," she said, looking around the lobby.

"This was a former beach cottage, and we've turned each of the rooms into displays. If you like the decorations, you can find them in the peach baskets at the base of the trees," Jade said.

"Sure, thanks," the blond said, smiling at Chloe.

"Aren't you with the fireworks competition?" Jade asked, hoping to get a conversation going.

She nodded and took the basket Jade offered. "I'm Brianna. I heard over at the coffee shop and the bookstore that you had a cute place. I wanted to stop by and check it out." The younger woman's gaze darted around the lobby like she was looking for someone.

"We had so much fun watching the fireworks show. Can't wait until Saturday," Jade said as Brianna snapped a selfie with the tall Christmas trees in the background.

"My family's pulling out all the stops for this weekend. It'll be spectacular. I think people will be really excited about what they see," Brianna said. "We have a good show. Hopefully, we'll dazzle the contest judges."

"Are you part of the fireworks extravaganza?" Jade asked, watching Brianna's facial expressions.

"I've done most of the jobs in our business through the years. That's what happens when you're born into a family like this. Right now, I do all the marketing and social media for the company. The boys handle the explosives. I had enough of that as a kid. My talents are better used elsewhere." Brianna pushed her long hair behind her ears and snapped more selfies.

"Didn't I see you with the one of the Zanettis on Saturday? I'm sure it was you," Jade said, prodding for information.

"Uh, no. Don't think so. I was really busy that night." She picked up her basket and strolled into the toy room.

Jade hoped she didn't roll her eyes or make a face at Brianna's denial. It's doubtful she would have admitted to being at the Pearl, either. Pulling out her phone, she tapped a quick message to Nick. **U still looking for Brianna? She's in the store shopping right now.**

Her phone dinged with his quick response: **Be there soon.**

About twenty minutes later, Brianna returned to the counter to check out at the same time as a foursome of seniors invaded the lobby with lots of giggles and chatter. Jade answered all their questions and gave them the ten-second tour and shopping baskets.

When the four women disappeared into the first showroom, Brianna inched toward the counter and set her plastic basket down as she continued to stare at her phone.

"Did you find everything all right? Jade asked, hoping to stall until Nick arrived.

"Yep. I've never been to a Christmas store before. I found some ornaments that looked like my cat Smokey. And one that looks like Cleopatra, my grandmother's Persian."

"Awww. These are cute," Jade said, holding up each ornament before she scanned the purchases. "Are you enjoying your time in Mermaid Bay?"

"It's okay. We visit a lot of towns with the firework shows. I'll kinda be glad to get back home for the holidays. Beaches aren't that much fun in the winter."

"Where's home?" Jade asked, deciding to double-wrap each of Brianna's purchases in tissue paper, trying to buy time for Nick to arrive.

"Philadelphia."

"I saw the Liberty Bell once on a school field trip and ran up the museum steps like Rocky."

Brianna stared at her blankly.

"The movie about the boxer from Philadelphia," Jade said. "You know, that's why everyone runs up and down the museum steps to see the statue of Sylvester Stallone."

After a long pause, Brianna said, "I must have missed that one." She tapped something in her phone and handed Jade a credit card.

When Jade couldn't drag out the conversation any further, she handed the young woman her receipt and card. "Thanks so much. I hope to see you again."

Brianna nodded and dropped her phone in her oversized, black purse. The bells on the door jangled as she pulled it shut.

Jade rushed to the window, hoping Nick was on his way. If not, at least maybe she could see where Brianna was headed. She let out a long puff of air when she saw Sebastian climb out of his SUV. Before Jade could step outside for snooping, the gaggle of seniors returned to check out.

After wrapping their purchases, Jade followed the last of the customers out to the porch. Brianna casually strolled down the sidewalk with Sebastian, watching her every move. When she approached Neptune Road, Sebastian turned to face Jade.

"Hey," he said. "Everything okay?"

She trotted down the stairs toward him. "Yep. I was going to ask you the same thing."

"All's well in Mermaid Bay." He looked over his shoulder and lowered his voice. "Had some questions for Ms. Pefferly about yesterday's altercation. She said she wasn't at the B and B and had no idea what I was talking about."

Jade raised an eyebrow. "Interesting. But why would someone say she was there? She denied seeing me after the fireworks when I talked to her and Paolo."

"Who knows? Maybe she was embarrassed. I know Josie didn't make it up, and she probably didn't get her days mixed up. But I guess that's always a possibility. I have a feeling Ms. Pefferly, and I will be talking again soon. Thanks for letting Nick know about this. I've been looking all over for her since yesterday."

"She didn't talk much inside except about her cat. And she didn't know who Rocky was,' Jade said with a chuckle.

"What? She's from Philly," Sebastian shadow-boxed and showed off his fancy footwork. He saluted and headed for his SUV.

Almost an hour later, Jade stood and stretched behind the counter as Patti held the door for a family with three small children to exit. "How's everything?" She stepped inside the store.

"It's been busy today," Jade said. "I'm glad you're here."

"Oh, good. I like it that way. Let me scooch out of my coat and put things away, and I'll be right back in a snap to help you."

Patti waltzed out from the back as the customer Jade was helping reached for her receipt.

When the door closed behind the woman, Patti whispered, "Have you seen the you-know-what this morning?"

Jade shook her head and pulled out her phone. "Nope. I've had a steady stream of people in here. And Sebastian stopped by. What's up?"

Patti leaned in closer and whispered, "Yesterday's tease and today's post hint that the murder of that poor Zanetti guy was linked to the families' feud and a big brawl over at the Pearl. Ruby will not like this. Is that why Sebastian was here?"

Jade nodded and skimmed through the latest on the blog site. "Hmm.

Interesting. Where is this person getting all this information? It seems like a small group of people would know what went on at the B and B. And according to Sebastian, most of them deny having anything to do with the fight."

"It could have been anyone. Lots of people have police scanners." Patti fanned her face with her hand. "These firework people have a lot of drama in their lives."

"Amy, Todd, and I were out with Nick when he got the call. We dropped him off and hung around Ruby's a bit. Nothing exciting happened while we were there," Jade said.

"He wasn't driving the death-mobile, was he?" Patti asked.

When Jade slowly nodded, Patti's hand flew to her mouth. "Well, that is kinda funny, I guess. Too bad the blogger didn't get a photo of the hearse parked in front of the Pearl. That would have been perfect for the sensational stories, even if Ruby would not have approved."

Jade rolled her eyes. "I hope no one took photos. Ruby would have a stroke. I promised Vivian a gift basket for the online contest the business council is hosting on its website. I need to assemble ours and take it to the library if you don't mind keeping things running here."

"Cool beans. Holler if you need anything." Patti hopped on the stool behind the counter.

Jade spent the next half hour gathering specialty snacks and ornaments and displaying them in a red basket. She added a firecracker and a mermaid ornament with wine glasses, mugs, a Christmas book, and Chloe's calendar. For this one, she chose an oversized, festive bow with sparkles to top it all off.

"Patti, I'll be back in a minute," Jade said.

"Sure," echoed from the lobby. "I'll text you if it gets crazy."

"You be good for Miss Patti." Jade pointed to the little dog in the puffy bed, and Chloe gave her a "who me" look.

Jade found a parking spot near the library and hip-checked the Wrangler's door as she juggled her purse and the giant basket. The four-building complex at the center of town housed the library, Sheriff's Office, jail, and town administrative offices. She had her choice of parking spaces. A normal day in Mermaid Bay. *Maybe all the excitement is over.*

An elderly man with a walking stick held the library door for her, and she made a beeline for the library's circulation desk. Before she could ask for the business council president, Jade heard a "Whoo-hooo" from the new book section.

Vivian hustled over and reached for the basket. "Oh, Jade, it's beautiful, as usual. Thanks for donating this for the contest. The lucky winner will be so excited. I'll email you a receipt for your donation. Look at all the goodies inside. This is fabulous."

"You're so welcome. How are things going?" Jade asked.

"All's quiet here, but I guess that's a good thing as we roll into the holiday season. We've had enough chaos to last us for a while." Vivian, usually high-strung and chatty, looked around like she was distracted.

"Everything okay with the fireworks contest?" Jade asked, trying to figure out why Vivian was out of sorts.

"Yep, the next bunch is getting their stuff ready. I hope we don't have any more altercations or worse…." Vivian's voice trailed off. "This wasn't at all what I expected when we planned this event. Those two families have caused ruckuses all over town. I wish they would act like adults."

"Brianna Pefferly came into the shop this morning," Jade said.

Vivian nodded and scanned the library like she was waiting for someone.

After an uncomfortable silence, Jade added. "Have you seen the new blog around town?"

Vivian's head jerked suddenly, and her countenance darkened. "Not you, too. I can't believe someone here would take jabs at our town and council activities. At least, Nell's gossipy column only comes out once a week. That blog thing is a constant barrage of garbage. Just what we need around here." She sighed loudly. "Uh, I've got to get back to work. Thanks again for the basket."

Jade strolled out wondering what had gotten into Vivian. Normally, she's raring to go on her latest project. *She seemed distracted today. Something's definitely bothering her. More than what usually bothers her.*

'Tis the Season's afternoon traffic slowed down, and Patti and Jade busied themselves with administrative tasks while Chloe spent her time snoring next to Jade's desk. Jade took a breath after finishing the sales tax, payroll, and new content for her newsletter. Then, she switched back to her Zanetti/Pefferly research. She listed all the players in her notebook and trolled social media for any additional information she could find.

"Everything's put away out front," Patti said, causing Jade to jump. "Oh, sorry. I thought you heard me cha-cha-cha in here. Need anything?"

"No, thanks. What exciting thing are you doing tonight?" Patti, who was always on the go, could give the Energizer Bunny a run for his money.

"Oh, I'm planning on a quiet weekend. Tonight is kitten and puppy yoga night. It's a fundraiser for the shelter. Then tomorrow, my sister and I are going shopping at the Outlets in Williamsburg. On Saturday, I'm having dinner with friends. Oh, I have a glass-blowing class on Saturday, too. And well, you know, the fireworks are Saturday night. Wouldn't want to miss the ones in the sky." Patti picked up her purse and winked. "What about you?"

Jade was exhausted after listening to Patti's packed itinerary. "Chloe and I plan to crash on the couch and take it easy. It'll be busy in here on Saturday with the artisans who will be in the multi-purpose room. I advertised it all over social media, so I hope there's a decent turnout."

"Sounds like fun. I'll try to stop by and check it out. See you next week." Patti flitted out the back door.

"Chloe, you about ready to head home, too?" The dog made a muttering sound and rolled over.

"I'll take that as a yes. I'm on a roll here with my information gathering. Let's go home. I want to see what else I can find on Paolo, Zeke, Brianna, and the rest of their gang. I'm doing a family tree to keep up with all the players. Oh, and I was pretty proud of myself. I looked up Mermaid Whispers on Domain.com and WhoIsThis.com. I couldn't see any personal information, but it did say the owner registered the site from Mermaid Bay."

Chloe raised her head and yawned.

"I know, it's not a ton of new information, but it confirms that the Mermaid is a local."

Chapter Ten

Early Saturday morning, Jade breezed through the store, unlocking doors and turning on all the Christmas trees. Yesterday, she and Bernie had spent the afternoon setting up tables in the multipurpose room to showcase local artisans and their holiday creations. She breezed in the back to make sure everything was ready to go for the guest vendors.

"Hopefully, all my advertising will work its magic, and we'll have a turnout today," Jade said to Chloe, who trotted behind her on the tour of the store.

As she set out trays of cookies and decorated the table with bouquets of candy canes, Bernie bounded through the front door with his hands full of shopping bags and an oversized gym bag. Bernie stopped suddenly in the doorway as Lorelei almost slammed into the back of him. She picked up the sack that he dropped as Neville pranced in like he was the guest of honor.

"Sorry about that, Lorelei. The alert on my phone went crazy, and I couldn't find it with all these pockets." He patted down his Santa suit and pulled his cell from one of the oversized coat pockets.

"Is everything okay, Bernie?" Lorelei asked.

"Yep. I'll be so glad when all this stuff is over. There's been way too much action at the pier." He looked around the lobby. "Hey, the snack table looks nice. I'll be back in a few for some samples."

"Morning, y'all. I'm hoping for big crowds today. Can I help you with anything?" Jade asked.

"Nope. I'm good. Running a tad late, but I'm raring to go," Bernie said with a fist pump.

"The vendors should be here by nine o'clock to set up their tables. I put name tags at each spot, so it should be easy to get them settled. They're responsible for their own sales, so it should be a low-maintenance event with lots of holiday cheer."

"I could do without the drama today. I had breakfast with the guys this morning, so I'm running a bit behind in terms of hair and makeup." Bernie chuckled and headed for the restroom in the back.

"What do you need me to do?" Her aunt asked, setting her red Coach bag behind the counter and stroking the black and white cat who had taken up residence by the cash register.

"How about you take care of greeting, and I'll jump in to help you after I get all the vendors situated? Tori will pop in at lunch for the afternoon shift. She's a little firecracker, and that'll give us a lunch break."

"I haven't seen Tori much since school started. This is her junior year, right? Wow, she'll be headed off to college soon. And I remember when she was born."

"I think she's still visiting campuses. She was really excited about Virginia Commonwealth University and James Madison," Jade said, restacking the flyers on the front counter.

"You'll have to get a new part-timer soon if she heads out of town for college."

The bells on the door jingled, and vendors with rolling carts and bags full of holiday crafts and jewelry started trickling in.

A half-hour later, Jade dropped onto the stool behind the counter.

"Whew. You look tired already. Are you okay? Were you out howling last night?" Lorelei asked as she leaned on the counter.

Jade laughed. "Not hardly. There was no rowdiness last night. Chloe and I had a quiet night doing research. But my eyes are burning from all the screen time." Jade blinked several times and suppressed a yawn. Everyone's set up and ready to sell their hand-crafted jewelry and ornaments. One lady has the prettiest tatted Victorian lace. You may want to wander back there and take a look at all the neat stuff. Oh, and Bernie's all transformed into the Jolly Old Elf. He's holding court with Neville by the fireplace."

"Neville, the Christmas cat. I love it." Lorelei's smile faded when she continued, "Any luck or the murder or your mystery blogger fronts?" Lorelei rummaged through her purse.

"Nope. Lots and lots of random facts, but so far, nothing stands out. Everything I've found points to the feud between the two families, but I can't find any neon arrows pointing to any one person. I did find out that the Mermaid Whispers person registered his or her blog from Mermaid Bay, so our blogger is someone who lives around here."

Lorelei raised one perfectly sculpted eyebrow and paused. "How did you find that out?"

"There's a website that shows where the URL is registered," Jade said as a group of visitors tromped through the front door. "Welcome to 'Tis the Season. We have over three hundred decorated trees, and today, we have thirty artisans in our multipurpose room showing off their handmade holiday specialties. And make sure to swing by and chat with Santa." Jade handed each person a basket. "Please let us know if we can help you with anything."

When the guests made their way toward the display rooms, Lorelei leaned over and whispered, "Who knew you could find out all that information online? And what else did you uncover about this blogger? Who is it? Everyone is dying to know."

Shrugging her shoulder, Jade replied, "I have no idea. Maybe she will reveal an identity soon."

"You think it's a woman?" Her aunt had an intense look on her face as she stared at her niece.

"I'm going with the 'mermaid' in the name," Jade said. "Just an assumption on my part."

"I think the mysteriousness is making it more popular than it would be otherwise. Interesting way to create a buzz," her aunt remarked, pulling out a small notebook and pen from her purse. "Plus, the person seems to have eyes and ears everywhere."

"And the teases that she drops ahead of the posts create a stir," Jade added.

"Everybody I've talked to is dying to know who it is and what she'll write about next."

"Amy's the only one I know who wants to be mentioned on the site. Everyone else is trying to fly under the radar," Jade said.

Lorelei laughed as she jotted down a note and returned her small notebook to her purse.

A little before noon, Tori Thomas flitted in the front behind a group of women in ski parkas. When the shoppers headed to the multipurpose room, Tori approached the counter. "Hi, Jade. Hey, Lorelei. What do you all want me to do?" Her brown ponytail swung as she bounced on her toes.

"How about you help Lorelei up here? She may want a break for lunch. I'll cruise through the store and check on the folks back there and Bernie."

"Perfect. Thanks for the extra hours. I love soaking up all the holiday feels here," Tori said, taking Jade's place behind the register.

"What's new with you?" Lorelei asked as Tori stowed her bag.

"Not much. I have a French test next week and a paper due before the holiday break. It's been pretty busy this semester. Oh, I'm on the ring dance committee, and next semester, I'm joining the newspaper staff. So stoked." She paused and looked around. "Speaking of writing articles and stuff, have you seen that new Mermaid Bay blog? All my friends are keeping an eye on it to see if she talks about any of our teachers or friends' parents," the teen said with a twinkle in her eyes. "We're all waiting for a juicy story."

Jade waved and left the pair to talk about the Mermaid as she headed toward Bernie's Santa Land in the next room. A long line encircled his throne, and it grew exponentially as Bernie spent time talking to each child. Jade caught his eye and mouthed, "Need anything?"

He waved and said, "Thanks, Jade. We're having a jolly time back here. Just hanging out with all these good boys and girls. I haven't seen anyone on my naughty list today."

"Did you hear that!" a little blond boy in line yelled as he tugged on his dad's sleeve.

Jade smiled and wended her way through the store's showrooms to the large room in the back that she added for classes and demonstrations. All the tables were decorated in red, green, gold, and white, and they sported all kinds of wares, from jewelry to handmade decorations. She walked through, greeted all the sellers again, and snapped a series of photos.

Stopping at a table all decked out in snowmen, she bought a pair of earrings. Eyeing cute dog and cat ornaments at the next table, she bought one of a white dog that looked like Chloe. Gathering her purchases, she lapped the room again and headed to her office when no one needed anything. There were always plenty of store tasks to do, even if the internet called her like a siren to do additional research on the firework families.

At five o'clock, Jade sunk into her office chair after her final walk-through of the store. All of the vendors had packed up, and the crowds had thinned out. Tori, Bernie, and Lorelei took off, and the store suddenly fell silent.

"Yay, Chloe. Another big day, and the vendors all seemed happy. That means great sales. We had a fabulous day. Let's go change into something warm for tonight."

Chloe heard the "G" word and toddled to the back door, waiting for her friend with thumbs to open it.

At home, Jade fed Chloe, made a peanut butter and honey sandwich, and poured herself a glass of milk. She stared at the suspect wall in her dining room when an idea flashed across her thoughts. She pulled out a black marker and a stack of sticky notes. Jade rearranged the colorful squares and added some new ones, but no a-ha moments caught her attention. She chewed on her bottom lip and looked for any hint or connection that would reveal the killer or even a key suspect. The two families were at odds and went to great lengths to annoy or attack the other. Brianna and Paolo were dating. Elio's phone conversation sounded menacing, and there was a fight on the beach and at the Pearl. Jade stood and rearranged the colorful squares. Not spotting anything else, she retreated to her bedroom to change into a thick sweater for an evening on the beach in December.

After she wrangled Chloe into her Christmas sweater, Jade added their light-up decorations and grabbed a blanket. "Let's see who's on the beach."

The pair made their way down the path and across the sand toward the pier as dusk settled over the bay. The sky had an ombré look at the horizon with gray, navy, and purple fading into each other. The briny smell of the bay danced on the breeze and reminded Jade that this was home with the flood of childhood beach memories it stoked.

Walking all the way to the pier this time, they picked their way around folks staking out prime viewing areas in the sand. Jade spotted Nick next to some barricades. Chloe trotted over and yipped at the sheriff until he picked her up for cuddles.

"How's everything going?" Jade asked. "I hope there were no problems this time."

"Nothing out of the norm. I had to bring in some guys on OT to help with traffic. People parked in every available spot, and some of the neighbors went ballistic when they blocked driveways or parked in their yards. There is always something. You here with Amy?" He set Chloe down in the sand, and she danced around his shiny, black boots.

"Nope. Haven't seen her today. Chloe and I plan to stake out the perfect spot. You need anything?"

"I'm good. Thanks," he said. "Wanna get dinner tomorrow? I should be fully recovered if I get to sleep in past breakfast. There's no telling when we'll get out of here tonight." Nick scanned the growing crowd.

"Excuse me, Officer, what time does the show start? I have to run back to my car for something, and I don't want to miss it," a man with round glasses and a toboggan said.

"About eight-thirty," Nick said, turning to face the man.

"See ya later." Jade picked up Chloe to keep her from underfoot in the growing crowd. Jade stepped carefully around beach chairs and blankets. It was almost time to pull out her flashlight. As she paused and looked for a spot to spread her blanket, Jade sensed someone behind her. A grab at her shoulder caused her to squeal and squeeze Chloe.

Jade turned to see Amy jump back. "Sorry," she said, taking a moment to catch her breath. I've been chasing you across the beach. You didn't respond when I called your name."

"Sorry. I must have been lost in thought. And all the people noises must have drowned you out. Where are you sitting?"

"Todd's deck filled up before I could stake out my claim. No girlfriend perks tonight. I set up a blanket in the sand over there. Come on." She waved and jogged off toward the base of the hot dog stand's deck.

Chloe curled up on Amy's blanket next to the picnic basket, and Jade plopped down beside her. When the wind shifted off the water, Jade draped her blanket over her legs, and Chloe buried underneath to snuggle.

"So, what's new with you?" Amy asked.

"Busy day. But a good day."

"I saw your parking lot. Jam-packed. I tried to get over there to see Bernie in full regalia, but I had a steady stream of folks today, too. Gotta love holiday shoppers. I'm planning one more big marketing push for next weekend. So far, it's been a great season. I'm liking my new role as bookseller to the beachgoers."

"You taking a break for the holidays?" Jade asked, watching hordes of people stream in across the dunes.

"Sort of. Todd promised that he'd help me move some of the heavy bookcases in the back. I want to open up the area, let in some light, and add a game and puzzle section. I plan for us to paint, too, but Todd doesn't know that yet. Shhh! Don't spoil the secret. But my plans aren't all work. Todd also agreed to go to Massachusetts with me, so that should be fun. Road trip with the boyfriend. Our first."

Like last week, the speakers crackled, and Bernie's voice boomed from the pier. "Ladies and gentlemen. Children of all ages welcome to the second weekend of Mermaid Bay's Fireworks Extravaganza. Tonight's contestant is the Pefferly Fireworks Company. So sit back and enjoy the show."

"No marching band this week," Amy said, sinking back on her elbows.

Fum, fum, fums sounded as someone lit the first salvo of shots. Colorful lights blossomed over the bay, and the crowd ooohed and ahhhed as the fireworks seemed to melt into the water.

An eerie silence fell over the beach. When nothing else happened, the crowd started fidgeting and talking, and then booms echoed over the water.

"Something's off with their timing," Amy said. "Last week, it was constant noise and flashes. I wonder if something is wrong or whether it's supposed to be like this."

"It does seem odd," Jade said, staring at the pier.

"It's not as polished as last week's show," Amy mused.

They watched the rest of the show with lots of pauses and silence. It was too herky-jerky to look like it was planned that way.

After a finale of about fifteen fireworks, the crowd paused, waiting to see if there was more. The only sounds were the waves hitting the sand and rustles from the crowd. Then the speakers crackled again, and Bernie announced, "Thank you, Pefferlys. And thanks, everyone, for coming out tonight. Be safe on your ride home. See you next Saturday for the final holiday show. Same place. Same time."

"Well, that was interesting," said Amy. "No wow factor with this one. Lots of fits and starts. And the message that airplane was dragging last week didn't come true."

"Thanks for letting us hang out with you," Jade said, standing and folding her blanket. "It did seem shorter than last week's show. And you're right. There wasn't anything that was stunning."

"I'm off to see if Todd needs any help closing up and then work on my next blog post," Amy said, shaking the sand out of her blanket.

Jade's head jerked toward her friend, and she froze, dropping one end of her blanket in the sand. She stared at Amy as she stooped to pick up her blanket.

"What, oh no, not that. I'm creating a blog on my website to build up interest in my events and the store." She laughed as she stood and gathered her things. "Nope. Sorry. I'm not the Mermaid. My blog is about cool, new reads, local authors, and anything book-related that I can think of. Gossip and scandal aren't my cups of tea. I don't know enough people here yet, so I'd have to make up most of the stories."

Jade laughed and grabbed the edge of Amy's blanket to help fold. "You're too funny. I'm gonna head home and see if I can find anything new on social media. Chloe, we'll take the long way home through town this time."

"Are you strolling home, or are you doing research? Good luck. We're counting on you and Nick to solve this thing. I hope you figure it out before the new year."

"It was really dark last week. The sidewalk may be a better option this time. But thanks for the vote of confidence." Jade picked up Chloe and hiked through the sand toward the lights of the pier. Hundreds of people tramped through the parking lot as she made her way to the pier's entrance and the traffic barricades. No Nick or deputies in sight. Everyone must be on traffic duty now.

Squeezing past one of the wooden sawhorses, the pair walked toward the decking. The chilly breeze whipped her hair around and caused her to pull her coat tighter around her. Spotting Bernie and some of his friends by the tackle shop, she hustled over and stood with her back to the wind.

"Hey, Jade. Whatcha doing out here? Enjoy the show? What there was of it," Bernie said, still wearing the pants to his Santa suit and a thick wool coat over top.

Looking over her shoulder, she replied, "It was okay. It wasn't as exciting as the one last week," she whispered as the Pefferlys packed crates and boxes at the other end of the pier. The men tossed and stuffed equipment into any available container.

"Hey, Jade," Cecil yelled as he approached. "You missed all the fun before this shindig got going. We had to go get Nick." Jade's eyebrows formed a "v" as he continued, "Some of the fuses didn't go off when the Pefferlys lit them. That tall guy—I think his name is Zeke—swore up and down that he checked everything. I thought he and that Goose guy were about to get into a fistfight. And the grandfather was livid. He was ranting that the two guys ruined their shot at a lucrative contract."

Bernie paused a moment and watched the crowd. "They started screaming that they'd been vandalized. Nick came over to investigate, and Cecil, here, checked out the new cameras we installed. And guess what?"

Before Jade could answer, Cecil, who was as round as Bernie, butted in. "Bupkis. Nada. The only people who had been on the pier since the evening before were the Pefferlys, me, and Bernie. And we didn't go near any of their equipment. We stayed in the shack where it was warm. So, unless something crawled out of the ocean, no one messed with their stuff."

"It's a shame that it happened during their part of the contest," Jade said.

"After all that bragging and boasting," Cecil muttered, patting Chloe on the head. "They couldn't put their money where their mouths were. I wonder if that Mermaid Whisperer will have something to say about the lack of sparkle. Today's show was a little disappointing, if I do say so myself. I hope next week is better," Cecil said, heading into the shack-like office. "I gotta lock up. See you all later."

"We've got to head home, too," Jade said. "See you next week, Bernie."

"I'll be there with bells on. Tell Patti to keep the cookies coming," her Santa yelled, patting his ample midriff.

Jade made her way to the sidewalk and mingled with the thinning crowd. By the time they got to the cottages past Hot Diggity Dogs, there was no one else out on the sidewalk. When a blast of wind hit, she hugged Chloe closer and pulled out her phone flashlight.

Hearing footsteps behind her, she paused and turned around. Nothing moved in the shadows. She waved her phone around. The white beam seemed to get swallowed up by the night. Jade shook it off as beach noises and picked up her pace. Chiding herself for being so jumpy, she stopped suddenly and swung around when she heard a strange noise.

"Hey," a guy said, and she almost jumped out of her shoes.

She flashed her phone at him, and Elio, the Zanetti from Ruby's garden and Paolo's cousin, covered his eyes with one elbow. She lowered her phone.

"I've been chasing you for three blocks. Can you hold up for one minute?"

Taking a step backward, she watched his face. *What did he want with her?*

He took a step closer. Not sure if she should scream or run, she waited a heartbeat to two to see what he would do next. The seconds seemed like they dragged on forever. Before she could respond, he continued, "You dropped these back at the pier. I thought you might need them." The thirty-something handed her a ring of keys.

"Thank you," she said sheepishly. "They must have slipped out of my pocket." Jade could feel the heat flashing in her cheeks. She hoped it was too dark for him to notice. *How embarrassing. At least she didn't scream or kick him before she found out what he really wanted.*

"No problem. I have to get back. I know the family's whooping and celebrating our victory over the Pefferlys this evening. What an amateur performance." He jogged across the street and headed back toward town.

Nerves took over even though it was an innocent encounter. Blood coursed through her veins, and her skin prickled as they race-walked the rest of the way home. Jade didn't relax until she slammed and locked her front door. She peeked out the front window several times to make sure no one else was out there.

Chapter Eleven

J ade and Chloe trekked to the store before the sun came up. She didn't sleep well again and decided it was better to do something than toss and turn. After downing an espresso and filling all the overnight orders, she settled in to check her social media sites, and of course, she had to take a peek at the Mermaid Whispers. The mystery blogger was at it again with details on the Pefferly/Zanetti feud. *Maybe there was some truth to the rivalries between the two companies. Elio and his team were hanging around town and celebrating the Pefferly's misfortunes.*

A "Whooo hooo" behind her made her jump. "I see you're following the work of the mysterious one, too," Patti said, standing behind Jade's chair. "There seems to be something almost every day. And I see you filled all the orders. Miss Productivity today. Anything else you want me to work on?"

"I put some catalogs on the front counter. There are some new collections for next year if you want to go through and highlight what you think our shoppers would like."

"Perfect," Patti squealed. "Let me gas up on some java juice, and I'll get right on it."

Jade scrolled through her Facebook and Instagram feeds and scheduled some posts for the upcoming week with photos of Bernie and the artisans.

Patti's infectious laugh trickled into the back room. Jade smiled. She, Bernie, and Chloe were perfect ambassadors for the store. She was glad to have them on her team.

A tap, tap, tap interrupted Jade's musings. It repeated before she could get to the back door without tripping over Chloe, who suddenly turned into an attack Rottweiler.

Jade opened the door, and a bloody Goose Jennings, Zeke Pefferly's cousin, stumbled in. "Are you okay? Here, sit down in this chair," she said, guiding him to the empty desk.

"I'm fine. I need to clean up and a minute to catch my breath." His gaze darted around the office.

"You need an ambulance," Jade said, pulling out her phone and closing the top part of the Dutch door.

"No, don't do that. I'll be okay. It's a little scratch." He wiped his lip with the back of his hand.

"A little scratch? Hardly. Here, let me get you a towel. Your temple and your nose are bleeding. And your eye's all swollen. What happened?"

"And the back of my head, but who's counting," Goose said, taking the dishcloth she offered.

"Do you want some ice?"

"No, but a drink of water would be good. Or something stronger if you have it. My mouth's bleeding, too," he slurred, moving his tongue around.

"What happened?" she repeated as blood dripped on her floor. She handed him a bottled water from the fridge. "I'm calling an ambulance."

"I don't want the hassle." He tried to stand but sat quickly back in the chair.

"No arguments. You're white as a ghost," she said, punching in 911. "Hi, this is Jade Hicks at 'Tis the Season. I have a man in my back office, a Goose Jennings, who needs some medical attention. He stumbled into my store, and he's bleeding from some head wounds. Yes. Yes, he's conscious. Please ask them to come to the back door. It'll be easier. Thanks. We'll be here."

She disconnected and glared at the man. "What did you get into?"

"I'm fine. I really need a ride to the hotel. I tried calling Brianna and Tank, but nobody's answering this morning. I'll be okay after some aspirin and a hot shower. And maybe some TLC." He winked and smiled a smarmy grin.

Ignoring his flirting, Jade said, "Just let the EMTs check you out. Did you get attacked?"

"Something like that. It was a little misunderstanding. You should see the other guy. Just kidding. It's no big deal. Hardly any blood at all. It looks worse than it is. I'll be fine with a wipe and a couple of bandages. And maybe a cute nurse."

Jade pursed her lips. "It wasn't one of the Zanettis, was it?"

"Uh, no. Though I should get medieval on them after what they did to us last night." He leaned over, and blood dripped on the floor and his white sneaker.

Jade pulled out her phone again and tapped a quick text to Nick.

"Where are your brothers again? And Brianna?" Jade asked.

"We're staying at the hotel over in Seaport. The big pink one with the seahorse out front. I don't know where they are. And they're my cousins. My Uncle Daniel is Zeke and Brianna's dad. I'm an only child." He leaned forward again and held his head with both hands.

The faint sound of a siren got louder, and Jade picked up Chloe and opened the back door. She waved with one hand to get their attention.

As two EMTs sprinted inside and surrounded Goose as the dividing door opened, and Nick stepped into the office and took off his hat.

After poking and prodding and two bandages later, the male EMT said, "You need to be transported to the hospital. You could be concussed."

"I'm fine. I need a ride back to my hotel. I'm good as new now. Could youse guys drop me where we're staying?" Goose said.

"We really recommend that you get checked out further," the female EMT said. "We're not in the ride-sharing business. We only provide trips to the hospital. Rules, you know. I think you need to get checked out."

"Is that your professional opinion?" Goose asked.

"Go with them, and I'll ensure you get a ride back to your hotel," Nick added.

"I'm fine. Really." Goose stood up and paused. What color he had in his face faded, and the EMT guided him back down to the chair.

"That's why you need to get checked out. Come on. It won't take that long." The female EMT batted her eyes, and Goose returned to his flirty mode.

"If you'll ride in the back with me." Goose showed almost all of his pearly whites.

"Deal. Now, let's get you transported." She eased him to his feet, and they guided Goose out the back door as Jade mopped up the blood on the floor and the chair with some paper towels.

"What happened?" Nick asked as the back door closed.

"I heard a knocking, and he almost fell inside when I opened the door. He said it was all a misunderstanding. I called y'all when he started dripping blood on my floor and slurring his words." She pulled out the antibacterial wipes and scrubbed the area.

"Who is it?" Nick asked, jotting notes in his pocket notebook.

"Goose Jennings. Not sure what his real name is. He's a cousin of the Pefferlys."

Nick nodded. "Anything else I should know?"

"Not really. He was cagey and didn't speak highly of the Zanettis. He said they did something to them on Saturday night. But the altercation wasn't with them. That's all he divulged. No other details."

"Thanks," Nick said, pocketing his notes and pen. "Time to head on over to the hospital to talk to him. And if that doesn't yield much, I'll get someone to check security cameras. Maybe he'll want to chat on the ride to his hotel." Nick's mouth formed a straight line.

Jade booted up her laptop and scanned through to see if her cameras caught anything.

Nick leaned in and watched over her shoulder, and she caught a whiff of his spicy cologne. Her camera captured Goose ambling up the sidewalk. She sped back through the feed. The only thing that looked odd was about a fifteen-second blur on the camera facing the street. Slowing it down and moving frame-by-frame, it looked like two cars racing down Neptune Road at about two in the morning. She made copies of both clips and emailed them to Nick.

The feed on her other camera was a black square. "That's strange," she said as Nick followed her to get a stepladder.

Outside, she looked up at the camera. "No light on it," she said as Nick climbed up to examine the device.

"Looks like someone shot out your camera with a pellet gun," he said.

She made a face. "Great. I guess I'll be ordering a new one."

Back inside the office, she headed for her laptop to see when the camera stopped working. Jade scrolled back through the camera's feed. In the wee hours of Saturday morning, two shadowy figures trotted around the side of the building to the back door. They looked around, and one of them jiggled the doorknob. The taller of the two motioned, and they jogged into the grass, where he turned and shot out her camera. No more pictures.

"Sent you what I have," Jade said, letting out a heavy sigh. "It's hard to identify the men from the feed, especially since they had hats on that covered most of their faces."

"Thanks. Gotta run. I'll call you later." Nick hurried out the back door as Jade refilled her coffee mug.

He waved to Patti, who looked like she got caught with her hand in the cookie jar. She stopped writing something in her notebook and pretended to look at her nails. *It was odd that she didn't fly in here when all the commotion started. Interesting.*

"Let's check on our insurance and find a new camera," Jade said to Chloe, who was not concerned in the least bit about the store's security equipment or deductibles. Patti returned to the front and didn't ask about Zeke or what happened. *Very out of character.* Jade took a deep breath and tried to push thoughts of burglars to the back of her mind. *Someone tried to get into my store.*

After an hour of searching online for a replacement camera, Jade rested her head on her folded arms.

"Why so glum," Patti asked when she drifted in the back for water.

"Someone shot out my back camera."

"Oh, wow. Do you think it was an attempted break-in?" Patti's eyes widened, and her mouth formed a small "o."

"Possibly. They pulled on the back door and then destroyed my camera. There was no sign of any other damage. I'm hoping it was kids being stupid."

"Any idea who it was?" Patti asked.

Jade shook her head. "It was dark. There were two figures in the shadows. I sent the clips to Nick. Maybe he and his guys can figure it out."

"What was up with the ambulance and Nick's visit? I had a bunch of people come in all at once, and I couldn't pop back here to check. Everything okay?"

"One of the Pefferlys knocked on the back door, and he was covered in blood. He was evasive about what happened, but a cute EMT talked him into getting checked out at the hospital. At first, he wanted me to drive him back to his hotel."

Patti's hand flew to her mouth. "What else is going to happen around here? First, the camera." Patti tsk-tsked. "I used to feel safe in this town. Now, marauding people are shooting out cameras and beating people up. Not to mention what happened to that poor Zanetti kid earlier. Mermaid Bay isn't like it used to be."

"Nick would say that the crime rate isn't really that higher than normal, and it's pretty low when you compare it to the towns around us. You know his mantra. Be alert and aware of your surroundings," Jade said.

Patti's mouth curled at the corners. "I do. But I'm always looking over my shoulder. And I took that self-defense class at the gym. Maybe Vivian and the council business council should sponsor a refresher course for all the business owners. Safety is everyone's business."

The bell on the door announced a visitor, and Patti hustled out front. "Hey, Lorelei."

Her aunt popped her head into the office. "How're things? I think I may have left my phone here. What was all the excitement?"

Lorelei rummaged through the drawers of the other desk. "You haven't seen my phone, have you?" She paused and stared at her niece. "Are you okay?"

Jade shook her head. "One of the Pefferlys showed up. He looked like he had been in a fight, and I called an ambulance."

"What happened?"

"His mouth, nose, and head were bleeding all over the place. He was vague about the details."

"Which one was he?" her aunt paused from her rummaging and stared at Jade.

"The one they call Goose. He's Zeke and Brianna's cousin."

Lorelei nodded slowly. "I guess I didn't leave my phone here. It might be in another purse. Since Steve and I were out and about, I thought I'd check here. Ciao." Her aunt waved over her shoulder. *Lorelei and Patti have been acting strangely. I need to poke around and see what's going on.*

"See ya," Jade said as her aunt slipped into the lobby. Jade's phone buzzed and distracted her. "Hi, Nick. How's Goose?"

"Not very forthcoming with any details. He keeps saying it was a misunderstanding, and he's not interested in an investigation or pressing charges. Do you need a copy of the report to file a claim on your camera?"

"Yep. Can you send it to me? Chatting with the insurance company is on my to-do list. There seems to be a lot of the wrong kind of interest in my store lately. Not sure if it's all related to the Goose thing or the murder."

"Dinner tomorrow?" he asked.

"Sounds good. How about if I make lasagna?" Jade peeked at her Facebook newsfeed.

"The meat kind?" Nick asked.

"Just for you."

"And garlic bread. I'm not in the mood for that eggplant stuff. My mom keeps trying out different vegetarian options on me. Don't forget the extra cheese, and I'll bring dessert. See ya after work. Love you." Nick said.

"Love you, too," she said, disconnecting.

Chapter Twelve

The Goose and camera incidents tickled at the back of Jade's thoughts throughout the entire workday. As soon as the last customer scooted out the door, she closed the store, took Chloe home, and fed her. *I feel like all this stuff is related to the Pefferlys and the Zanettis. I need a way to get some more information. Let's see if this works.* Jade changed clothes, dabbed on some extra makeup, and ran a hot comb through her long red curls. Selecting a tailored jacket and a chic purse to match her tall boots, Jade drove to the Sandcastle Motel in Seaport. The flamingo-pink high-rise dominated a corner between the main thoroughfare and the bay.

Scoring a parking spot near a privacy fence that separated the hotel's parking lot from the mini-golf course next door, Jade checked her makeup one last time. A quick glance at the back of the lot at the four trucks and two logoed trailers confirmed that the Pefferlys were still in town. Jade dialed the front desk and asked for Goose Jennings. After four rings, she got the standard guest room voicemail message. Clearing her throat, she said in her breathiest voice, "Hi, Goose. This is Jade Hicks from 'Tis the Season. I'm calling to see how you're feeling today. I wanted to make sure you were okay after what happened."

Jade disconnected and waited. When there was no return call, she climbed out of the Jeep to see what she could find inside the hotel. The sliding glass doors to the lobby swooshed open, and a wave of heat and antiseptic smells greeted her. She cruised through the lobby filled with mid-century couches tucked away behind giant palm trees that had seen better days. The desk clerk stared at his phone while a handful of guests wandered around the lobby. Cruising toward the bar, she spotted Goose on a barstool, staring at a basketball game on a large TV with no sound.

Fluffing her long curls, she slid onto the stool next to him. "Well, hi, Goose. Long time no see," Jade said.

He turned and stared. He grinned and slowly nodded. "Hey. I remember you." His swollen face sported medical tape across the bridge of his nose and a couple of scary-looking stitches in his top lip. A couple of Frankenstein stitches poked out of his temple where his blondish hair had started to recede.

The bartender in a bright pink polo approached. "What'll you have? Our drink specials are over there on the chalkboard." He pointed haphazardly toward the faded board near the door.

Jade glanced at the smudged board that listed five-dollar shots and frozen margaritas before six. "A ginger ale to start," Jade said. Turning toward Goose, she cooed, "How are you feeling?" She patted his arm for good measure.

"Uh, better. It's nothing." He took a long swig of his beer. "You should see the other guy." He laughed loudly. His glance darted around the almost empty bar.

"You never did say how it happened? Or who the other guy was." Jade reached for the glass the bartender handed her.

"Just a little altercation. It's over. Uh, nothing worth harping on. Let's talk about something fun. What are you doing tonight? It doesn't seem like a hopping place," he said, changing the subject.

"I'm meeting friends after work, and I was surprised to see you sitting over here." She batted her eyelashes.

"This place doesn't seem to be a hip place. Everything's pink. From what I can tell, this whole place is dead," Goose mused. He looked around again at the empty tables.

"It's off-season," Jade added. "I'm surprised that you all are still in town."

"Yup. The team wanted to stay and see the thing on Saturday night to see all the competition. It's winter, and since we have no shows booked until New Year's, we decided to stay for a little R and R. Plus, I rode down with them. Can't leave if my ride isn't ready to go." He let out another belly laugh. When she didn't join him, he continued, "Might as well hang out at the beach before heading back to Philly, even if it is the dead of winter. Hopefully, we'll be back here next summer when the weather is nice and there's stuff to see, like bathing suits instead of coats. I like summer at the shore."

"By the way, how is Brianna doing? She came by my store last week. She seemed a little distracted," Jade said.

Goose paused for a moment. "Who knows with her. She does what she wants. Even if it's stupid."

"Shopping is stupid?" she asked, putting on her best puzzled look and hoping she appeared offended.

"Uh, no. Not shopping. I meant she's normally a dingbat. She's not known for making good decisions. But she's her dad's favorite, so she does what she wants, and everyone keeps quiet. Me and Zeke don't like her hanging out with that Paolo kid. He's bad news. And he better watch out if he knows what's best for him. We'll show him who's boss. Trouble. All the Zanettis are. They messed up our show this weekend. They're trying to ruin our chances of landing that huge contract. Big disaster. We've declared war. We'll get our revenge. Just you wait." He paused and looked around the room like he was expecting someone. "Be back in a sec."

Jade watched him stagger through the restaurant toward the back. He used nearby empty chairs to steady himself on the short walk.

Movement in the doorway caught her attention. Zeke Pefferly watched Goose's progress. He ran a hand through his longish hair. When Goose rounded the corner, Zeke wended his way through the empty tables to where his cousin had disappeared around the corner.

Dropping enough cash to cover her drink and a tip on the bar, she picked up her purse and followed the other two. Pausing outside the restroom doors, she heard muted voices. With nowhere to hide, she scooted closer to the women's room in case she needed to duck inside for a quick escape.

"Shut up. You're always running your mouth. There's no leaving this alone," came from behind the men's room door. "You said you had this. Why do I trust you?"

Jade didn't catch the mumbled reply, but she clearly heard, "You're going to help me. You have to. We can't sit back and let it happen."

The door muffled the reply. Their conversation sounded like the adults in a Charlie Brown cartoon. Jade strained to pick up any more of the conversation.

Another waiter in a pink shirt strode down the hall and pushed the bathroom door open. Before ducking out of the line of sight, Jade heard Zeke say, "Be smart about it," before the door swung shut.

Jade hesitated, trying to figure out what to do next.

The men's room door flew open and banged against the wall. Jade casually wiped her hands and pretended she was exiting the room across the hallway.

Zeke stormed out toward the restaurant without even a glance in her direction. Goose toddled out and took more than four or five heartbeats to remember where his barstool was.

Jade arrived back at the bar in time to witness Goose's multiple attempts to climb on the stool. *The third try's the charm.*

"Everything okay?" she asked, sidling up next to him. "You were gone a long time. I got worried. I thought you ditched me."

"Uh, nothing like that. I'm fine. I told you it was no big deal. Zeke needs to get off my back and let me take care of things. Dang micromanager." A shrill ring interrupted his rant, and he fumbled with the holster on his belt for his phone. "What? You serious?…I saw you, like five minutes ago. I mean, we literally just talked. Okay. Fine." He drained what was left of his beer and threw some money on the bar. "It was nice to see you. Gotta go," he said, sliding off the stool and heading for the lobby.

Jade slipped out of the bar and watched Goose board an elevator on the other side of the lobby. When the door closed, she stepped closer to see if she could figure out where he was headed. With only arrows above the door, she had to settle for up and no indication of what floor he was visiting.

Chapter Thirteen

The Goose and Zeke conversation at the bar created more questions than answers. Jade paused on the sidewalk and then turned toward the boardwalk. The ocean, always her place of peace, called her. This was her spot to think and to block out the rest of the world. She walked along Seaport's cement boardwalk as the breeze whipped her curls in all directions. Pulling an elastic loop from her purse, Jade tamed the curls into a messy ponytail and continued her walk to think about where to go next.

She turned and spotted a guy leaning on the metal railing. Her breath caught in her throat. Zeke's friend stood staring out at the bay. The bald guy, with the physique of a professional wrestler, watched something on the horizon. Wracking her brain for his name, she stepped closer.

"Hi. I'm Jade. Didn't I see you at the fireworks last weekend?"

The man turned and nodded slightly. "Yup. I'm Tank. I work for the Pefferlys."

"I thought I saw you on the pier. Fun show. Y'all are still in town?" She asked, turning so the wind was in her face to keep the stray curls at bay.

He nodded like a bobber with a fish on the line. "Checking out the competition on Saturday. I like to see what others are featuring."

"It seems like a cool job. How long have you been in the fireworks business?" she asked.

"Since high school. It started out as a part-time job, and I hung around." He raised one shoulder dismissively. "I knew Brianna and Zeke from the neighborhood. I like this better than all the other jobs I've had, like bouncer, roadie, and warehouse security guard. I can't stand the thought of sitting in an office every day for eight or ten hours. This is outside. I have my schedule, and the rest of the time is mine."

"It sounds so interesting," she murmured with her best radio voice. "I mean all the science and technology that goes into it. How hard was it to learn? It sounds very dangerous." She opened her eyes wide, hoping it gave her a curious look.

"Yup. If you don't know what you're doing, you can blow your fingers off or worse. It's gotten better over the years. A lot more safety features. Let's say there's a ton of OTJ training. Ephron and Daniel are good teachers. They've been in the business for years, and they know their stuff, even if they're old school."

Her brows furrowed. "I don't know them."

"Ephron founded the company with Daniel, Zeke and Brianna's dad."

She nodded. "I'm fascinated with all the colors and the setup. I didn't realize how much time it takes to make it all come out right. There's so much work that goes into a show that lasts about thirty minutes."

The sun sank further behind the trees, and the light faded to a dull gray. The pair stared out at the bay and watched a trawler with white and red lights creep across the horizon.

After a long pause, he asked, "It's getting cold out here. Wanna get a drink?"

Jade nodded and followed him back to the hotel. She hoped Zeke and Goose were long gone. *That would make for an awkward moment.*

Settling into a booth near the window, he continued, "That's better. We can still see the ocean from here, but it's warmer." He blew on his hands and looked up at the TV over the bar.

"What can I get you?" The bartender yelled.

"Coffee black," Tank hollered back.

"I'll have a hot chocolate," Jade said.

"So, what do you do?" he asked. "This town looks a little sleepy in the winter."

Jade laughed. "It's off-season. But it's my busy season. I own the Christmas Shoppe in town. Brianna came by this week. She popped in to buy some decorations."

"By herself?" he asked as the bartender set two mugs in front of them.

Jade hugged the steaming mug with both hands and nodded. "She said she was doing some holiday shopping. Why?"

"She's been sneaking out with that Zanetti kid like a lovesick teenager. Her family's not too thrilled about it, especially after all the trouble they've caused recently. Goose, Zeke, and I try to keep an eye on her."

"I only talked to her that one time, but she seemed pretty level-headed. She was by herself when she came into my store."

"She was probably there taking selfies to use later as an alibi. She schedules posts to make it look like she's somewhere that she's not," he muttered. "She's smart. Well, crafty. Her dad wants her to take over the business one day. But she can be a brat. We spend way too much time looking out for her and making her mistakes go away."

An eerie shiver slid down Jade's spine. *What kind of mistakes? And how far would they go to make something go away? Did they have something to do with Lorenzo's death?* She shook it off and tried to not look panicked. "So, tell me about Zeke and Goose. Y'all seem to work as a well-oiled machine."

A slight frown crossed the large man's face. "They were born into the business. They've been at it all their lives. Not sure how close they are, really. Me and Zeke have a routine. We check behind each other. And Goose is well, Goose." He shrugged a shoulder. "He's fun to hang out with, but he's kind of a loose cannon."

"How did you all meet the Zanettis?"

He took a swing of his coffee. "It's a small industry. There aren't that many companies that do professional fireworks. We see each other on the circuit. Vie for the same contracts. Plus, there are trade shows and demos. We run into each other all the time. Brianna and Paolo met at a trade show. Her father and grandfather blew a gasket when they found out they were getting friendly with each other." He took another drink and stared out the window. Tiny dots of light from the boats offshore bobbed in the inky darkness.

"I need to be heading back soon," she said.

"I'll walk you out." He reached for his wallet and flashed a room key at the waiter.

After signing the receipt, Tank followed Jade to the lobby. A blast of arctic air hit them when the main door slid open.

"Brrr," she said, pulling her jacket closer around her. "I'm a beach girl. Can't wait for spring. This feels like winter and a possible freeze tonight."

"Where you parked?" he grunted, scanning the lot.

"Over by the fence."

He followed her to the Jeep.

Tank pointed at her license plate and laughed. "NO GRNCH. That's funny."

"The Wrangler reminded me of the color of the Grinch when I bought it, and it's perfect for the Christmas Shoppe. Thanks for the hot chocolate. See ya around."

Jade climbed into the Jeep and locked the doors. She let out a long puff of air. *Did one of these guys have something to do with the murder? And what happened to Goose? Did they turn on him, too?*

Jade sped home and double-checked that she'd locked the front door behind her. Her mind and her heart raced a mile a minute.

Not feeling like TV tonight, she added notes from what she learned today about the Pefferly team to her spreadsheet and murder wall. There seemed to be enough anger between the two companies, but would business rivalries lead to murder? She needed a way to find out more about Lorenzo. He seemed to fly under the radar. Why was he the target? Nobody ever talked about him. Maybe if she could figure that out, she'd find the killer.

Jade reached for her phone and clicked on Nick's contact.

"Hey, what's up?" he asked. It sounded like he was chewing on something.

"Hi. Just checking in. You still at work?"

"Yup. Lots of paperwork this week. I have to work on Saturday. Wanna grab dinner on Friday? That way, it'll save you from cooking."

"Afraid I'll make you try something new? You're afraid of eggplant, aren't you?"

He chortled. "Nah. Thought we could both use a break."

"Sounds good. Have your guys found anything out about the victim?" she asked.

"Which one? And why?"

"Lorenzo. I talked to Brianna when she came into the store. Then I ran into Goose and a guy who works for the Pefferlys today. They all talked about the two families, but nobody ever mentioned a word about Lorenzo. He seems to be invisible. I was curious."

"Uh-huh. Curious." Nick sounded distracted. Jade heard his police radio in the background. "He seems to have been fairly quiet. He's Paolo's cousin and Elio's brother. But he looks like his cousin. Folks teased them about being twins, even though their personalities were exact opposites. Hey, I've gotta run. See you soon. Love you."

"Love you, too. I'm the one who needs to remind you to be safe." Jade laughed nervously and disconnected.

She stared at her wall and moved a couple of the sticky notes around. *So many bits of information and no way to connect most of it. There are way more questions than answers. Why does this puzzle look like it's missing a handful of pieces?*

Chapter Fourteen

J ade lay in bed as rain spattered the window. Every little noise from the storm sounded like an intruder. Her wild imagination and thoughts of burglars and murderers drowned out all hope of falling back asleep. If she couldn't rest, at least she could scour the internet for stuff about Lorenzo and Goose. Both had secrets she wanted to know about. Why was Lorenzo targeted? That had to be the key to all of this. And who did Goose get in a fight with? He seemed to be pretty mouthy and hot-headed, not the kind to forgive and forget if he felt he was wronged. Then there was Brianna, who scheduled social media posts as alibis.

When her alarm echoed from her bedroom, Jade jumped in the shower and turned on the water as hot as she could stand it. She felt better, but a dull ache behind her eyes still distracted her. A double shot of espresso was next on her to-do list.

Running out of time for research, she stuffed all of her notes in her messenger bag. "Chloe, we need to double-time it. I kinda dawdled this morning."

The dog gave her a judgy look and marched toward the door.

Jade boosted Chloe into the Jeep and hopped in beside her for the short ride around the block. Rain continued to pour and made visibility difficult. The water pooled in the gutters and on the streets.

Once safely inside the store and slightly drier, she brewed a mug of hot tea and settled in at her desk to check emails.

"Whooo-hoooo. A perfect day for ducks," wafted through the store as Patti hustled in and hung her all-weather coat on the spare chair. "How are things?"

"When you get settled, wanna start with the overnight orders? And how are you on this blustery day?" Jade asked.

"Life is good. I love the holiday season. Too bad all this rain isn't snow. Wouldn't that be awesome? I don't ever remember a white Christmas here. Thought it did flurry on Easter once. Let me get the coffee maker chugging, and I'll get right on those orders."

Jade's phone alerted and drew her focus. **Still on for dinner tonight? I'm knocking off at 5:30 tonight.**

I'll bring pizza, quickly followed the first text.

Sounds great. Still afraid of veggie lasagna? Jade added.

Nick sent a green-faced barf emoji. **See you around 6**.

Jade stifled a laugh and pocketed her phone. "Patti, I'm off to Ruby's for a minute. Can you and Chloe mind the store?"

"Not a problem," she said, pushing a cart full of ornaments to the workroom. "We'll get these orders boxed lickety-split. Try to stay dry, though it may be hard to do. The rain looks like it's coming down sideways. Say hey to the gals at the Pearl for me."

"Call me if you need me." Jade slid into her jacket and ducked out the back door. Dodging puddles and street flooding, she cut through the neighborhood and parked in front of the bed and breakfast. Pulling up her hood, Jade made a dash for the side door.

After a couple of knocks, Ruby opened it. "Hi, Jade. What brings you out in this mess today? It's a hot tea and a good book kind of day. Come on inside."

"Thought I'd stop by to see if any of your guests were around on this glorious morning." Jade stomped her boots on the mat and tried to shake off the rain from her jacket before stepping into the warm kitchen.

Ruby cracked a smile. "What are you poking at this early in the day? Though you did pick the perfect day to see people since everyone is trapped inside."

Jade gave her a half-smile. "I haven't found much on Lorenzo. I was hoping someone here could give me some insight into him. I have no idea why he was targeted. Any ideas?" she whispered.

"He barely said two words when he was here. I always got him mixed up with that Paolo fella. I think the patriarch of the bunch is in the library, where he usually hangs out. The rest of his team doesn't show up until later. They're night owls who bang around and keep everyone else up and then sleep until lunchtime."

The outside door creaked, and both women stopped their conversation. The door inched open, and Paolo stepped inside, carrying his boots. Rain from his coat puddled on the mat.

"Good morning," Ruby said. "Can I get you anything besides a towel?"

"Coffee," he said, flashing his pearly white smile at the pair. "I got caught in a downpour on my way back this morning." He took the towel Ruby offered and closed the door. "Thanks."

"Here's a mug. Breakfast is on the buffet in the dining room. Let me know if I can get you anything." Ruby picked up the wet towel he dropped by the door.

"I'll join you, if you don't mind," Jade said, guiding him toward the dining room.

"Jade, I'll bring you some coffee in a jiff," Ruby yelled to their backs.

After Paolo loaded a plate with croissants, mini-quiches, and fruit, he sat at the head of the Victorian dining table that could seat twelve and started shoving the food into his mouth.

Jade took a bite or two of fruit. "I'm so sorry to hear about your cousin. Any word on when you all can leave town?"

He shrugged and continued to wolf down his food. When he paused for a breath, he replied, "They plan to release the body soon. Grandpop wants to stay and see the show on Saturday. We'll head back to New Jersey sometime on Sunday."

"That's positive news," Jade said. "Tell me about Lorenzo."

Paolo paused a second or two. "He was quiet. Always had his nose stuck in a book. He did a good job, but I always got the feeling that his heart wasn't in the business. He wanted to be a writer, but that wasn't an approved job in the Zanetti family. Grandpop didn't want him to waste money on a college degree."

Jade chewed on her bottom lip. "So, he was going to stay with the job even though it wasn't his passion?"

"Blood's thicker than water," he said, shoving three tiny quiches in his mouth. "Plus, everyone does what Grandpop says," he said, chewing with his mouth open.

"Maybe he was doing his writing on the side," Jade suggested, trying to prompt him for more background.

Paolo made a sour face. "Grandpop was afraid he would give away the family secrets. Can't have that. It's been banged into our heads since we were little kids. Family and business first. And do not talk about our business to anyone. It takes a lot of time and money to create our show, and he doesn't want it stolen." He reached for the salt and shook it over his home fries like a flurry of snow.

Jade got a chill. *Could trade secrets be worth killing over?*

Shrugging off the melancholic feeling, Jade said, "I'm so sorry about your family's loss. I hope you all will be able to take him home soon and find some peace."

Paolo made a second pass at the buffet. "I hope so, too. This town looks like it would be fun in the summer, but it's kind of a drag in December. I'm missing friends and parties back home."

After a long pause, Jade put her napkin beside her plate. "Thanks for breakfast. I better let you get back to starting your day."

"Ha! I just got home. I'm headed straight to bed. No plans until Saturday night. So I guess that'll give me time to catch up on some Zzzzs." He picked up his shoes and his coffee and disappeared into the foyer.

Jade stuck her head in the library where Aldo sat, snoring softly in one of the wingchairs. She tiptoed back to the kitchen. "Thanks, Ruby. The fruit was tasty."

"Hope you found some nuggets," she said, loading the industrial, stainless-steel dishwasher. "I wish you and Nick would hurry up and solve this thing. And tell us all who this crazy new blogger is." She rolled her eyes. "Rumor at the beauty shop is that it was Josie. Not a chance. She has too much to do here to mess around with the gossip mill. You know who it is?"

"I don't have a clue about the blogger's identity. And as for the murder, there are a lot of disparate bits of information. Nothing's falling into place. Maybe Nick will have better luck," Jade said with a sigh.

"Not sure why a town this size needs more than one gossip monger. Nell is fit to be tied," Ruby muttered as she wiped down the granite top of the island that dominated the room.

Jade waved and pulled the door behind her, picking her way around the puddles. Inside her Wrangler, the blast of warm air felt good until it fogged up the windows. The defroster worked overtime to clear enough windshield for her to be able to see enough to drive to the store.

Could fireworks really be at the center of this mess?

Chapter Fifteen

It finally stopped raining by the time Jade returned to 'Tis the Season. She shook out her coat and hung it on the hook on the back door.

"There you are," Patti said, heading for the refrigerator. "I didn't hear you come in. We've had a steady stream of walk-ins, but the overnight orders outnumbered the in-person sales today. Oh, and I put the new catalogs on your desk. Lots of cute things, especially with hearts on them. They'll be perfect for next year's *My Coastal Valentine* premier. I can't wait for the big day. I want to see what I look like on TV. And I know I'll watch it a million times to see all the local places and familiar faces. We're gonna be on the Love Channel!" Patti danced around with her water bottle. "And we can cover this place in Valentine's decorations. It'll be a perfect way to celebrate a normally gray and drab February."

"It'll be fun," Jade said. "I heard some of the actors may come back into town for our premier."

"Ooooh. Exciting! I want to see Raphael Allard up close again. I wonder what he and Elle Valentine will wear to that hoity-toity event. I'll have to buy something fancy. I wonder if we can hold it in one of the swanky hotels in Seaport." Patti paused, and a dark expression clouded her face, "Did you see the blog post this morning?"

"Nope. I was doing some research. What's up?" Jade asked.

"Whoever the mystery blogger is, she's teasing us again. Hints of more hookups and breakups are coming. There was a recap about Trish and Jarrod and how devastated she was that he was seeing a younger woman. According to the Mermaid, she snuck out of town and is spending the rest of December in Miami. There's also a snarky comment about Todd's surf-mobile hearse, and maybe it can be put to good use if there are any more murders before the holidays. The Mermaid said she's not a fan of the horn."

Jade let out a puff of air that fluttered her bangs. "I have no clue about the Mermaid's secret identity. At first, I thought it was Vivian, but she's usually a cheerleader for the community. She doesn't like anything that puts her or the town in a bad light. Amy says it's not her, and it's sooooo not me."

"I don't think Ruby even knows how to blog. She just learned how to text. I think it would be unlikely that it's anyone who works for the town. Do you think it could be a guy?"

"Hmmmm. Probably not. I agree with Amy, the tone sounds female," Jade said, starting at her computer. *How could she find out who the blogger was? Would it be possible to plant a story?* Jade's thoughts drifted to ways to catch the mysterious person.

Patti dumped several boxes and an envelope on the counter.

"Jade. Earth to Jade. Did you hear me? You look lost in thought. Are you okay if I head out a little bit early tonight? I'm meeting my book club for drinks, and I have to swing by my house. I forgot the book. Though I don't really need it. We hardly ever get around to talking about what we were supposed to have read. And half the group never reads the book anyway."

"That's no problem. Have fun tonight." Jade opened a Word file and jotted down some outlandish story ideas that popped into her head. Maybe there was a way to catch the Mermaid. Some of her thoughts sounded like they belonged on the front of the tabloids in the grocery checkout line. She would plant some of these around town and see if anyone took the bait. *For now, this is my little secret. It's crazy enough that it might work.*

A little after five, Jade and Chloe packed up and headed home. She had enough time to pick up the living room, add today's sticky notes to her wall, and change outfits twice before Nick knocked on the door.

Handing her the pizza box with a white paper bag on top, he leaned over and picked up Chloe, who melted in his arms. "I got a calzone to mix it up since you had pizza the other day. Close, but not exactly the same."

"Come on in. It's good to see you. And no worries. Pizza is the one food I could eat anytime. And the calzones at Pizza D'Action are great." Jade kissed him and set the box on the table. "What can I get you to drink?"

"Water's fine for now," he said, staring at her wall. "So, what's new here?" Nick pointed at the rainbow of sticky notes.

Returning with two glasses and plates, she said, "Paolo said that Lorenzo didn't like working in the family business. He wanted to be a writer, but their grandfather didn't want him to leak any trade secrets. And that college was a waste of money."

Nick raised one eyebrow and pulled some pepperoni out of his calzone. He popped it in his mouth, and Chloe gave him a side-eye. He reached for another piece and slipped it to her under the table.

"The Zanettis told me you had told them not to leave town," Jade said.

"Not in those exact words. I told them the M. E. is the one to release the body, and I said we may have questions for them as the investigation progresses. They decided on their own to hang out and check out their competitors." A slight scowl darkened his face.

"Paolo did mention that they were hanging around because they wanted to see the competition's show. There seems to be a healthy little feud going on between some of the players." Jade pointed to her suspect wall. "So, what have you uncovered recently? Anything exciting?" She eyed him over her forkful of calzone.

"Not as much as I would have liked. The preliminary autopsy report came back. Lorenzo was stabbed, and he died from his wounds. It was a pretty brutal attack. Up close and personal. We don't think he was killed in your lot. There's evidence to suggest that he was moved. And before you ask, we don't know from where yet or how. The guys are still slogging through hours of all kinds of camera footage in hopes of getting a glimpse of something useful." He paused and stared at her wall.

"Something bothering you?" she asked.

"Nope. Wanna go for a walk to let dinner settle before we eat dessert? The exercise and fresh air will do me good, even if it's freezing out there. I need to clear my head."

Before Jade could answer, Chloe tore through the living room and danced at the front door. "Sounds like that's a yes from my sidekick."

Nick grinned and took the harness and leash Jade handed him.

"I'll be back in a sec. Let me put these in the kitchen and change my shoes."

By the time Jade returned, Chloe pranced around, showing off her blingy harness.

"Y'all ready?" Jade asked, pulling on her coat and checking for her gloves.

Nick wrapped one arm around Jade's waist, and they headed toward the beach, following the enthusiastic dog who couldn't wait to see what was going on outside. The sounds of the wind and the waves created a Zen-like moment, blocking out the rest of the world. The pair walked in silence as the little dog churned up sand in her wake. Jade licked the salty tang from the air off her lips. As the shadows crept toward them, Nick flipped on his phone's flashlight, and Chloe dug in the sand when she spotted a family of tiny white crabs.

"It's nice out here except for the temperature." Jade scooted closer to Nick as her teeth chattered.

"You wanna head back?" he asked.

"Nah, let's go see why all the lights are blazing at the pier." Jade pointed down the beach to what looked like a beacon ahead of them.

They walked past the darkened deck at Hot Diggity Dogs and spotted two Crash Boom Bang semis in the parking lot next to Amy's store. Every light on Suggs Pier blazed in the inky darkness where the night met the edge of the bay. Plastic hurricane fencing outlined the pier and blocked access to the sand and the area under the worn wooden beams.

"This company has gobs of toys and a huge crew," Nick said.

The pair stood and watched all the activity. It looked as chaotic as an ant hill as guys in red jackets stacked crate after crate and made towers that lined the entire length of the pier.

Nick paused and stared at the wooden structure. "Be back in a sec. Stay here."

He jogged toward the fencing. Pushing the orange mesh into the sand, he stepped over it.

Jade paused and stared at the pylons. No sounds except the waves and an occasional snort from Chloe. *What caught Nick's eye?*

Something moved under the pier, and Nick sped up. He darted toward the darkness under the pier. Jade's pulse raced. She leaned over the plastic fencing to get a better view.

Chloe started digging in the sand drifts that were about as tall as she was. Jade picked her up and brushed the sand off her stomach and paws.

Inching closer and hoping Nick didn't notice, Jade watched him flash his badge at three men by the pylons. One had a camera with a huge lens. She caught her breath. Were they the Pefferlys?

"What are you all doing down under here? Didn't you see the fencing?" Nick asked.

"Yep. The one we climbed over," Goose said. Zeke elbowed him in the ribs.

"Sorry, officer. We were watching them set up," Zeke said. "We didn't think anyone would care at this hour. We thought this was a public beach. That's what the sign over there says. We aren't bothering anyone."

Tank dropped a cigarette in the sand and crushed it with his foot. He shifted his stance.

"It's not an issue for you to watch. I need you to move back behind the barriers," Nick said, pointing behind him.

"Of course, officer. We didn't mean any harm," Zeke replied, reminding Jade of Eddie Haskell. "Come on, guys. Let's make sure we're complying with all the rules. We don't want to wear out our welcome here. Especially since youse guys will see a lot more of us this summer when we win."

Goose snickered, and he and Tank followed Zeke to the fencing. As Zeke stepped on the plastic netting. Tank turned and stared at Jade. It was hard to tell in the dark, but she thought she saw a flash of recognition.

The three men wandered around the temporary fencing and continued to stare at the activity above, looking over their shoulders occasionally to see what Nick was doing.

The sheriff moved closer to Jade and then stopped suddenly enough to kick up sand. "And you come out, too." Nick bellowed.

They waited for what felt like an eternity until Elio stepped out from the pier's shadows. "I wasn't doing nothin'. I saw the Pefferly guys run under there, and I wanted to know what they were up to." He stuffed his hands in his coat pockets and rocked back and forth on his heels.

"I'm sure you heard me tell them that this area is off-limits. You need to move on." Nick took a step forward.

"Not a problem. I'm headed out, too." He pulled his hood up and jogged toward the parking lot in the opposite direction of the Pefferlys.

"The pier's a popular place this evening," Jade said when Nick returned to where she was standing.

"You ready to head back?" Nick scanned the area until the Pefferlys moved to a more public space.

"Date night is always fun with you." She set Chloe down in the sand, and the chubby Frenchie trotted around Nick's feet.

At the cut-through to Jade's neighborhood, Nick paused and stared back toward the pier. Jade scanned the empty beach, too. There were a few lights on in nearby cottages and on the boats offshore.

Pulling out his phone, Nick clicked a contact. "Driscoll here. Could you send a patrol car to Suggs Pier and add it to the rotation tonight? I ran off four guys from under the pier. The company is setting up for Saturday, and I don't want any problems. Yep. Thanks. You, too."

He disconnected and followed Jade and Chloe to her bungalow. "Who wants cannoli?" he asked.

Jade nodded, lost in thought about what the Zanettis and Pefferlys were really doing, slinking around under Suggs Pier.

Chapter Sixteen

Not finding anything in her kitchen that was breakfast-worthy, Jade and Chloe took a walk on the beach toward the Busy Bean. On the stoop outside the coffee shop, she dusted the sand off her boots, and she and Chloe made their way inside. James and Sophie's Christmas tree twinkled with white lights. The silver and aqua ornaments matched the store's décor and gave off a beachy vibe.

"Hey, Jade. And Chloe. What can I get for you all today?" James, half of the brother-sister team who owned the hip spot, asked.

"I hope all's well. We're getting excited about this weekend's fireworks. How about a lemon muffin and a large, extra caffeinated mocha for me?"

"Always a good choice. This weekend's group brought an army with them. I watched their fleet of trucks pull in yesterday. It looked like the circus had arrived. They were blocking Amy's parking lot this morning. It's like they descended on us. Luckily, Sophie and I could get in around back to open on time. I'm glad they moved them before our customers started arriving."

Sophie, James's sister, breezed in with a large aluminum tray of scones. "Morning, Jade. How are things? You're right in the middle of your busy season. I hope you get time to enjoy some of the festivities. Based on all the trucks and equipment, this weekend's show should be spectacular." She arranged the bakery items in the glass display case in a way that would make waiting customers drool.

Jade smiled. "It's been a crazy season. I hope this week's sales are like the recent ones. It's been impressive. I'm enjoying the shows. I wasn't sure about a winter fireworks competition when Vivian announced it, but it's been fun. I like that the council is doing off-season events." *That story plant was benign. But if it shows up on Mermaid Whispers, I'll know where it came from.*

Sophie nodded as James handed Jade a drink and the bag. "There's something in there for you, too, Chloe," he said.

"She'll enjoy her treat. Thank you." Jade and Chloe stepped outside, and the wind whipped around the building that the Busy Bean shared with Mermaid Books.

Turning her head for a double-take, she spotted Nick and Sebastian at the end of Suggs Pier. Making a quick detour, despite the chilly morning, Jade and Chloe headed in the direction of all the activity.

"Good morning," Jade said as she approached.

"Hey, Jade," Sebastian said. Turning to Nick, he continued, "I'll go check on that and then swing by the Pearl." He saluted with two fingers and jogged down the wooden decking.

"Morning. What brings you out this way?" Nick asked.

"We stopped in to see James and Sophie. Can I get you anything?" Jade held up her Busy Bean bag.

"Nope. We're wrapping up here. It seems to be my second home lately." His glance drifted to the movement at the end of the pier.

She paused, and before she could ask what was going on, he continued, "The Crash Boom Bang folks reported some suspicious activity near their equipment last night. The cameras showed a guy sneaking around. It looked like things were moved, but so far, nothing is missing. So we'll spend the morning chasing down our usual suspects."

Jade pursed her lips. "I never would have guessed that the fireworks industry was so cut-throat."

"It's big money, and they're always looking for the newest and coolest thing. According to Will Adkins, the owner of Crash Boom Bang, drones are the hottest things right now. His folks take great care to protect their investments. Those trucks have almost the same security as an armored vehicle. They brought cameras and all kinds of gizmos with them."

Jade's eyes widened. "If all that's for the prep, I can't wait to see the show this weekend. It sounds like they know what they're doing."

"Time to check on a couple of things and head out. I'll call you later. Stay out of trouble." Nick winked.

"You, too." Jade smiled and wiggled her fingers at him. The wind whipped off the bay, and Chloe didn't dilly dally on her way to 'Tis the Season.

A thunderous rumble caused Jade and the Frenchie to pause on the sidewalk in front of the realty office. About twenty bikers rolled down Neptune Road on mammoth motorcycles decorated for the holidays. Many had large teddy bears in holiday garb as passengers. Chloe yipped and retreated behind Jade's legs. She picked up the little dog and waved as the mini parade rolled by. When they roared out of town, Jade had an idea for another Mermaid Whispers story plant.

Jade stepped through her opening routine in record time and settled in at her desk for her Busy Bean breakfast and a quick check on her social media. She handed Chloe the dog treat James had added to their bag.

"Mmm, huh. We'll have to let James know you approve. You ate it before I could get a picture for him," Jade mused as Chloe smacked her lips and sniffed around for more.

The bells on the front door jangled, and she heard a "Hey, there" as Lorelei breezed in wearing a full-length winter white coat and matching hat. "Good morning, all."

"What are you doing up so early? You're not on the schedule today," Jade said.

"I know. Steve and I are headed to Richmond for some luncheon thing, and I can't find a list I was working on the other day. Just wanted to see if I had left it here." Lorelei rummaged around the second desk. "You didn't spot a little teal notebook, did you?"

Jade shook her head as her aunt continued to dig through the drawers.

"Maybe I left it behind the cash register. What's new with you? I haven't talked to you in a bit."

"We've been busy with the online orders. I'm hoping the foot traffic will pick up as we get closer to the weekend. Oh, I saw the guys setting up for Saturday. It looks like the next show will be amazing."

Her aunt paused and then did a quick check of the back counter. "Hmm," she replied. "Yep, it's cold out there."

She's not listening to me. Jade looked over at her aunt, who continued to rummage through the drawers near the counter. Lorelei turned suddenly and ducked behind the counter in the lobby. "Any luck?" Jade asked.

"No. It bugs me when I can't find something." She looked behind stacks of ornament catalogs and holiday flyers.

On a whim, Jade decided to see how distracted she was and to continue her Mermaid Whispers investigation. "I heard that there's a motorcycle gang in town. Chloe and I saw them cruising up and down Neptune Road this morning. I think they're looking for a new home base."

"Really?" Lorelei said, standing straighter and staring at her niece. "In Mermaid Bay? Seaport would be more to their liking. That's news."

Jade shrugged. "Maybe we're attracting a different crowd these days."

"Interesting. I hadn't heard that one." Her aunt's eyes widened. "I thought we were too quaint. I still can't find that notebook. This is driving me nuts."

"Did you check all your pockets and whatever bag you used last? Whenever I'm missing something, it's always between the door and the passenger seat of my Jeep. Stuff slides down there," Jade said.

"You take the turns too fast, speed demon," her aunt mused. "Well, it doesn't seem to be here either. I tore up my kitchen and living room looking for it this morning. Wait. Voila! There you are, you little booger. I'm glad I didn't lose you." Lorelei reached deep into the shelf behind the counter. Pulling out her small notebook, she flipped through the pages and slid it into her coat pocket. "See you this weekend," she said, waving over her shoulder.

"Have fun in Richmond," Jade said as her aunt waltzed out the front door.

After refilling her mug with tea, Jade plopped down in her chair and rested her head on her arms. She was making zero progress on who killed Lorenzo and who was behind the Mermaid Whispers. "Okay, time to concentrate on what you can control," she said aloud.

Printing out the ten pages of orders, she spent the morning packing them and updating her inventory.

Her stomach rumbled around one-thirty, reminding her that she had missed lunch. Grabbing a power bar and a water from the back, she scrolled through her email. "Emergency Business Council Meeting Today" caught her eye. "Well, Chloe, I now have plans for after work."

The white butterball of a dog yawned and rolled over in her bed, not interested in anything political or council-related.

Vivian's meeting email was vague. Jade dashed off a quick text, hoping to get some details from her, though she was pretty sure it was fireworks-related. And why was the pier suddenly the center of all the police action? *I guess that's better than it being my store.*

Her phone alerted. **It has come to my attention that some of our vendors may have violated our code of conduct. We need to agree on our course of action.**

Jade let out a breath she didn't realize she was holding and tapped back. **See you at 6.**

Chapter Seventeen

Jade snagged one of the few remaining parking spots and jogged toward the brick building. The conference room, filled to capacity, already felt muggy. She glanced around and spotted Amy waving from the third row of folding chairs.

As Jade approached, Amy elbowed Todd in the ribs. "Move over one, baby, so I can sit beside Jade."

A slight smile crossed Todd's face, and he stood, so Jade could take his seat. "My pleasure. Wouldn't want to block two besties. Y'all keep it down over there and behave."

Amy smirked and blew him a kiss. Then, doing a fake pearl clutch, "What and incur the wrath of Vivian. We will be on our bestest behavior. I don't want to be called to the carpet as a local miscreant." Then she dissolved into a fit of chuckles.

"I don't know about her, but I'll behave," Jade said, sitting between the couple.

"So, what's new in your world?" Amy asked, squirming in her seat to get comfortable.

"Gearing up for Christmas and hoping for some amazing foot traffic this weekend. I heard you had some action around your place," Jade said.

Amy nodded. "Those semis surrounded my lot like they were setting up a perimeter or some kind of fortress. It felt like we had been invaded. Nobody could get in or out. The guys, Trey and Will, were nice about it, and they fixed it. It looks like they brought an army to town. Makes me want to see the show even more to see what comes out of all those trucks." Reaching behind Jade, she tapped Todd on the shoulder. "Hey, can you reserve a table on your deck on Saturday for us. Last time, we got squeezed out and had to sit in the sand. Pretty, please. You gotta take care of your biggest fans. We like sitting on your deck. It's a perfect viewing spot." She batted her eyes at Todd for good measure.

"Anything for you two. I'll put out my best hot dog stand reserved seating," Todd said with a salute.

"You have that?" Jade asked. Amy nodded as Todd shook his head and offered a half-grin.

Jade cracked a smile as Vivian approached the lectern with her oversized gavel. Several bangs and the noise in the room subsided.

"Hello, members. Thank you so much for coming out on short notice. The council and I want to keep you abreast of recent events and the council's stance. When we release any future statements, we want to make sure everyone is aware. You all know of the horrific murder of one of our vendors. After that, we've had numerous reports of vandalism, fights, and other unprofessional behavior. We had a board meeting yesterday, and we wanted to inform you all of our plan." Vivian paused and scanned the room. "The council has decided to disqualify contestants who are unsportsmanlike and do not demonstrate fair play. So, the council will remind our vendors that they signed our code of conduct. We do not want anyone to be surprised if the board decides to disqualify any participants. We are in discussions with the county manager and our legal advisors, and information will be available next week about how we will proceed." Vivian pursed her lips and scanned the room for reactions.

Mumbles emanated from the audience.

A voice in the back yelled, "This is the reason for the emergency meeting? This coulda been an email." A murmur of agreement rippled through the crowded room.

"I totally agree," Amy whispered. "We have a lot of emergency meetings around here."

"The board and I thought it was important to meet and make sure everyone understands our position. Our events and activities are designed to promote

Mermaid Bay and our businesses. We want to represent the values of our community. Council rules require us to notify our members and provide an opportunity for comment. It's hard to do that via email and to give everyone a chance to respond if they want to. It's a logistical nightmare to manage responses and ensure that we preserve all records." Vivian glared at someone in the back of the room.

Several people exited the meeting amidst the crowd rumblings.

Vivian rapped her gavel. "I'd like to open the floor for comments. So our secretary can record them properly."

Amy waved her hand and bounced in her seat. "Have we disqualified anyone yet?"

"Not yet," Vivian replied. "We want to be fair and to ensure we have our processes in place. And provide you, as council members, an opportunity to address any concerns with our plans before we take action. Let the minutes reflect that this will be our process going forward for all events, and all our vendors will be required to sign our code of conduct."

"So, do you anticipate eliminating anyone?" Amy followed up.

"Possibly. We're waiting on an update from the sheriff's office before making our final decision. This is a valuable vendor contract, and we want to cross all our t's and dot all our i's." Vivian paused for a brief minute. "Any other questions or comments?"

"I have a question." Martha Vanderbeek waved her tiny arm in the air, trying to get Vivian's attention. Jade's neighbor may look fragile, but hidden behind the white hair and laugh lines, she was a steel magnolia that the other neighbors were a little afraid of. Her wit was as sharp as her tongue.

Martha cleared her throat and continued, "What happens if you disqualify more than one of the contestants since we only have three? It sounds like there are multiple issues."

Vivian paused and looked at the Town Manager, Tom Berryman. When he nodded, she pulled the mic toward her. "If we disqualify two, then the contract will most likely be awarded to the third company, if they follow all the rules."

"And if they're all eliminated," Tom Berryman interrupted, "Then we'll put the fireworks contract out for an RFP bid like we did last year. We want the best possible vendor for our summer celebrations."

"Thank you, Tom. Any other questions?" This time, Vivian didn't bat an eye before continuing, "Okay. Then can I get a motion to close this discussion?"

"Ayes" echoed from the room.

After a voice vote, Vivian continued. "Kelly Jamison of the Pirate's Chest is heading the winter activities committee. Do you want to come up and give folks a preview of what's coming in the new year and where folks can help?"

Kelly made her way from a row in the middle of the room. She paused at the lectern and raised the microphone. Looking out over the audience, she smoothed her slacks and cleared her throat. "Thanks, Vivian. Hi, y'all. I'm Kelly, and my team, Amy Pemberton, Ruby Ellis, and Vivian are working on our own version of Winter Wonderland. We'll be hosting a rummage sale at the high school in January for all those who want to make decluttering a New Year's resolution. So, Marie Kondo, your stuff and think about getting a table or two at our sale. And if you want to donate your items, the 4H Club will be glad to sell them at their booth. After that, we are working with the Love Channel's publicist to have our own screening of *My Coastal Valentine* in February. We expect to have a series of events leading up to the big night that coincides with the network premiere. We are looking for volunteers, so please reach out to one of us. We could use your help. The Love Channel's premiere is a big deal for Mermaid Bay. And we want to make a big splash. Uh, thanks," she said, returning to her seat.

"Okay, Ruby will be at the back door as you leave, and you can sign up to be a volunteer. Any other business we need to take care of?" Vivian asked, adjusting the microphone again.

From the back of the room, Nell Jones yelled, "So what's the scoop on this blogger who's specializing in all the rumors and gossip? The one who calls itself Mermaid Whispers. This doesn't quite present the image that we want for our town. Does this council have any plans to respond?" Nell's voice trailed off as she glanced around to see who was looking at her.

Vivian made a harrumphing sound. "Unless he or she does something illegal, there's not much we can do. And I don't plan to spend my day offering a retort to every post I don't agree with. I have better things to do than to roll around in the muck with a gossip-monger. Nell, you, of all people, should have known that we don't usually respond to negative or unflattering stories."

The local reporter's cheeks turned red. "Just curious," she said. "This one seems to cross the line a bit. And doesn't follow any journalistic standards." Nell glanced around the room again. "I think they should identify themselves and be open about what's said. It's too easy to hide and take potshots. I personally don't think it represents our community well."

"You'd know," came from the back of the room, followed by a series of snickers.

"Okay then," Vivian said. "If there are no other questions or items for discussion. I'd like to thank you for joining us today and doing your council duty. Don't forget the fireworks from our last contestant start around sunset on Saturday. Come out and support your fellow business owners."

"Sounds like the fireworks have been going on with the vendors for quite a while," Todd mumbled.

Amy leaned over Jade and punched him lightly in the arm. "And so you know, both of you are going to help me with the Love Channel thing, right? This is my first volunteer effort here, and I want to show Vivian my crazy mad organizational skills," she whispered.

"Of course," Jade said.

"Oh, good. I'm so excited. Todd has to help me cause it's in the boyfriend code." She winked and gave his arm a light pinch. "Too bad Nick works for the town. We could drag him along, too, but he's probably doing official police business."

"As long as I don't have to sing or dance," Todd said, rising.

"Would I do that to you guys?" Amy pouted.

"Yes," Todd and Jade said in unison.

"I'm the fun one, and you love it. Your lives are so much more exciting since I moved here. How about we go grab a pizza, my treat, and we'll brainstorm some ideas or just gossip about everyone here? I'm hungry."

"You had me at pizza," Todd said. "Jade, wanna meet us over there?"

"I need to talk to Vivian, but I'll be right there. Save me a seat."

"Will do," Amy said, shooing Todd toward the exit.

Jade felt like she was swimming upstream against the people traffic as she made her way to the front of the conference room. "Vivian, do you have a quick minute?" she asked.

"Hi, Jade. Did you sign up to help? We could use you and your energy. What's on your mind?"

"Amy recruited Todd and me. I'm looking forward to it. Hey, I read online that the big-name actors, Elle Valentine and Raphael Allard, may show up here for the premiere. Are they really coming back? That would be fabulous for our marketing." Jade felt a little guilty for starting rumors, but she was still trying to find out the secret identity of the Mermaid.

"I hadn't heard that one per se. I'll have to check into it. The Love Channel did offer us a publicist to assist with our efforts. They want us to create a buzz. We'll see what that turns into. Oh, there's Tish Taylor's friend, Farrah. Excuse me. I need to catch up with her to see how Tish is doing. After…well, you know." Vivian bustled off after the stylish Realtor.

Jade headed for her Jeep, one of the remaining vehicles in the lot next to the library. A lone figure who looked out of place in the empty lot stood in the grassy area. The man hunched over. Jade's curiosity peaked. *Was he okay?* As she approached her Wrangler, the person straightened up and jogged over to a truck parked at the tree line. The headlights popped on, and she used her arm to shade her eyes. The truck started to move toward her. Jade's heart rate jumped off the charts. She blinked a couple of times to get her eyes to adjust. With all the craziness, Jade was on high alert. Not wanting to hang around, she ran for the security of her Jeep.

Once inside, she locked the doors and started her engine. The truck picked up speed as it bounced across the field. Not sure if she should move or stay put, she hesitated. The truck continued to approach.

Then, at the final second, it swerved and skidded. Dust and grass flew around like a mini tornado. She let out a deep breath and willed her heartbeats to slow down to something closer to normal. She took a deep, cleansing breath, all the while waiting to see what he would do next.

Before she could reach for her phone, the truck guy jammed his vehicle in reverse and sped backwards, slamming on his brakes when he was parallel to her vehicle with his driver's door near hers. He rolled down the window and yelled something.

"What?" she asked, rolling her window down a crack, hoping that he would apologize for his crazy driving.

"I thought it was you when I saw you. It's me, Zeke. Zeke Pefferly." He stuck his head out the window and waved with one hand.

Jade waited a few heartbeats and stared at the driver's side window. *Was he for real? And what was he doing here? Did he crash the council meeting?*

"Tank said he saw you over at the hotel and at the pier the other night. He enjoyed talking to you. You should call him," Zeke said.

Jade almost said she didn't have his number, but she hesitated. Why would he chase her down in a menacing way to tell her that? Is he really that clueless?

When she didn't reply, he said, "Anyway, I thought I'd let you know in case you're interested. He's a good guy. You should call him." Zeke put the truck in gear and sped away toward town.

Jade rested her head on her steering wheel for a moment as all the adrenaline seemed to seep out of her.

Chapter Eighteen

After her weird encounter with Zeke, Jade's pulse rate finally returned to normal, and she no longer heard the pounding in her temples. After another deep breath, she zipped over to Pizza D'Action, where she found Todd and Amy snuggled in a cozy booth in the back. "Hey, guys," she said as she approached. "I hope I'm not the third wheel on your date."

"Oh, it's not a date," Amy said, getting a side-eye from Todd. "He's hungry, and we're out here supporting our fellow business owners. What are you thinking of having tonight? Come sit down." She patted the booth's vinyl bench.

"I want to try their subs. Patti said that he toasts them, and they're good," Jade said, looking at the menu board above the counter.

"I think I'll have that, too." Todd put his menu behind the napkin holder and arranged the salt, pepper, parmesan, and pepper flakes in height order.

Amy rolled her eyes. "Fine. I'll get a couple of slices of pie. I thought we were having pizza. No worries. Is there a waitress, or do we need to order at the counter?" Amy looked around the dining area.

"I don't see Mrs. Rossi. She usually takes care of the tables," Jade said.

"Then, it's the counter," Amy said, hopping up. Her dark ponytail with the purple ends bounced as she sashayed to the front.

After placing their orders, the three settled in the booth. Jade asked, "Any idea who this mystery blogger is?"

Todd shook his head. "I have enough to worry about with my restaurant without trying to keep up with the latest chatter about who's doing what.

Plus, I get all my spicy updates from my Gen Z staff or her." He pointed to Amy with both index fingers.

"But the blog's gossip nuggets are so good," Amy said. "And now I'm always looking at people to try to figure out if it's them. I think it's Vivian or Josie. Or maybe it's you," she pointed at Todd. "You act all nonchalant. Maybe that's a cover, and I've been kissing the Merman all this time. Or should I call you Aquaman?"

"Nope. Sorry. Not your guy. Jade, what about you or your staff? Patti seems to have her finger on everything," Todd said, changing the subject.

"She said it isn't her. You know Peppermint Patti likes to stay in the know, but I don't see her stirring up controversy on purpose. You know she's Miss Harmony, hugs and cupcakes with sprinkles."

"Love, Peace, and all that. What if it's James or Sophie? You always have to watch the quiet ones," Amy whispered. "They talk to just about everyone in town every day. Hmmmm. As their landlord, I'm going to have to watch them. I could be harboring the Mermaid." Amy's dimples peeked out of the corners of her smile.

"Numbers twenty-two, twenty-three, and twenty-four," Anthony Rossi yelled from the counter.

"Come on, Jade," Amy said. "Let's get the grub."

After claiming their dinners, they dug into their food. "I didn't realize how hungry I was," Jade said, wiping brown mustard off her chin. "I got busy today, and lunch was a granola bar."

"Oh, I can't do that," Amy said. "That wouldn't turn out well, especially for those around me."

"She gets hangry and turns into a three-headed monster," Todd said with a laugh.

Amy jabbed him in the ribs with her elbow. "But I'm an adorable mess."

"That's it. That's the Mermaid's next story. Transylvania has its Dracula, the Pacific Northwest has its Sasquatch, and Mermaid Bay has its own sea monster. Watch out," Jade said. "It may be the next hot topic."

"Oh, perfect. I already have the dragon mural in the kid's section of the store. I think I'll name her Hangry Amy. And I'll warn unruly patrons that she eats bad children for breakfast. I think I've got a new social media idea. Too bad, I'm not the blogger. I could do a thing on sea serpents and dragons. Maybe I'll still do a cool window display. I have a dope dragon puppet somewhere. I could get two or three blog posts out of that topic."

"And if dragons and sea serpents aren't enough, I heard in town that some ghost hunters were coming to Mermaid Bay. It was something about it being home to shipwrecks in years gone by, and there was some kind of paranormal vibe going on," Jade said.

"Ooooh, that's exciting," Amy said. "I wonder if another one of those shows will come to town. Todd, we could do all kinds of cool promos and drag out the hearse again. It would be perfect. I wonder if I could schedule some of the ghost hunters at the store for some creepy events. You all got me started on the cool ideas." Amy's eyes sparkled, and she whipped out her phone and started tapping.

Todd shrugged and added. "Now you've done it. She's got a new project. And that means that I have a new project." He turned in the booth and smiled at Amy as he continued, "But you do know Mermaid Bay has its share of creepy over the years. That weird suitcase turned up on the beach last summer with the odd collection of bones. Lots of whoo-whoo stuff has gone on around here through the years." He paused and raised his eyebrows. "My grandfather used to scare us with all the local lore. And we're not too far from the Civil War and the Revolutionary War battlefields. Just saying. There may be something to it. And some of the older houses on the outskirts of town have been the focus of ghost stories for years. Death is all around us," he said with a maniacal laugh.

Jade chided herself for another fib, but she was trying to see if any of her planted stories ended up in Mermaid Whispers. *Let's see if this experiment works.* Shaking off the guilty feeling, she changed the subject. "So, what is planned for the Love Channel premiere around Valentine's Day? What have I gotten myself into?"

Todd laughed. "Just smile. No matter how crazy it is, you know she's going to beg, wheedle, and nag until we do it."

Amy laughed and put her index finger to her lips. "Now, would I do that?"

"Yes," Jade and Todd replied, loud enough for the couple at the next table to look up from their meal.

"And you know you love doing fun stuff for the business council. It's for a wonderful cause, and this is our chance to get a first glimpse at *My Coastal Valentine*. We can stir up some business for everyone because we all know that their fan base is rabid, and they dumped a chunk of change when they were here last fall. The team's been brainstorming. We're thinking about doing a death-by-chocolate fundraiser where people pay to gorge on decadent sweets. We were also thinking about some kind of hoity toity ball. And Kim wants to do something like a blind date thing, or a meet and greet for singles. You know, like a speed-dating thing. We'll have to see what that morphs into. And then, of course, there will be the big movie premiere." Amy paused to take a sip of her drink. "I'd like to think up something book-related. Maybe I could have a bunch of romance writers at the store. Jade, you could teach us how to decorate for the holidays."

"Too bad it's in the middle of winter. The premiere would have been fun to do out on the beach. When we were kids, they'd put up a screen on the pier and show family movies on the weekends," Todd said.

"Maybe we could revive that in the summer. That would be a fun evening on the warm sand." Amy tapped on her phone. "What else can we do for the premier? We need something for the kids." Amy set her phone on the table.

"What about a 10k or a scavenger hunt?" Todd asked.

"You could have a family-friendly progressive dinner at restaurants and businesses. The ticket sales could go to a charity. Or you could have an auction," Jade said.

"Make it an online auction, and you could capitalize on the show's fans across the country," Todd said, popping a bite of his sub sandwich in his mouth.

"All great ideas. Love your energy. We make a great team," Amy said.

The trio chatted and finished their dinners as a steady stream of guests and take-out customers flooded in and out the front door like the tide.

A little after seven-thirty, Todd stood and cleared the table. "Anyone want refills or to-go cups?"

The women shook their heads.

Jade picked up her purse. "This has been fun. Thanks for inviting me. I need to get home and check on Chloe."

"And call handsome Nick to find out what's going on with the criminal element in Mermaid Bay." Amy winked. "He and Sebastian hung around the pier today. I saw them every time I passed by the windows. They'll be glad when all this fireworks stuff is over with. See if you can worm any good four-one-one out of him. Ciao, baby."

Jade waved and hustled to her Jeep. She spent the ride home thinking about the mysterious blogger since her research on Lorenzo's murder seemed to be at a dead end.

Chapter Nineteen

What a difference a day and Santa made. Jade easily exceeded her ten thousand steps before lunch as she and Lorelei greeted customers and rang up purchases as the calendar inched closer to Christmas. For most of the afternoon, the line to see Bernie stretched through the store and out on the porch.

"Whew," Lorelei said, sinking down on the stool behind the register. "This could wear a gal out. I think this has been the only time all afternoon when somebody wasn't holding that front door open."

"I know. It was a tad chilly. But I promised myself I'd never complain about a busy day. It's a good kind of tired." Jade leaned against the front counter.

"Your grandma would be so proud. She worked hard to get this store going, and you've been able to take what she rooted to the next level." Lorelei smiled at her niece.

"I took a gamble when I put all that money toward the new website and the online shopping. But it paid for itself, so it was worth it. My goal for the new year is to find some different activities that will draw folks to the store. I need to do another order for Valentine's decorations to go along with the business council plans for that show's local premier." Jade scribbled on a sticky note. "If I don't write it down, I'll forget it."

"I'm right there with you. I searched high and low for my notebook, phone, and glasses this week," Lorelei said, rifling through her purse again.

Jade straightened up and stretched her arms and neck.

"Was that your back popping?" Lorelei asked as her smile shifted to a look of concern.

"Yep. I need to stretch more." Jade grabbed her head and tilted it slowly side to side until it popped too."

"Eww. Don't do that." Lorelei rolled her eyes.

"Maybe I'll sign up for your yoga class. Want some tea?" Jade asked.

"Nah, I'm good for now. Hey, where did you hear that thing about the motorcycle gang in Mermaid Bay? Did that come from Nick?" She paused and stared intently at her niece.

"I don't remember. I heard it at either Todd's or the Busy Bean. Why?"

"I was talking to Steve last night. He hadn't heard anything on the subject. His law firm handles a bunch of criminal cases, so I was surprised he hadn't gotten wind of it. He said he planned to talk to Tom and Nick to see if the town should address it before it becomes a summer issue."

Jade pinched the bridge of her nose, hoping her plan to out the mystery blogger didn't cause problems for the town councilman and his team.

"Just curious," her aunt said. "Mermaid Bay has never been hip enough to attract the party people. I wonder what's changed? I could see it attracting characters like John Travolta and his Wild Hogs gang. We're more of a William H. Macy kind of town instead of a Sturgis."

Jade raised one shoulder and made a face. "Some days I see so many people. Not sure where I heard it. I did see a group of bikes thunder through town the other day." Changing the subject, she said, "Watch out. Amy's on the planning committee for the Valentine's Day events, and she's looking for volunteers."

Lorelei rolled her eyes. "She and Patti will have us all dressed up like Cupid or dancing hearts before this is over. Though, I am looking forward to seeing how our town appears on the Love Channel. I had fun being an extra. I've told everybody, so I can't wait until it finally airs. I hope we do something special. It is kind of a big deal."

Before Jade could comment, the bells on the front door jangled, and Nick stepped inside.

"Not a customer, but it's still good to see you, Sheriff." Lorelei winked. "I've got to do something in the back with Chloe. See y'all around in case you want some privacy."

"Hey, Lorelei. Hey, Jade." Nick took off his hat and stood next to the Christmas tree.

"Long time no see," Jade said, leaning across the counter. "What brings you by these parts?"

"Heard you had a sizable crowd today. Glad I didn't have to send someone over to direct traffic or break up a fight or worse."

Jade glanced at him. "And I was going to offer you something to drink. Don't tell me that I'm one of the town's problem businesses." She tried to project a perturbed scowl, but she cracked up when he grinned at her.

"You can never tell with all those Christmas fans. They could be trouble. We saw how crazy all those Love Channel folks were," Nick said.

"Lorelei and I were talking about that a few minutes ago. You want some coffee?" She offered.

"I'm good, thanks. Just wanted to see how you're doing. I'm leaving work on time tonight, and I'm in the mood for some seafood. Wanna go to the Red Herring?"

"Of course, she does," floated in from the back workroom.

Neville the Devil cat heard his favorite person and strutted through the lobby in search of Lorelei. He jumped on the ledge of the dividing door, eliciting a long, guttural growl from the chonky Frenchie.

Ignoring the circus around her, Jade said, "Of course, I'd like to go. Shrimp is always a favorite."

"How about if I pick you up at your place around six?"

"Sounds like a date," Lorelei yelled again from the back.

"Wanna join us?" Jade asked.

"No, thanks. I've got class tonight. I'm taking a social media workshop at the community college, and it's been a long time since I've had group projects and homework. I didn't realize it was such a time suck. It's become my life for the last few weeks. I've been so distracted," Lorelei said. "Plus, I hate to be the third wheel."

"Lorelei, you're always welcome," Nick yelled. Turning toward Jade, he said, "I better get back. The Pefferlys have been blowing up my phone today.

It seems Brianna is missing again."

Jade chewed on her bottom lip. "Any reason to suspect a problem or foul play?" she whispered.

"Don't think so. She's an adult. We're on the lookout for her, but right now, we're not even sure that she's missing. Zeke and his bunch want me to arrest Paolo and throw him under the jail."

"For what?" Jade asked.

"Lately, for existing and talking to Brianna. He seems to be their scapegoat for anything that's wrong in their world. Sebastian had to calm them down this morning. They had their own little hunt for her going on around town. If you see or hear anything out of the ordinary, call me."

"Will do. See you tonight," Jade said.

He nodded and slipped out the front door as three seniors in thick jackets approached the cash register with overflowing baskets.

"Hi, ladies. Did you find everything okay?" Jade asked.

"Oh, yes. We are so glad we found you. Love your store," the taller woman, who resembled Bea Arthur, said.

"While we focus on Christmas, we like to have decorations for every holiday, so make sure you stop back by for New Year's and Valentine's. I put some flyers and coupons in your bag, too," Jade said.

The shorter woman with the silvery bob said, "And you could throw in the name and number of that Santa cutie. He was a hoot. I'd love for him to do a party for us."

Jade smiled, pulled out three of Bernie's business cards, and passed them to the women, who left the store giggling like school girls.

"Sounds like Bernie has a fan club," Lorelei said, slipping behind the counter. "Hey, Bern, I didn't know you did private parties."

"If the price is right," Bernie said, poking his head through the doorway. "I am the jolly old elf who makes everyone's visit special. And if I'm free, I love a good party, especially if there are eats."

"And I know you'll clear your calendar for those three lovely ladies," Lorelei said.

"The consummate professional," Jade said. "I gave them all your card. You definitely impressed them." She winked as he returned to his special spot by the fireplace.

"If I didn't know he had makeup on to create his rosy cheeks, I would swear he was blushing," Lorelei said. "I've got this out here if you have other things to work on. It looks like the flow of people has slowed down a bit. I have to finish my homework."

"Thanks. Time to finish the orders before the delivery driver gets here," Jade said.

Jade spent the rest of the afternoon packing orders and printing shipping labels. After Lorelei, Neville, and Bernie left, she and Chloe zipped through the store, making sure all the doors and windows were secure, and the lights were twinkly.

Gathering her things and juggling an armload of stuff, she managed to hold Chloe's leash and lock the front door. While she fiddled with the doorknob, Chloe let out a shrill yip and pulled on the leash. Pulling loose from Jade's grip, she dashed down the wooden steps and tore off toward a man in the parking lot.

Panicked, Jade dropped her stuff and ran after her. Zeke Pefferly patted the dog's head and straightened up to his full height as Jade approached. Chloe jumped at him to get his attention.

Ignoring the dog, he said, "Hey, your pal here is friendly."

Jade stepped forward and picked up the butterball of a dog. Hugging her close to her, Jade cleared her throat and tried to prevent her voice from quaking. "She's our store greeter, and she loves people. But I worry about her running toward the road. What are you doing out here on a cold evening?"

"I'm looking for my sister. I was hoping you've seen her recently." Zeke looked around like he was waiting for someone.

"No, sorry. Just that one time when she came in to do some shopping. If I see her, is there a number where I can reach you?" Jade asked.

Still distracted, Zeke pulled out his wallet and fished out a crinkled business card. "Use this one," he said. "If you see Paolo, call me. I know he's with her. Hanging out with that slime will ruin her life. I need to put an end to that once and for all." He turned and stalked off toward the road.

Keeping him in sight, she hustled back to the porch to gather her things. On a whim, she decided to see where Zeke was going. She helped Chloe inside and put the Jeep in gear. They rolled out of the parking lot. It was a chilly night to be out walking around. And something didn't quite feel right. His story sounded a little fishy. He could cover more ground in a warm car or truck.

Zeke walked across the street to Hot Diggity Dogs. He looked like he was going inside, but he changed his mind and ambled toward Amy's bookstore, where he stood looking in the front door. Turning suddenly, he jogged back across the street toward the pizza parlor.

Jade made a U-turn as Zeke disappeared around behind the Pizza D'Action building. What was behind the store he would be interested in? Last time she checked, it was a small paved area and a trash dumpster.

Glancing at the time on her dashboard, Jade pulled into the lot. Before she could decide whether to go home and get ready for her date or follow Zeke, a white truck zoomed out from behind the brick building. Not pausing to stop at the street, he gunned it and headed toward Seaport.

Jade let out a heavy sigh. Why was he walking around looking for his sister when he had parked his truck behind the businesses? His behavior seemed erratic.

"Not sure what just happened, Chloe," Jade said. The little dog looked at her and turned her head. "Definitely weirdness. I'll mention it to Nick. We better get a move on. I need to find something to wear other than my shop T-shirt."

Chapter Twenty

Nick slid into the vinyl booth next to Jade. A spark of excitement tingled down her spine as their legs grazed each other. He could still send her into orbit and make her feel like a teenager. He scrolled through his phone as she took in the atmosphere of the restaurant. Not much had changed around here except the clientele. It tended to be a mix of an older crowd and families with kids. A few tables near the window were full.

"Hi, Sheriff. It's good to see you again," cooed a twenty-something waitress with multiple piercings in each ear and her lip. She zipped around from behind the bar and batted her thick, long eyelashes for several seconds before handing him a menu.

"Uh, hi," he said, reaching for the plastic menus.

She pushed her aqua-tipped hair behind her ears. "It's been a hot minute since I've seen you or your guys. Please tell Sebastian that Anji says hello. You all must be busy. I haven't seen him around here in weeks. Are you working him too hard? Oh, are you all still solving that murder? The one that happened next to that funny store. I saw it on the news."

"'Tis the Season," Nick added. "It's a Christmas Shoppe across from Hot Diggity Dogs."

"Well, a murder doesn't sound very Christmasy," she snickered. "What can I get you guys to drink?"

"I'll have an iced tea," Nick said.

"Me too," Jade added, scooting a bit closer to Nick.

"Nothing stronger? You're both off duty, right?" Anji asked.

"Tea's fine," Nick said.

"Same for me. The Christmas Shoppe closes at five, but you never know if Santa's watching." Jade winked at the waitress. "So, I guess that means I'm never off duty either."

A surprised look crossed the younger woman's face, but she recovered quickly. "Do you all know what you want to eat? If not, I'll be back with your drinks before you miss me."

"We need a few minutes," Nick said, setting his menu on the table.

"Be back in a flash." Anji trotted off toward the bar as she glanced back over her shoulder.

"Friendly sort," Jade said. "What are you having?"

"Jealous?" he asked with a mischievous grin. "Or just offended by the funny store comment?"

Jade offered a wry smile and shook her head. "Any specialties on the menu tonight?"

"Steak and shrimp." Nick winked and draped his arm around her shoulders as the waitress appeared with their teas and a basket of hushpuppies.

What can I get you all this chilly evening?" she asked.

"I'll have the mushroom-smothered steak and the grilled shrimp with the baked potato," Nick said.

"Loaded baked potato and salad?"

He nodded and said, "With ranch."

Anji stared at Jade. "And what about you?"

"I'll have the popcorn shrimp with a baked potato and house salad with French dressing."

"Very good. These will be out soon. Let me know if you need anything." She wiggled her fingers at Nick.

When she was out of earshot, Jade asked, "So, anything new with Lorenzo Zanetti?"

"Not really. He hasn't said anything. Sorry, warped cop humor," he said, lowering his voice. "He was stabbed and moved to where he was found. Alcohol and weed came back in his tox screens. I looked into your book theory. He was taking writing classes and in some online groups. No indication that he ever published anything. His cousin confirmed that he was writing a thriller about a family who ran a fireworks company. Write what you know, I guess. He also mentioned that the grandfather had gotten upset a couple of times when Lorenzo talked about his manuscript. Like you said, the senior Zanetti was insistent that he shouldn't write about the family or the business. Obviously, the fireworks world is a lot like that of the magicians, where it's sacrosanct to keep all tradecraft confidential."

"I never realized it was such a cut-throat business. I thought it was one of those happy jobs like amusement park owner."

"It's expensive to stay on the cutting edge, and everyone seems to be a copycat. You have to keep changing up your act to wow people. And some of these contracts are quite lucrative. Sebastian and I talked to the Adkins brothers, Trey and Will, from Crash Boom Bang. They've diversified to include a drone light show with some serious techno-wizardry and a ton of technicians to pull it off. Will promised that Saturday will be eye-popping. Their operation looks like it's done with military precision and security that rivals Camp Peary or Ft. Knox."

"Interesting. The Zanettis had a good show, but it was only with traditional fireworks. Very old school. I think Zeke's crew was the same, but theirs didn't come off as polished," Jade said. "Technology is the wave of the future."

"The first two families are still pointing fingers and accusing the other of all kinds of despicable deeds," he said. "My guys will be glad when they all leave town."

"Did you all ever find Brianna?" Jade asked, popping part of a hushpuppy in her mouth.

Nick shook his head. "Nope. She disappeared, and Zeke couldn't tell what, if anything, was missing from her room. He couldn't say whether or not she took anything with her."

"I saw Zeke this evening. He asked me if I had seen her." She neglected to mention Zeke's weird behavior after the business council meeting.

A slight frown crossed Nick's face. "Did he say anything else?"

"Not really. He was kind of jumpy. He gave me his card and said to call if I saw Brianna and Paolo."

"How jumpy?"

"It was kinda weird. Chloe had gotten loose. She ran to him in the parking lot. I was kinda having my own personal crisis at the moment. I was worried that she would run into the street. Zeke kept looking over his shoulder. He walked up to the store, and when he left, he went behind the realty office and the pizza parlor to retrieve his truck. It was odd."

"Stay clear of them. Call me if they come around again. He's got a temper and a record that goes back multiple years. He's obsessed with Paolo and the Zanettis. And he fancies himself as his sister's protector."

Before Nick could elaborate, the waitress approached with a tray of steaming plates. "Be careful. These are hot." She set them down like she was slinging hash at a diner. Steak sauce and ketchup are on the table. Can I get you anything else?"

Jade shook her head, and Nick replied, "Nope. We're good. Thanks."

He waited until Anji disappeared in the kitchen, and then he answered. "The Pefferlys said they hadn't heard from Brianna. I'll see them again if she's not back soon. They're itching to file a missing person's report. They've been bugging the heck out of my deputy today. Now, they're speculating that Paolo kidnapped her, and they want to press charges."

"Do you think it's foul play?" Jade asked, mashing her baked potato and spreading the butter around.

"Doubtful. My gut tells me she ran off to meet someone or to have a fling. I've got one of the deputies monitoring her social sites. So far, nothing. I sent Sebastian over to talk to the Zanettis this afternoon. No one has seen Paolo all day, so that kinda leads me to the theory that they're off somewhere together."

"Were the Zanettis as worried about Paolo?"

Nick shook his head. "Nope. They acted like it was normal for him to disappear."

"Hmmm. What did the Zanettis have to say about Brianna?" she asked.

"They were sorry that she was missing. They had nothing to do with it, and they try not to have any contact with that family. Sebastian said it was like pulling teeth to get any information from them. One of the cousins did mention that the family knew Paolo was seeing her, but they hoped it was a phase. And if it got serious, Aldo, the grandfather, planned to cut him out of the business and the will. He had made that perfectly clear to Paolo and the rest of the family."

Jade's eyes widened. *That could be a motivation for a murder. But Lorenzo had been murdered, not Paolo.* "Sounds like the Hatfields and the McCoys. The end of the festival can't come soon enough."

"Agreed," Nick said. "But we'll have to steel ourselves for the chaos if one of them gets the fireworks' contract."

The pair fell silent and focused on their dinners.

When Nick's steak and Jade's shrimp had almost disappeared, she set her fork down and asked, "Is your spidey sense tingling? I mean, do you think Brianna is in any danger?"

Nick shook his head. "From what Zeke said, she's done this before. She usually makes contact after a couple of days when she feels like it. He said she's gone jetting off with friends on ski strips and shopping extravaganzas before without telling anyone. Then, in the next breath, he insisted that Paolo was trying to corrupt her and take her somewhere against her will. He said Paolo was even trying to brainwash her. Then he gave me a ten-minute explanation of how Paolo was trying to force her to shun her family." Jade rubbed her eyes, and Nick continued, "They're both in their mid-twenties. They are adults."

When the couple pushed their plates back, Anji swooped in like a seagull after a French fry. "Did you two save room for dessert? We have a whole list of yummy stuff."

"No, thanks," Jade said. "Dinner was delicious."

"Just the check next time you're by." Nick took a swig of his drink.

"Okey dokey," Anji said, giving him a sly smile.

When she returned, Nick pulled out his wallet as a shrill tone came from his pocket. He tossed his credit card on the plastic tray for Anji and fished his phone out of his jacket pocket.

"Driscoll, here. Gotcha. Interesting. Nah. Meet me at the office. What time is it now? Let's say eight, and I'll go over with you. Yep. Nope. Thanks for calling."

A sheepish look crossed his face as he pocketed his phone.

"I know," Jade said, smiling. "The hazards of dating a cop. Dinner was nice. Why don't you come over on Sunday, and we can watch football? I'll make game-day food."

"Deal. Sorry to cut tonight short. That was Sebastian. One of the deputies on Facebook patrol has an idea where Brianna and Paolo are, and it doesn't look nefarious."

Chapter Twenty-One

After Nick dropped Jade off, she and Chloe decided to burn some pent-up energy on a brisk walk. The wind off the bay whipped her hair around in all directions and chilled Jade to the bone, despite her big coat. Jade glanced around at the beach, populated only by a few gulls. "Let's go, Chloe. It's a wee bit frigid out here tonight. I'll race you back home."

Challenge accepted. The little Frenchie took off, kicking up sand and galloping toward the cut-through.

Back inside her cozy cottage, Jade fluffed the lap blanket for the little dog. Jade said, "That's better. Let's snuggle on the couch and see what's on TV after I make a cup of hot chocolate. That wind was something out there," Jade said. Chloe burrowed under the fuzzy blanket on the couch as Jade tried to tame her wild curls into a ponytail. Giving up on her unruly hair, she snuggled with Chloe for an evening of true crime documentaries.

A series of beeps echoed in the quiet room. Jade sat up on the couch and tried to sort out where she was. Turning off the TV, she picked up her phone. *Twelve-thirty.*

Her cameras on the front of the store picked up three guys prowling around the porch. They moved around in jerky motions. Then they shoved a guy into one of her rocking chairs. In the next clip, two guys made their way down the steps and disappeared. No sign of a vehicle. No other movements.

Jade's heart leapt into her throat, and her mind raced. *Was this a break-in? What is going on at the store?*

After texting Nick the clips, Jade stared at her live camera feed for a few moments. Nothing else happened. Where did those guys go? And it looks like somebody is still on the property.

Waiting impatiently for a response from Nick that never came, Jade slid on her coat and rummaged through the junk drawer for her pepper spray.

Pocketing her phone and keys, she slipped out the door and jogged to the store. Her hand had a death grip on the can of pepper spray. Her heartbeat pounded in her ears like the rough surf crashing on the shore. Hoping that walking would be a stealthier way to arrive, she tried to stay in the shadows as she neared the store.

Pausing beside a huge bush on her neighbor's property, she peered at her store's porch. Someone was still sitting in one of the chairs. No movement. Adrenaline surged through her entire body, making her ignore that little warning voice in her head that sounded an awful lot like Nick. *Where are the other two guys?*

She took a deep breath and tiptoed closer, hoping the other guys were long gone. An eerie quietness had settled on the property.

As she approached, the figure in the chair slid down. His head and arms dangled over the arm of the wooden rocker. She pulled out her phone and tapped 911.

"Mermaid Bay 911, what's your emergency?"

"This is Jade Hicks. I'm in front of my store, 'Tis the Season on Neptune Road. My security cameras alerted me to people on my property. When I went to check it out, there's a guy slumped over in one of my chairs on my front porch," she whispered.

"Is he breathing?" the dispatcher asked.

"I can't tell. I didn't get close enough. There were two other guys who left him there. I'm not sure where they are. I'm scared they'll come back. Could you send police and an ambulance?"

"They're on their way. Are you in a safe place?" the dispatcher asked.

"Sort of. I'm near the front of my store. I don't see anyone else around." Jade glanced over her shoulder for good measure.

"Okay, stay where you are. Emergency is en route. They're estimating that they're about two minutes out. The police are coming, too. Is anyone else there?"

"Just the guy on the porch," Jade whispered.

She took a deep breath. Every little noise sent her imagination into overdrive. The wind rustled through the pine trees, and an occasional tree frog croaked. She tried to will her blood pressure to return to normal, but her heartbeat pounded in her ears. Who's on her porch? *Please let him not be dead.*

"You doing okay?" the dispatcher asked, jolting Jade from her dark thoughts.

"I'm fine. Just a little creeped out."

A crack and a crunch made Jade jump. She heard footsteps approaching. Jade looked around frantically as her pulse hit Mach 1. In the faint light from the neighbors' houses, Jade thought she saw movement. A large figure approached. Another one stood off to the side of the lot.

Jade tried to scream, but only a squeak came out.

"Jade, are you there? Are you okay? What's going on?" the dispatcher asked.

"Why are you poking your nose in this?" the closer figure asked. "This doesn't concern you," he growled.

Jade opened her mouth and closed it again. Gritting her teeth, she was determined not to show the panic that welled up inside her. Her fingers closed tightly around the phone, where she could hear the dispatcher trying to make contact. *I hope she can hear this. He had to be talking to me, right?*

Chapter Twenty-Two

"This is family business, and he should have kept his mouth shut and his stupid brother in check." The figure turned his head toward the guy on the porch.

Jade didn't reply. Her pulse thundered in her ears, and she gasped when the figure took a couple of tentative steps toward her. Her nose twitched when she got a whiff of alcohol and cheap cologne. Jade caught a glimpse of Zeke Pefferly's face as he stepped out of the shadows for an instant. She sucked in a mouthful of cold, night air.

"Everything would have been okay if his slimy brother hadn't brainwashed my baby sister and convinced her to run away with him. I can't believe Bri would fall for his fast-talking and schmoozing. I thought she was smarter than that. But she left with him. I still don't get it." He paused and looked around. "Maybe she didn't, though. I still don't buy what the cop said. I think Paolo tricked her. He needs to be arrested for kidnapping."

Jade heard a faint siren in the distance. Trying to stall, she mustered her courage and yelled, "Why would you attack him if his brother was the problem? Paolo isn't even around."

Zeke took a step toward her. "They're all the problem. Constantly trying to steal our stuff. They're trouble. This is the icing on the cake. And it was a fair fight. He mouthed off and got what he deserved. He should be smarter than taking on more than one of us at a time. It proves my case. They ain't too bright."

"Come on, man," the other hoodie guy said. "We gotta get out of here."

"Remo, make sure you tell the old man that we're not going to stand for this. We're fighting back this time and every chance we get. We don't plan to rest until Brianna is back safely where she'll never see your brother again."

The other guy approached Zeke. "Now. We need to go. Now." From where he stood in the shadows, Jade couldn't tell if it was Goose or Tank.

"It doesn't matter. And I don't really care. They know who we are," Zeke said, swatting the other guy away. "Her cop friend will be around to talk to us again. If he can find us." He turned toward Jade and said, "Tell your boyfriend that we're tired of waiting for him to do his job."

The two disappeared in the darkness. Jade let out a long breath and closed her eyes for a moment.

"Jade, are you okay?" The dispatcher repeated for what seemed like the twentieth time.

"I'm fine. Sorry. The two guys came back, but now they're gone again. Oh, wait, I see flashing lights. I see a deputy. Thanks for all of your help." Jade disconnected as a police SUV pulled into her lot. Red and blue lights bounced around and filled the lot with light, and brought Jade a sense of relief. Sebastian climbed out as Jade hurried toward him.

"Hey. My cameras alerted. There were three guys. Two of them left that guy on my porch. And one of them was Zeke Pefferly. I'm not sure if the guy in the chair is sleeping it off or if he's hurt," Jade said, pausing to catch her breath.

"Are you okay? Where are the other guys?" Sebastian asked.

"They dumped him and hightailed it that way. Then Zeke and some other guy came back. Zeke was angry that Paolo had run away with his sister. They disappeared into the darkness, over that way." Jade pointed over her shoulder.

"Stay here," he said, opening the back door of his vehicle for her. "You can sit here."

Sebastian jogged to the porch as Jade heard another siren. He checked the body for a pulse as the siren screamed louder.

Shielding her eyes to block the oncoming glare of the ambulance's headlights, Jade bounced up and down and pointed toward the porch with her free hand. The ambulance skidded to a stop, and two EMTs bounded up the wooden steps.

Minutes dragged by. She craned her neck to see what Sebastian and the two EMTs were doing. They blocked the body that they had moved from the chair and onto the porch. All she could see were the three men hunched over Remo. She said a silent prayer that he was okay.

As her legs started to twinge, she plopped down in the back of the SUV. Sebastian walked the perimeter of her store as the EMTs continued to assist the guy on her porch. What was taking so long?

A flash blinded Jade momentarily. She heard a door slam, an engine whir, and tires squeal. Nosy Nell zoomed out of the parking lot in her Fiat. *Great. I hope I'm not Nell's latest story for the Beachcomber Gazette. Not my most flattering photo in the back of a police vehicle. I'm surprised she didn't ask any questions about what was going on.*

The EMTs hoisted Remo on the gurney and maneuvered it down the steps. As they loaded him in the back of the ambulance, Jade tiptoed closer for a better look.

Remo Zanetti, his face swollen and cut, lay unresponsive on the gurney.

"Is he going to be okay?" she asked.

"He's breathing on his own. That's always a good sign. He'll be sore for a while, but I'm hopeful. We'll see if he has any broken bones. Please tell the deputy we'll be at the emergency room entrance."

"Will do. Thanks." *Remo, what were you doing messing with the Pefferlys? This didn't look like a fair fight.*

Nick's SUV flew into the parking lot, kicking up sand in a mini storm visible in the glow of his taillights. "Jade!" he yelled.

"I'm fine. It's Zeke. You need to go find him before he does anything else. Zeke and another guy beat up Remo and left him here."

"What are you doing here?" he asked, letting out a heavy breath and adjusting his gun belt.

Before she could answer, they heard footsteps, and Sebastian trotted around the other side of the building. "No sign of anyone else." He nodded in Nick's direction. "Jade, can I see those clips?"

"The alert from the cameras woke me up. I came over to see what was going on. And before you fuss at me, I stayed clear of the porch until Sebastian got here." Jade tapped the app on her phone and handed it to him.

Nick nodded and took the phone that Sebastian handed him.

"I'll have a couple of deputies canvas the area and check security cameras of homes and businesses when it's daylight," Sebastian said.

"One of the EMTs said to tell you they were headed to the emergency room entrance," Jade said as the ambulance lit up and pulled out onto the street.

Two shots rang out, and the retorts echoed in the quiet of the night. Nick shoved Jade behind the SUV, and he and Sebastian drew their weapons and took cover behind the vehicles. *Could it have been a car backfire?* Nick and Sebastian's reaction disproved her theory. *This is like a bad dream.*

Jade crawled under Sebastian's vehicle and tried to see where the shots were coming from. Afraid that Nick or Sebastian didn't have time to call it in, she wiggled until she could pull out her phone. Punching in 911 again, she yelled into the phone before the dispatcher got her message out. "This is Jade Hicks again. I'm still at 'Tis the Season. Someone is shooting at the ambulance and Sheriff Driscoll and Deputy Sanchez. Please send back-up now! Hurry!"

"Shots fired. Officers are on the way. Ma'am, are you safe?"

"I'm under the police vehicle. Nick and Sebastian are looking for the shooter. I can't see where they are at this moment." Jade jumped when more gunfire echoed. She tried to shield her head with her other arm. It was hard to tell where the shots came from. Jade was sure it was a handgun, but the proximity made it sound like a cannon. Her phone started alerting. Ignoring the incoming texts, Jade said, "Nick and Sebastian took off with their guns drawn. The ambulance floored it and drove over the curb. It's gone."

"Can you get to a safer place?" the dispatcher asked.

"No. Too much open space. I don't know who's shooting or from where." Jade tried to swallow the bile that was rising in her throat. She took a couple of calming breaths.

"Okay, stay put. And do whatever the officers tell you. Two other units are almost there. I'll let them know you're under the police vehicle. Anyone else there?"

"No. Not that I know of. The ambulance left with the injured guy. Please tell the deputies to hurry." Jade tried to get control of her panicked voice.

"Can you tell me what's going on? Do you see anyone?" the dispatcher asked.

"No, it's quiet and dark. I haven't heard anything for a while now. I don't know where Nick and Sebastian went," Jade whispered.

Chapter Twenty-Three

Thundering footsteps distracted Jade from her conversation with the dispatcher.

"Jade, Jade," Nick yelled.

"The sheriff is back. I've gotta go." She clicked the red button on her phone and crawled out from under the SUV.

Nick's strong arms pulled her the rest of the way out and helped her to her feet.

"Did you find the shooter?" she asked as Sebastian ran around from the other side of her store.

"No. Are you okay?" Nick asked.

"I'm fine." Jade dusted sand and pebbles off her clothes.

"Go lock yourself in the store and stay away from the windows. I'll let you know what we find." Nick jerked open the door to his vehicle, and Sebastian climbed in the other SUV.

She nodded as Nick and Sebastian sped off in different directions.

Full of adrenaline and panic, Jade was in no mood to go wait in the office, but she didn't want to be a sitting duck if the shooter came back to the store. She needed to check on Chloe. Ignoring Nick's order, she jogged home, constantly looking over her shoulder for any movement.

Once deadbolted inside her bungalow, she picked up Chloe for hugs. The little dog was interested in going back to bed than she was in Jade's midnight adventures or the cuddles.

Too pumped to sleep, Jade did a load of laundry and sat down with a glass of milk at her dining room table with her laptop. There had to be more out there on the Pefferlys and their crew. She pulled up their website with bios on all the team. Buried deep in the Google pages, she found details including their full names, Abner "Tank" King and Walter "Goose" Jennings. *Interesting.*

Jade spent hours scouring the web and social media sites for any information she could find on the fireworks teams. Most of the Pefferlys and the Zanettis were kin. Crash Boom Bang was the only company that had a larger crew of employees. She decided to do a deeper dive into the Zanetti family. Maybe Lorenzo had some deep, dark secret that caused all this?

Stopping to rub her eyes, Jade was about ready to wrap it up. *Lots of little bits of information, but no clue about the murder or the attack.* Deciding to check another site before hitting the shower and starting her day, Jade scrolled through TikTok.

"Well, I'll be," Jade said aloud, causing Chloe to jump. "Sorry, puppy. But I think I found something. Well, lookie here. There's Brianna and Paolo living it up in the Bahamas at some club, showing off a new pair of left-hand rings." She copied the link and sent it to Nick. "I guess Zeke can stop searching for them now." Chloe rolled over and snorted, not interested in the pair's love life or their elopement.

Jaded added her notes to her wall and headed off for a much-needed shower. *I'm going to feel this today. All-nighters are for college kids.*

The hot shower and double shot of espresso seemed to get her moving a little faster. After feeding Chloe, she said, "Come on, might as well get some real work done instead of fretting about all this craziness and going down so many rabbit holes on the internet."

She and Chloe settled in the Jeep and made a quick detour to the Busy Bean before heading to the store. The lights in the coffee shop's windows welcomed early risers. "Let's go see James and Sophie. I need another high-test jolt to stay awake today. My home brew has already worn off."

They wandered into the brightly lit store that exuded calmness. Just what Jade needed after all the stress of this morning.

"Hey, you're up early," James said, creating a drink for Cecil Jacobs, one of Bernie's fishing buddies, who waited at the counter.

"Hey, Jade. Hey, Chloe. I think we're the early birds today." Cecil looked over his shoulder at the quiet dining room.

James laughed. "Cecil, you're here when we open every morning."

"I've slept in once or twice," Cecil remarked. "Today, I'm headed over to the pier to see who shows up. We've been watching who comes and goes since all this nonsense started with the fireworks. A couple of the guys spent the night in case there were any shenanigans. We're each pulling shifts on guard duty."

James handed him his to-go cup and a bag. "Sophie wants y'all to try out some new sweets. Let us know what you think."

"'Preciate it," Cecil said. "The guys will love it and be glad to tell everyone how great they are."

"Y'all fishing this morning?" Jade asked. "Brrr."

"Nah, it's mostly chewing the fat. Bernie calls it networking. And like I said, we're keeping a watch out on the pier for people trying to mess with the equipment. See you around." Cecil tipped his ball cap and waddled out the front door.

"What can I do for you?" James asked.

"I'll have a ham and cheese croissant and a chocolate mocha to get my mojo going. I need the caffeine and sugar today." Jade stepped closer to the register.

James said, "I saw on Facebook that there was some activity down your way. Everything okay?"

Jade had been too busy with her research that she neglected the texts and alerts from her own social sites. "It was kinda hectic and a rude awakening in the middle of the night. My store cameras woke me up. There were some trespassers. I kinda got tied up with the police after that." Jade made a mental note to catch up on the missed messages.

"Some people posted that they heard gunshots. Anybody hurt?" he asked.

"Just the guy who was dumped at my store. The ambulance took him away." Jade pulled out her phone and started scrolling. When she noticed James's surprised look, she added, "But he wasn't shot. The gunfire happened when the ambulance was leaving."

After swiping her card, James handed her a bag and cup. "Sorry you got dragged out of bed. You may want to check out Nell's post," he said, raising one eyebrow. "Her version sounded like it was the shootout at the O.K. Corral."

Jade rolled her eyes. "Thanks, just what I need at a Christmas store." She and Chloe found a table near the front window. Over fifteen texts and a bunch of Facebook messages about the crime spree in Mermaid Bay greeted her. Letting out a heavy sigh, she spent breakfast responding to comments and letting folks know she was okay.

Not hearing anything from Nick, she sent him a link to Nell's exaggerated account of what happened and a frowny emoji. "Fingers crossed, Chloe. Maybe he'll have a real update for us soon."

"Chloe, I'm so sorry," James said, scooting around the corner. "I forgot your treat this morning. I don't know where my head is lately. Sophie made these yesterday, and you get to be the first taste-tester. They're peanut butter bites, but I think I'll rename them Chloe's Peanut Butter Blossoms."

The round dog woofed her approval and danced on her hind legs for the treat.

"I think that's five stars," Jade said, picking up her trash. "Let's go get the store ready for this weekend."

"All of the fall and winter events have been fun." James wiped down the counter. "But I'm kinda glad the fireworks business will be over soon. Way too much drama for me." Jade waved as a blast of frigid air greeted them when she opened the door.

Jade drove deliberately around her store's parking lot. No sign that this was a crime scene earlier. She shook off a shiver and drove around to the back. Nothing looked out of place.

She parked and hurried around to the passenger side to help Chloe down. The pair hustled inside, where the unlit trees cast a spooky, shadowy pall on the store. "What we need is some happy music." She flipped through her playlists and turned on the Eighties Christmas songs. "Last Christmas" by Wham! floated throughout the store as she added some dance moves to her store-opening routine.

"There, that's much better. Now I'm getting into the holiday spirit," she said, plopping down in her chair and booting her laptop. "Peppy music and twinkly lights make everything better."

She printed the night's orders and got distracted by some Facebook posts on the neighborhood page about the goings-on at her end of Neptune Road. Lots of comments about how crime is out of control.

The shooting had to be related to Zeke and Remo. It was too much of a coincidence that a shooter came along after the other violence. The possibilities made Jade's head start to throb. And why would Zeke or his pal be stupid enough to shoot at the police and an ambulance after they had already left the scene? That would take the fight and dumping Remo to a whole other level. Why shoot at law enforcement? Or were the shots meant for someone else? Jade wrapped her arms around herself to stave off the shivers. Fumbling through her desk drawer, she found a bottle of aspirin and popped two in her mouth as she rubbed her temples.

Ignoring the online orders, she Googled more information on the Pefferlys. Typing Walter "Goose" Jennings, she found a few hits on Zeke's cousin. Most of the pictures of him were of his drinking buddies or shots with young blond women. A quick search for Abner "Tank" King yielded even less. He flew under the radar with no social media presence. She clicked down near the bottom of the list of results and whistled when she found a local news story about Tank's sports scholarship to a prep school and then another report of an arrest in his twenties for his part in a bar fight. He also did time for driving a get-away car after a liquor store robbery.

"Well, at least this is more than I had," Jade said. She printed copies of all of what she had found. *Goose seems to be in the middle of things. Maybe I should focus on him.* She spent the better part of an hour searching with nothing else to show for her efforts.

As a last-ditch attempt to find something, she opened a website full of electronic yearbooks and searched for all the players. Maybe she could find something from their younger years. It didn't take long to locate the three at a prep school in Philadelphia where Tank got his scholarship. Zeke and Goose dotted the pages of their senior yearbook with track team and lacrosse pictures. Both seemed to be the life of the party. A sullen Tank appeared in two or three shots for the wrestling and football teams.

After another hour of searching that yielded only a smattering of clues, Jade closed her web browser and grabbed a cart to fill the online orders. "Time to get up and move around," she said to Chloe.

The bells on the front door jangled, and Jade poked her head in the lobby. "Hey, Lorelei and Neville. How are you all doing?" The tuxedo cat wove in and out of her aunt's legs and hopped on the counter to show his best majestic pose.

"We're fine. How about you? Are you okay?" Concerned flashed across her aunt's face. "Your text this morning was a little cryptic. I heard it was a bit tense around here. I was surprised that there wasn't any police presence this morning when I pulled up. It looks pretty normal out there. No trace of what went on earlier. With a shooting, I expected crime scene tape at the very least."

Jade shrugged a shoulder. "Nick and Sebastian went off after whoever was doing the shooting. It was all terrifying. The ambulance hauled Remo to the hospital. There was some fight earlier with him and the Pefferlys. I never did figure out what that was about or who did the shooting. I guess they're done with their investigation here."

"The violence around here has increased exponentially. We all knew that Mermaid Bay couldn't stay isolated forever. New folks are moving in, and the big city ills are approaching, if they're not here already," her aunt mused. "I hope the gunfire has nothing to do with the gang sightings you mentioned the other day. That's the last thing we need here." Lorelei stowed her black Gucci bag behind the counter and stroked Neville's neck.

Hoping that she didn't start something with her rumors to out the Mermaid Whispers blogger, Jade raised one eyebrow. "I gathered all the orders. I need to give Chloe a quick walk, and I'll be back to box them."

"Neville and I can work on that until the crowds roll in." Her aunt dusted her hands and followed Jade to the workroom.

After slipping on her coat and the harness over the little dog, the pair made their way across the back field. The cold didn't seem to bother Chloe this morning. She pranced around, sniffing every clump of grass and searching for the elusive and often-phantom squirrels.

There was no sign that anything sinister happened here. It looked like it did every other morning. Chloe tugged on her lead and pulled toward the oleander hedge and the fence at the back of the property. The little dog snorted and buried her nose in a patch of clover. As Jade tried to guide her toward the store, the Frenchie yanked harder, determined to find whatever she was searching for.

"What is it, baby?" Jade said, leaning over. Picking up a silver and white thing that looked like it belonged in Dr. Frankenstein's lab, Jade turned it over in her hands. It had a plunger like a hypodermic needle and some sort of sparkplug-looking thing on the other end. Several wires dangled from the middle. "What did you find? And how did it get here?"

Chloe looked disappointed that Jade had taken her new toy. "Let's go figure this out. It's cold out here." The pair headed for the door and the warmth of the office.

After a treat that the bag billed as a Chunk of Joy, Chloe returned to her bed, the weird plaything all but forgotten for the moment.

"Whatcha got there?" Lorelei asked, stacking the boxes in the bin for pickup.

"I don't really know. Chloe found it near the fence." Jade turned it over in her hands, and the wires flapped like some kind of weird party favor.

"That is some kind of contraption. You think it's drug paraphernalia? That's all we need is a spike in drug use, and it's not even the summer season." Her aunt planted both hands on her hips.

"I don't think so." Jade snapped a picture and asked Google what this was.

Pictures of medical devices and lawn mower sparkplugs popped up. "This isn't helpful. I'll post a picture on Facebook. Maybe the collective hive will know what it is. Somebody's bound to be able to ID it. And once I know what it is, maybe I can figure out who it belongs to. It's too weird to be random trash."

"I'd try Bernie. He knows everything gadgety." Lorelei said.

The bells jangled, and Lorelei switched into greeter mode. "Let's start our day." She clapped her hands and sashayed toward the lobby.

"What is this thingy?" Jade asked Chloe. "I should go wash my hands, huh?"

Chloe turned her head, still miffed that Jade had taken her find.

Chapter Twenty-Four

The next morning, Jade finished the remaining drops of her coffee and checked her social media sites. The weird contraption that Chloe found received a ton of comments, mostly from people cracking jokes or providing possible uses for it. None were that helpful. She picked up the device and turned it over sideways. "What is this? This is some kind of electronic thing. Maybe I should go talk to Bernie." Chloe raised her head. Not seeing any treats, she decided to return to her nap.

"I have no idea. What are you talking about?" Lorelei breezed in with Neville.

After one yip and a snarl, the chase was on through the store before any of the humans had a chance to close the dividing door.

"I hope they don't knock anything over," Jade said, listening to the dog and cat race through the showrooms.

"I'll check on it in a bit. Coffee first. Did you ever find out what that thing was?" Lorelei slid a mug under the coffee maker's spout.

"I have no idea. I posted it, and so far, nobody has any serious ideas. Late night for you?"

"Nah. Not a fun one. I've been working on a project. I'm too old to stay up past midnight anymore. That'll teach me." Lorelei stirred in enough creamer to turn her coffee beige.

Jade sent Bernie a text to see which of his favorite hangouts he was currently haunting.

A quick reply from her part-time handyman affirmed he was hanging out in the pier's office.

"I need to see Bernie for a few. Be back in a sec." Jade pulled on her coat and stuck the device in her pocket.

Pausing when the icy breeze off the bay hit her in the face, Jade pulled her scarf tighter around her neck and picked up her pace. The fresh air and the exercise might help to clear her head. She crossed the empty street and hustled toward the pier.

Jade ascended the ramp to the pier's entrance and watched the fireworks guys mill around, stacking crates and black boxes. All the equipment made her curious about tomorrow's show. This looked like a major production. Jade picked her way around all the Crash Boom Bang stuff.

The tiny office that looked more like a shack or a 1950s kids' clubhouse sat alone at her end of the pier. Jade knocked on the weathered blue door. Not waiting for an answer, she turned the knob and stepped into a sauna. "Wow, it's tropical in here," she said to Bernie and Cecil. "How are y'all?"

"Toasty. We like it snug in here. Close that door before old man winter creeps in with you," Cecil said, pointing to the small space heater on the floor.

"Mornin', Jade. What brings you out on such a perfect beach day?" Jade furrowed her brow, and Bernie continued, "Every time an out-of-towner calls about tourist information, I always tell that it's a balmy eighty-five degrees. And the fishing's great."

Jade smiled and pulled out the mystery device. "Hope they don't get mad when they find out we have all four seasons in Coastal Virginia. I was walking Chloe last night, and we found this. Any ideas on what it is?" She waved the mystery thing in the air, and the dangly ends clacked like some kind of noisemaker.

"Hmm," Bernie said, pulling out his reading glasses.

Cecil reached for it as Bernie held it up to catch the light from the office's only window that had a film from years of grime and salt spray.

"I have no idea. Maybe it's one of those new, fangled electronic car parts that you need a computer degree to understand," Cecil muttered.

"It's some kind of switch," Bernie said. "Like an igniter, but it's not a spark plug." He pointed to the metal and ceramic piece that stuck out on top.

Handing it back to her, he said, "I don't think it goes on an engine."

The door opened, and a blast of frigid air filled the tiny space.

"Woah, Nellie. Close that door," Cecil sputtered.

A tall man and his border collie entered. "Sorry," he said, shuffling inside and closing the door behind his black and white dog.

"Hey, Jade. You might ask Will here if he knows what this is," Bernie said. "He's the resident expert on gadgets these days. You should see all the stuff they hauled off those tractor-trailers. Tomorrow's show will be epic. Did you know he has drones?"

Jade shook her head and handed Will the device. "My dog found it in a field yesterday. Nobody on Facebook seemed to know what it was. I've gotten answers that range from boom box converter to a Tesla sparkplug." Jade let the dog sniff her hand, and then she patted his head.

A grin crossed Will's face. "That's Roscoe. He's part of the team."

"I've seen you all around town. I'm Jade Hicks."

"Yep, we've been here for a while checking out the competition. Our turn is tomorrow. That's an igniter. I haven't seen one quite like this before, but it's used to control fireworks when you're sequencing them. You plug this into the board, and this plug is to daisy chain it to the next set of explosives."

"Interesting. I have no idea what it was doing in my yard. But it's probably linked somehow to either the Zanettis or the Pefferlys," Jade said.

"Mind if I take a picture of it?" he asked, whipping out his phone and clicking three or four shots before she could object.

"If you hear of anyone missing one, send them my way. I own the Christmas store down the street," she said. He handed her the device, and she stuffed it in her pocket. "Thanks, y'all. I'm going to get out of your way."

Will stared at the photos on his phone. "It's not one of ours. We brand all our equipment. I've not seen anything that looks like this before." He stared at the photos on his phone.

"It's nice to have an idea of what it is. I almost trashed it. See you all tomorrow at the show," Jade said, patting Rosco again.

"I'll be at your place all decked out as the Big Guy in the red suit bright and early tomorrow morning," Bernie yelled.

"See ya," She waved over her shoulder and made a quick exit, so Cecil wouldn't fuss about her holding the door open too long.

Interesting. What was a firework igniter doing on her property? It was too far back in the lot to have been thrown from a passing car. Someone dropped it or hid it near the bushes. Was someone planning to light off fireworks from her lot?

On the way to the store, Jade's phone played a snippet of Frank Zappa's "Library Card." "Hi, Vivian. What's up?" she asked after clicking the green button.

"Jade. This was supposed to be a fun holiday season, and it's turned into a regular crime spree. Since those firework guys have been in town, we've had fights, vandalism, a murder, and now a shooting. People won't come here if they think it's not safe. I'm wondering if we should have another emergency meeting and have the sheriff give us an update. We all need a refresher on personal safety and active shooter drills."

Jade pictured Vivian wringing her hands and pacing as she talked.

"Mmmm. It's over tomorrow night. Why don't we see how that goes, and then your committee can announce the winner? Maybe that will sort out everything. Don't worry. By the time Memorial Day and summer roll around, the tourists will have forgotten all about it. It'll be a distant memory."

"I hope you're right. But this will get bigger and bigger and blow up in our faces. And we're not going to be able to control the spin." Vivian let out a long puff of air. "And if I have my way, I will disqualify the two that have done nothing but cause trouble. My nerves can't take having either of them back twice next year. Here's hoping that tomorrow's crew is head and shoulders above the rest. I want it to be an easy decision. This event has caused way more problems than I ever imagined."

"Vivian, it'll be fine. I vote that you pick a winner and send out the council's choice after tomorrow night. We'll all be sure to blast it out on our social media sites to create a buzz. Plus, everyone is getting ready for the holidays. They're too busy to think about the bickering and unfortunate events that seemed to be centered around my store. Soon, it'll be a footnote. People will have moved on to the next big thing." Jade closed her eyes for a moment and hoped her voice sounded confident.

"Well, my dream is that the next big topic of conversation isn't that new blogger. Just what we need is for someone to be stirring up the stink around here. I've had enough of him or her to last me a long time."

"It's new and juicy right now. But people are fickle. I'm guessing that if we don't make a big deal out of it, it will flame out on its own," Jade said.

"I hope you're right. It's good to talk to you. You're always a voice of reason. See you tomorrow, if not before." The librarian clicked off. *I hope she doesn't blame me for the string of incidents. 'Tis the Season seems to be connected to everything.*

Chapter Twenty-Five

Lorelei tapped a quick message on her phone and then rummaged behind the counter for her purse. "It's time for Neville and me to head out. I've got a couple of things to do before Steve picks me up tonight. You okay?"

"We're good. Chloe and I have it all under control. What cool thing are you two up to? I'm living vicariously through you and Patti since Nick is still working on his case."

"Poor babies. You two work too much. We're going to a concert in Williamsburg. All the instruments are made of crystal. It should be interesting. And then we'll swing by that new tapas place near Yorktown," Lorelei said.

"Have fun," Jade said, opening her internet browser.

Her aunt slipped on her puffy white coat and matching hat. Pulling on her red leather gloves, she picked up Neville and stroked his head. "Come on, puddin'. We need to get a move on."

The bells on the front door jingled behind them, and then all Jade could hear was the air blowing through the heating ducts. Locking the door, she made the rounds and checked all the windows and doors again. Setting the tree timers, she gathered her things and did another walk-through to reassure herself everything was secure. All of the recent incidents made her second guess almost everything lately.

By the time she and Chloe walked to the Jeep, the sun sank behind the cluster of spindly pine trees. Shivering in the night air, she zipped her coat. "Come on. Let's go make some soup and grilled cheese for dinner."

The chubby dog's ears perked up, and Jade gave the little butterball a boost into the passenger seat. Jade pulled out onto Neptune Road, unusually void of cars at this time of the evening. She cranked up the Christmas carols on the radio.

A loud engine roared behind her, and high beams cut through the Jeep. "Pass me already. There's no one in the other lane," Jade said to the rude driver. She rolled down the window and waved her hand outside for him to go around her. The headlights bore down on the Wrangler.

The truck sped up, and the driver flashed the headlights, filling her Jeep with a blinding light. Jade tapped her brakes, and the truck behind her squealed tires and fishtailed.

Pulling over to the edge of the road, Jade willed the creep to pass her. The driver gunned the engine and pulled up on her bumper again. Half of his big truck was in the lane, and the other part was on the road's shoulder. *Where is a deputy when you needed one?*

Trying to stay calm, Jade squinted to see the road ahead. She floored the Jeep and zoomed toward her neighborhood. Nervous about showing this idiot where she lived, she formulated a quick plan to do a U-turn at the next street and head back toward town, maybe to the police station. "Hold on, Chloe." She accelerated again and put her arm across the small dog to brace her for the upcoming turn.

The truck slammed on brakes, squealing tires for several seconds. Then, the truck's driver did a three-point turn and tore off toward the pier.

Jade took a deep breath to quell the bats that were banging around in her stomach. Not seeing the truck anywhere, she hurried home. Nothing near her empty driveway looked out of place. She sat in the Wrangler for a couple of moments, waiting to see if the person would come back. All was quiet on her end of the street. She gathered her things and picked up Chloe for the short run to the porch. She skipped checking the mailbox today. It could wait until daylight tomorrow.

Jade slammed the front door and locked the deadbolt behind her. Leaning on the door, she tried to will her heartbeats back to something other than the staccato they pounded in her temples.

"I think he's gone, Chloe." Jade peeked out her front window. No cars or trucks outside. The only lights were from the nearby houses where folks had settled in for dinner. Holiday displays cast faint twinkly lights across the street.

A loud rumble sounded outside, and Jade darted back to the window. In the streetlight's glow, a truck sat at the end of her driveway. The exhaust formed a cloud behind the vehicle. Grabbing her phone, she punched Nick's contact.

Jade tapped her foot on the floor. Seconds seemed to drag on with every unanswered ring. After his sheriffy voicemail, she yelled, "Nick. Someone followed me home from the store in a truck. He tailgated me down Neptune Road, and now he's back at the end of my driveway. He's sitting there in a truck. I guess it's a he. Can't tell. Anyway, if I don't hear from you soon, I'll call dispatch."

Jade doused all the lights in the house and watched from the window. No movement. It was hard to see inside the cab. The driver had turned off his headlights, and the windows may have been tinted.

Her phone rang, and she jumped.

"Are you okay?" Nick asked. "Sorry. I was on the other line with the forensic unit."

"I'm fine. Just a little rattled. The jerk sped up on my tail and blinded me with his high beams. There was no one else on the road. He could have easily passed if he didn't like my driving." Jade hoped her voice didn't sound as panicked as she felt.

"Did you get a plate or a good look at the truck?" Nick asked.

"No, it was an older truck. A big one. I think it's white." Jade lifted the slats on the blinds for another quick look. "He's gone. He sat out at the end of my driveway for a while. I have no idea what he was doing out there."

"I'm tied up here with the town lawyer and councilman. I'll send a car by. Don't go anywhere. Stay in the house until you see my deputy. Promise."

"Promise. I've had enough excitement for one night." A wave of relief washed over Jade.

"Call me if anything else happens, or he comes back. Love you." Nick said.

"I'm fine. We'll wait here for the deputy. Love you, too," Jade disconnected and let out a long breath.

Running into the spare bedroom, she dug through the closet for her old softball bat. On her way back, she paused in the kitchen. Jade grabbed the largest steak knife she could find.

Chloe stared at her and her weaponry.

"Hey, no judging. I want to have something handy in case the truck guy comes back."

Chapter Twenty-Six

A loud engine rumbled from her driveway, and Jade's blood pressure jumped off the charts. The engine stopped, and she heard footsteps on the sidewalk. Clutching the knife's hilt, she moved the blind slats for a closer look.

She let out a breath. The air escaped from her like a punctured beach raft. A Mermaid Bay Sheriff's Office SUV sat in her driveway, and an officer shown a flashlight around the mailbox and her Jeep. Jade flipped on the porch light.

"Jade. It's me, Sebastian." He tapped on her front door.

Jade pulled open the door with a little more force than needed. "So glad to see you. The jerk hasn't been back after his little road-rage incident. Did you find anything out there?" Sebastian shook his head slightly. "I checked all around your house. It's kinda dark in here," he said, leaning down to pet Chloe.

Jade flipped on the living room lights. "I wanted to watch from the window, and I didn't want to be backlit. Come on in."

"No sign of anyone. If he did come back, he didn't get out of his truck. Any idea who it was?"

Jade shook her head and set the steak knife down on the dining room table. "It was an old white truck. I couldn't figure out why he was so mad. I was doing the speed limit, and if he didn't like it, he could have passed me. Nobody else was around."

"Nowadays, you never know what's going through someone's head. We're going to step up our patrols around here. If he comes back, call 911. Nick needs to get you a better weapon than a steak knife." Sebastian snickered.

"And a softball bat." She pointed next to the door. "Use whatcha got." Jade could feel the heat rising in her cheeks.

"Try to have a good rest of the evening and call us if he comes back," Sebastian said, glancing around the room.

"Thanks. It's not how I expected to spend my Friday night. Chloe and I were planning for a quiet night to get ready for tomorrow's festivities."

A slight smile crossed the deputy's face as he focused on her dining room wall. "Oh, wow. Nick said you had your own murder wall. This is better than some we do at the station. And now I know why you and Nick are perfect for each other. If you see the guy again or have any other issues, call it in. Keep the steak knife in the kitchen and save the bat for softball season."

"Funny," she smirked.

"Yeah, but looks aren't everything," Sebastian said, opening the door. "Deadbolt this behind me. I'll do one more pass around your yard and then take off. You should keep your outside lights on."

"Ten-four. Thanks for coming by."

Jade double-checked all the doors' locks. On her way back through the living room, she picked up the bat and set it next to the couch. Even though her pulse had returned to almost normal, a sense of uneasiness still blanketed her thoughts.

The little white furball hopped up next to her. She squeezed the dog until she grunted. "I feel like all the blood has rushed out of my head, and now I'm exhausted." Chloe wiggled free of the embrace, circled the couch cushion three times, and snuggled on top of the lap blanket.

"Maybe dinner would help. If it doesn't, we may want to call it an early night. How about grilled cheese?" Chloe's ears shot skyward. After heating a can of tomato soup, Jade settled in at the dining room table and stared at her suspect wall while the Frenchie stood guard under the table for any crumbs.

"Okay, somebody lost or threw some weird igniter device in my lot. That has to mean something. We found Remo nearby after a fight with some of the Pefferlys. So, did one of them steal it from the other? Was that what this was all about? And maybe the Brianna/Paolo thing was fuel for the fire?"

On a whim, Jade found the contact me section on both companys' websites. She dashed off a friendly note that she enjoyed the fireworks in Mermaid Bay and that she found something that might belong to them. "Let's see if that stirs anything up,"

Chloe turned her head. Not hearing any food words, she retreated to the living room.

Flipping the top of her laptop closed, Jade moved to the couch to find something interesting to binge-watch. Settling on a documentary about serial killer connections to a hotel in California, Jade laughed aloud when she realized that she was watching a true crime show about murder to relax.

A sharp trill echoed in the house and made Jade jump. Eleven thirty-six. It took a moment to figure out where she was. She shook off the groggies and said, "Hey, Nick. What's up?"

"Sorry, I couldn't get over there when you called. Sebastian said he didn't see anything at your place. We've got regular patrols going by. Any other sign of your road rager?"

"Nope. It was very weird and unexpected."

"I want you to be careful, and until all this settles down, keep the walking by yourself to a minimum."

"I hate that I have to change my behavior when I didn't do anything wrong. How come I'm the one being inconvenienced? Sorry if that sounded whiny. It's been a long day."

"I know. I finally made it home. It's been a hectic this week. You need to be hyper-vigilant until we figure out what's going on. Call me if anything looks fishy or if anything makes your spidey senses tingle," he said.

"I will. We're almost at the end of the busy season. The plan is to cut my hours back after Christmas," Jade said.

"Speaking of that, my mom wants us to stop by Christmas Eve for dinner," he said.

"Aww. That sounds nice. What can we bring?"

"She said nothing but ourselves."

A warm tingle coursed through her. It was nice to be part of an extended family. She made a mental note to get gifts for Nick's mom and family. "Will Cecilia be there?"

"Yep, she, Zac, and Zoe have been staying with Mom while her husband's been deployed to the Middle East. Mom's been helping her with the twins," he said, chewing on something.

"That'll be fun. I haven't been around kids at Christmas in a long time," she said.

Nick paused, and Jade could hear his police radio in the background. "What happened to Remo?" she asked, changing the subject.

"We rounded up Zeke, Tank, and Goose for questioning. All of them clammed up and swore it was a fight between drunk, mouthy guys with too much testosterone and not enough sense. Nobody had a gun or a knife, but that doesn't mean anything." Nick blew out a long breath. "Remo wouldn't talk either. Then, after hours of questioning, no one wanted to press charges, even though Remo looked like he tangled with a pack of hyenas."

"That's frustrating," she mused. She could almost see Nick rolling his eyes.

He cleared his throat. "There was nothing to charge any of them with unless you want to press trespassing charges. And hopefully, none of them will be back any time soon."

"Let me think on the trespassing thing. What about the shooting?" she asked. "Any idea who was behind it? Do you think it was the Pefferlys?"

"I have no idea," he said as his radio continued to squawk in the background. "And all of them denied hearing any gunfire."

"I couldn't figure out why they were shooting at us or the ambulance. It didn't make any sense," she said.

"Sebastian and I will get to the bottom of it. Forensics didn't find any shell casings. Just a couple of cigarette butts and an aluminum can. After all this, I kinda miss our routine summer problems."

Jade laughed. "I talked to Vivian earlier."

"Did you have to scrape her off the ceiling? She's called me about three times in the past few days about the increase in criminal activity and how it's ruining the town's image," Nick said.

"Yep. Same story. She mentioned disqualifying some of the fireworks contestants for their bad behavior. From the last meeting, it sounded like the council members agreed with her."

"I'm hoping that this third company knocks everyone's socks off, and they're the clear winner. It'll make everything easier." Nick's voice faded off as his police radio crackled and chirped in the background.

"That would solve everything," Jade said, straining to listen to his radio's chatter. "I went over to see Bernie this morning about that weird thing Chloe found in the yard and met one of the Crash Boom Bang guys. He said the thing was an igniter for fireworks. I'm still wondering who dropped it in my empty lot. My guess would be either a Zanetti or a Pefferly. I hope they weren't planning to shoot off anything next to my store. Do you think the gunshots were fireworks?"

After another pause, he said, "It's not likely, but I guess we can't rule anything out right now. Save the igniter thing for me. I'll swing by tomorrow to pick it up. It may be another weird piece in all of this."

"Will do. Try to get some sleep. You've been putting in some serious hours," she said.

"It'll calm down soon. I'm looking forward to Christmas and New Year's," Nick said.

"Are you off for New Year's Eve?"

"I'm on call, but yes, technically, I'm off. But you never know what'll happen around here. I'm hoping for peace on earth and goodwill for all."

"We should plan something. Maybe a nice, quiet dinner?"

"Sounds perfect," he said. "See you tomorrow. Love you."

"I love you, too," she said, disconnecting as excitement fluttered inside her.

"Okay, Chloe, we've got to get a move on with this Christmas thing. I don't have anything for Nick's sister or the kids. I need to make a run to Amy's and see what she has for five-year-old twins. And then I've got to get everything wrapped."

Chloe opened one eye and pretended to be interested.

"Let's call it a night. We'll figure out the details tomorrow."

Jade's mind raced with things to do for the holidays, but thoughts of the

Pefferlys and the Zanettis kept creeping in and taking over until she finally fell into a restless sleep.

Chapter Twenty-Seven

After what felt like hours of tossing and turning, Jade settled on her couch and flipped through the channels, landing on an episode of *Expedition Unknown*. Maybe someone else's mystery will take her mind off the ones here, and she wouldn't feel so on edge. Little guilty thoughts niggled at the back of her brain. She should have told Nick of the contacts to the two fireworks companies about the weird thing Chloe found. But she didn't want to send law enforcement on a goose chase if it wasn't relevant, and he had enough real problems to worry about. Blocking doubts and what-ifs from her internal monologue, she tried to concentrate on the show.

Jade's phone alerted with a series of beeps and caused her to jump. Something set off the camera at the store. *Not again!* She watched and caught a glimpse of something moving by the back door. *Was it a human? She'd feel stupid calling the police about a stray cat or a raccoon.*

Jade replayed the clips, trying to figure out what was at the back of the store. Deciding the shadow was too big for an animal, she sent a text to Nick and dialed 911.

"Mermaid Bay Emergency, how can I help you?"

"Hi, this is Jade Hicks. Something set off my cameras at my store. I can't tell who or what it is, but something is moving around my back door. Could you send someone to check it out? We had an incident earlier."

"We'll have a deputy go by there. What's the address? Are you there and in a safe place?"

"I'm at home. The store, 'Tis the Season, is at 4585 Neptune Road. I'm not sure if they're trying to break in or not. We've had some issues there lately. I can't tell from the cameras what's going on."

"I'll send a deputy over to the store. She should contact you after she checks it out. Is this the best number to reach you?" The dispatcher asked.

"Yes. Thank you." Jade disconnected and sunk back into her couch. "Chloe, what else is going to happen? This is supposed to be the happy Christmas season. You and I are due a vacation after this." She let out a long puff of air as the Frenchie snorted.

Her phone jangled, and she quickly connected with Nick.

"Hey. You okay?" he asked.

"I'm fine. The store's back door camera alerted, and I called it in. They're sending a deputy by. I couldn't tell from the clip who it was."

"The deputy is on her way now. You should hear from her as soon as she knows something. I'm on a case right now. We had a couple of bad accidents tonight and a runaway. The street team will patrol Neptune Road regularly. This time, stay put. You don't need to go to the store to check it out. We'll take care of it and let you know what we find. We have guns and no baseball bats." She thought she heard a snicker.

"Very funny. Okay," she said as the bats still banged around in her core.

"It'll be okay. If it's anything, the deputy will take care of it. Don't worry until we know something," Nick said.

"Thanks. You get home as soon as you can and get some sleep. Tomorrow will be a long day for your team."

"But then we should catch a break. Hopefully. See you sometime tomorrow night."

"Hugs and kisses," she said, disconnecting.

Time seemed to move in slow motion. Her thoughts bounced around like ping-pong balls in a lottery machine. When her phone finally buzzed again, Jade tensed. Taking a deep breath, she punched the button. "Jade Hicks."

"Ms. Hicks, this is Deputy Corinne Amos. I did a complete search of the perimeter of your property. There is no sign of a break-in, and whatever set off your camera is gone. This is on our regular hourly patrol watch, so we'll continue to be vigilant for anything out of place. All of your doors were locked, and there were no cars in your parking lot."

"Thank you so much for checking. I appreciate it," Jade said, rubbing her eyes.

"My pleasure," the deputy said, disconnecting.

Jade scanned through her camera feeds and saw the deputy check the store's doors. Back to a silent night. *Why is my store ground zero for all the trouble?* "I guess I should feel relieved. But now I feel jittery and like I have a target on my back. Let's call it a night."

Chloe bounced off the couch and followed Jade through the house as she checked all the locks for the umpteenth time. She left the porch light on and set the baseball bat next to her bed, just in case.

Jade thought she heard footsteps and breaking glass. *Was I dreaming?* She sat bolt upright in bed. The darkness seemed like a blanket around her. Her warm and cozy room suddenly felt stifling and oppressive after the freaky sounds. She lay in the dark, listening for any little noise. The walls felt like they were closing in. Two-fifty-eight. She clutched her phone in case she heard anyone outside. Chloe rustled in her bed but didn't bark. *Maybe I was dreaming? Did I hear glass breaking?*

Straining to hear anything out of the ordinary, she tiptoed toward the window. Nothing but darkness. Lights dotted her neighbors' porches. All quiet until a truck with a loud muffler sped by. Then silence. She waited, holding her breath. No traffic. No other sounds. No breaking glass.

Chloe didn't stir. Maybe it was a bad dream. Jade sat on the edge of her bed, still on high alert, listening intently for any sound. She chided herself for being so antsy.

Chapter Twenty-Eight

At six, the alarm blared, and Jade sat up again with a jolt. The sun streaming in between the blind slats made the room a friendlier place than it was in the wee hours of the morning. She stretched and tried to ward off some of the kinks from a fitful night's sleep. The adrenaline had escaped her body, leaving her with a sense of restlessness and a crick in her neck.

Jade peeked out the window, and life looked normal in Mermaid Bay. "Chloe, it's the final fireworks weekend. Let's get this day started. I'm hoping we have a good turnout. I've advertised today's events anywhere I could think of. Let's keep Bernie and Patti busy." The dog rose gradually and stretched like she was doing yoga.

After a long, hot shower, Jade donned her favorite Christmas sweater and leggings. "You need something festive, too." She pulled out a red and green harness with jingle bells for Chloe, who posed for a photo in her holiday garb.

Balancing her messenger bag, coffee, purse, and Chloe's leash, Jade pulled the front door behind her and stepped on something that crunched. Broken glass. *It wasn't a dream.*

Jade scooped up Chloe and stepped gingerly on the stoop. Someone had broken the bulb on her porch light. "What now! It is one thing after another."

Setting her things on the sidewalk and Chloe inside, Jade retreated to the house for a broom and a dustpan. Chloe watched all the activity from the doorway. "What is going on around here? I'm afraid to ask what's next."

With nothing to offer to the conversation, Chloe yawned and trotted toward her bed.

After a quick cleanup and a bulb replacement, she picked up Chloe again and headed for the Jeep. "Let's hope this is the worst thing that happens today."

After they parked behind the store, Jade and the chonky Frenchie walked the perimeter of the property. Nothing out of place, and the camera didn't catch anything else except the deputy's patrols of the building before dawn.

After whizzing through her opening routine, she sprayed cinnamon air freshener in all the rooms. "There, that makes it festive. Let's check the overnight orders, and then it should be time for Patti and Bernie to arrive."

Not interested in work, Chloe plopped on her bed and settled in for an early morning nap.

While Jade gathered the remaining orders, she heard the bells tinkle. Still being cautious, she made her way to the lobby.

Goose stood in the lobby with his hands in his jacket pockets.

"May I help you?" Jade set several ornaments on the counter. She hoped she didn't gasp or look startled.

"Hi. Nice place you got here. Tank said you owned a Christmas store. Never heard of such a thing before." He looked around and zeroed in on the front door. "Not very crowded. You'd think you'd be busy this time of year." He continued to scan the room like he was casing the joint.

"We're expecting a crowd today for the last day of the festival. And my team will be here any minute. If you hang around, you might get to meet Santa."

Goose scrunched his mouth and laughed. Jade paused when he stepped closer to the counter.

The hair on the back of her neck stood at attention, and a jolt of adrenaline coursed through her body. Picking up her phone, she pasted on a plastic smile. "Can I help you with some Christmas gifts or souvenirs to commemorate your time here in Mermaid Bay?"

"Uh, no," he said, looking over his shoulder. "Zeke and his dad sent me over to see that thing you found in your yard."

"Oh, that. I wasn't sure what that was, so I gave it to the deputy when he was here the other day. You know, when Zeke and Remo were here. Were you here that day? I can't remember." Her smile felt like a fake, toothy grin.

"Uh, no. I have no idea what you're talking about. Zeke said you had something for us to look at. He must have misunderstood. I guess I'll swing by the police station. Sorry to have bothered you." He looked over his shoulder again. After a long pause, he turned the knob and jerked the door open. The bells chimed frantically for a few seconds after he slammed the door behind him.

Jade let out a long breath and pulled out her phone. Tapping a quick text about the broken bulb and Goose's visit, she neglected to mention her fib about the device to Nick.

Nick replied, **Thanks. Patrols are checking regularly. Keep an eye out for anything unusual.**

Before Jade could dwell on Goose's strange visit, a "Hello, Christmas people" made her jump. Patti flounced in and set a tray of cookies on the counter. "I tried out some new ideas last night for the final day of the fireworks festival. I've got my Peppermint Snowballs, and Sophie's Busy Bean Vanilla cookies. I couldn't find any recipes for anything that looked like firecrackers.

"Mmm. Those look yummy. Thanks for bringing them. That may be my mid-morning snack since breakfast was a long time ago."

"My book club taste-tested the first batch and gave them a thumbs up." Patti moseyed toward the coffee station.

"Your creations are always a hit. And you know that Bernie's your biggest fan."

"Looks like you're working on orders. Let me stow this stuff, and I'll help you get it all boxed and ready to ship. Morning, Chloe. Lookin' sharp there in your holiday finest."

As the pair finished sticking on the remaining mailing labels, Bernie tramped through the front door with a suit bag and a makeup case. "Morning, gals. Time got away from me this morning. I was over there sipping my java and listening to the guys yammer on, and I forgot where I was supposed to me. I'll be dressed lickety-split."

"We've got time. Everything okay at the pier?" Jade asked.

"Yep. Those Adkins boys are crackerjacks. They have a whip-smart team. They think of everything. Their security guys and crew work together with military precision. Between us, I hope they win the contest. They're pretty cool. The other two families were trouble who stirred up way too much nonsense. Who has time for that? Let me get a move on. It takes a while to perfect my look." He winked and tightened his grip on the suitcase.

"It's good to see you, Bernie," Patti yelled as he walked in the back toward the restroom.

"Save me some of those cookies," drifted in from the back.

After they packed the orders in the carton for the delivery driver, Patti let out a squeal. "Busses! Plural. Bernie, are you ready?"

"All set to greet the visitors. Ho Ho Ho" boomed from the next room.

"Wow. This looks like a better start to the day," Jade said as the tour guide trooped in, leading a long line of senior citizens in brightly colored coats and knit hats.

A couple of hours later, after the second bus pulled out, Patti headed to the back for coffee. "Can I get you anything?"

"I'm good for now," Jade said as the bells on the door chimed. The door opened tentatively.

Remo, sporting stitches and two bandages across his nose, stepped inside and looked around. "Hi," he said.

"How are you feeling?" Jade asked. "I'm glad you're up and around."

"Oh, I'm fine. This is nothing. Uh, did you find one of our devices in your store?" he asked, shuffling toward the counter.

"Uh, out in the field, but yes. I didn't know what it was. I gave it to the deputy the night of your, uh, altercation."

"Oh, oh good. I'll check there to see if I can retrieve it. We're packing all our stuff and heading out early tomorrow. Lorenzo's funeral is scheduled this week." He hung his head.

"I'm so sorry. I hope you all have safe travels home." Jade's smile faded to a look of concern.

He stood there for several heartbeats, and when the pause became uncomfortable, he said, "Well, I guess I'll swing by the police station. Gotta pick up my stuff. Time to get everything ready to hit the road. Thanks."

"Who was that?" Patti asked, settling on the stool behind the counter as the front door shut.

"Remo Zanetti, Paolo's brother. He wanted that device Chloe found in the yard."

Patti's eyebrows formed a "V." "I read about his fight with the Pefferlys on that blog. It sounds like they've been at each other's throats the entire time they've been in town. Rumor has it that they've both worn out their welcome." Patti winked and picked up the latest ornament catalog.

"I'll be back in a sec," Jade said as she headed to the office to call Nick.

She heard the bells jangle and a familiar ringtone in the lobby. Popping her head over the top of the Dutch door, she spotted Nick chatting with Patti. "Hey. I was calling you, and then you appeared."

"The perfect boyfriend. You all are on the same wavelength." Patti giggled.

"Come on back. I have something for you," Jade said as Patti made googly eyes and kissy faces behind Nick's back.

"Yep, that's what I stopped by for," Nick said, covering the lobby in three strides. "My deputy said a strange guy came in looking for something lost that you turned in."

"Whoops. Something I meant to turn in. It got kinda busy around here. I got distracted. Then I tried to find out what it was," Jade said, making a dash for her desk. "I thought it was trash at first."

Nick pursed his lips. "My deputy said that Goose was pretty insistent about getting his property back before they left tonight."

"Will they?" Jade asked, rummaging through her desk drawer. "What if it's not his?"

He frowned and shook his head. "Get their property back? Not anytime soon. All interested parties will have to file a claim if they feel it belongs to them. It'll stay in our evidence lockup during the investigation. Will they leave town? We can only hope."

"Speaking of that, Remo Zanetti came in here looking for the same item. One of the Adkins guys from Crash Boom Bang was at the pier the day I showed it to Bernie's gang. He said it's a fireworks igniter, but not one of his. He kinda hinted that it was something new, and someone had created it like some kind of prototype."

"I'll have my guys do some research. It's new and cool, and obviously, the Zanettis and the Pefferlys are interested in it. We'll figure out who it belongs to."

"The Zanettis told me they brand all of their equipment. Here. I didn't see any kind of logo on this." She pulled the contraption out of her desk drawer. "Do you see any markings on it?" She handed the device to Nick.

"And of course, you've touched it."

"Along with about ten other people," she said with a sheepish grin. "I thought it was trash when I wrestled it out of Chloe's mouth. You're lucky I didn't throw it away. I hope it doesn't have the Frenchie's teeth marks in it."

His lips formed a single line, and he stared at her. "Jade."

"What? I'm always picking up trash from the empty lot."

He let out a long breath through his nose. "Do you have a mailing envelope or something I could put it in?"

Jade handed him an oversized mailer from her bottom desk drawer.

"Thanks. Anything else you forgot to mention?" Nick asked.

"No. Not that I can think of. Vivian said that she's looking at disqualifying some of the contestants. That should create a stir."

"She's always on a tear, but disqualifications would have opened a can of worms. I think Tom Berryman talked her out of that," Nick said. "Right now, she's fretting over the possibility of rain tonight and whether we'll have to use tomorrow as a rain date."

Jade checked the weather on her phone. "Channel 10 only has it as a thirty percent chance. I'm glad the town council talked her out of the other idea. She was fixated on getting rid of the troublemakers."

"The effects would be worse than not doing anything. She needs to leave it alone. Tom and the lawyers told her to wait and see what happens with the voting. It might make the decision for them."

"True." Jade opened her eyes wide. "But, at least, we may have figured out why the Zeke/Remo fight happened, and I don't think it was over a girl."

"No. It was something more valuable to them," he said, waving the envelope. "Gotta run. It's all hands on deck today and tonight. I'll call you tomorrow after I've slept for longer than three hours."

"Bye." She finger-wave as he stopped to pet Chloe.

Whew. He's not that mad at me, and I can always count on Chloe to smooth things over.

Chapter Twenty-Nine

"My face hurts from smiling," Patti said, taking a swig of her hot chocolate.

"That's something, coming from you," Jade said, locking the front door. "You are always Miss Mary Sunshine."

"Not all the time," a slight frown crossed Patti's face. "But I try to be. I lost count of the buses and people who filed through here today, but it was stellar. I'll have the receipts and the reconciliation for you in the twinkle of an eye."

"It's what we need to end this year on a bang," Jade said, fist-pumping the air.

"Ha! I think we already did that with the fireworks and all that drama that came with them. We'll have to see how everything shakes out tonight. Hopefully, they'll be a clear winner, and we can put all the chaos behind us." Patti pushed the button on the register, and it spat out a tape that rivaled a CVS drug store receipt. "Here you go. And here's the bank bag."

"Thanks," Jade said. "I'll lock it in the safe and make the deposit on Monday when Lorelei's here. I have a couple of things to do tonight before the fireworks."

"I'm picking up my sister and her brood, and we'll head over to the pier after we get a bite to eat." Patti slid into her fuchsia puffy coat. "It will be an adventure. I love the kiddos, but they're a handful."

"I'll look for you all. Amy talked Todd into reserving her a table on his deck. We'll see if he remembers." Jade winked and took the receipts and bag to the back office. "If not, we'll be somewhere near Hot Diggity Dogs. Come and find us."

"The little ones can be terrors," she whispered and made a face. "They are so full of energy and mischief. Hopefully, we can keep them contained and entertained until the show starts. We need a spot way away from all the other people," Patti said with a sigh.

A voice boomed from the other room, "Bye, Jade. Bye, Patti. I'm heading out to the pier to check on things with Cecil and the gang. See ya tonight," Bernie yelled.

"See ya later, Santa," Patti called behind him. "He is the best. That's about wraps it up for me, too. Need help with anything else before I scoot out of here?"

"Nope, we'll be on our way, too. Have fun tonight." When the door shut behind Patti, the store's silence was almost eerie. "Let's get a move on, doggo. It's time to go meet Amy," said Jade.

After triple-checking the locks and the safe, Jade and Chloe trotted down the front stairs to the Jeep. She did a quick check under the vehicle and in the backseat before she climbed in. Shaking off the tingly feeling that something was about to happen, she settled Chloe in the passenger seat.

Jade checked her mailbox at home and shooed Chloe toward the house. She couldn't ditch the urge to keep looking over her shoulder. She hated feeling like she had to be constantly on guard.

Jade heated up leftover ravioli in the microwave and ate it while standing in the kitchen. "You excited, Chloe? We need something fun to make us forget about this chaos. I can't wait to see the drone show. Let's go find something warm to wear."

The dog turned her head and hopped on the couch, where she made a bed on top of the lap blanket.

"You can stay here if you're tired." She patted the little dog's boxy head and covered her with the edge of the blanket.

After pulling on warm socks and boots, Jade grabbed her phone and keys and slid into her puffy coat. Not finding anything in her coat pockets, she made a beeline to the closet for her thickest gloves. "You settled in for the night? Maybe it's a good idea if you stay here and guard the place. I'll be back as soon as the fireworks are over." She kissed Chloe. "I'll leave the lights on for you."

Jade jiggled the handle when she pulled the door behind her. The icy wind whipped off the ocean. Wrapping her scarf around her neck, she tucked the ends in her coat.

Despite the chilly temperatures, the crowd had already gathered around the pier. Many people huddled close together in the almost freezing temperatures. She trudged through the sand toward the hot dog stand. Jade zigzagged around blankets and beach chairs to Hot Diggity Dogs, where Todd and Amy sat at the far picnic table. "Hey, Jade," he yelled. "Come on up."

Sliding in the seat across from them, she said, "Thanks for saving me a spot. It's a bit chilly, but at least the weather held out." She glanced at the clouds toward the west.

Todd nodded. "It looks like it's a go. I heard you had some excitement around your place. You seem to be a magnet for police activity lately."

Jade scrunched her nose. "It's been a little too exciting. I could live with a bit of quiet. Hopefully, after this weekend, things will calm down, and we can roll into the holidays. I'll settle for a week or two of boring." Jade turned so that the bay breeze was at her back.

"I'm not used to long hours in the off-season. I'm ready for some R and R, too. Though I'm not complaining about the sales," he added.

"Don't forget our road trip. It'll be an adventure and relaxation all rolled up into one fabulous week," Amy said. "He's going with me to Massachusetts for New Year's. So excited. We'll get to play tourist, and he can see all the places from my past. It'll be the Amy tour."

"I can't remember the last time I took more than a couple of days off for fun," Todd said.

"Y'all aren't taking the hearse, are you? That would be an awesome first impression," Jade said with a smile.

"Nah, I'll save that for later when I really want to be the talk of the town," Todd said. "We're both closing up the week after Christmas. Hopefully, they'll have some snow up there. I'd love to try snowboarding." Todd glanced at the growing crowds that filled almost every inch of space on the sand.

The Crack Boom Bang guys scurried along the pier, moving boxes and stands into place. The sun dropped behind the pine trees, and a few stars twinkled as clouds moved through. Lights from some boats bobbed on the bay.

"Be right back," Todd said.

When he was out of earshot, Jade leaned forward. "So, first trip home with the new boyfriend. You excited?"

Amy giggled. "Can't wait. We're taking it slow, but we both needed a break. And I need to get some of my stuff out of storage while I'm up there. It always helps to bring another pair of strong arms. Plus, it's in the boyfriend agreement. He has to help me carry the heavy stuff and kill the bugs. And before you say anything, yes, he knows he's the muscle."

Jade laughed. "Nick never knows what I'll drag him into. But he's always a good sport."

"Speaking of tall, dark, and handsome, I saw him over by the pier with his guys. It looks like they're out in full force tonight. And super sexy in their official gear. I'm kinda glad it's the last night for the fireworks. It's a little cold for this. I like them better in the summer." Amy shivered and wrapped her arms around herself.

Todd hip-checked the door and set a tray of steaming to-go cups on the table. "I thought hot chocolate would be a treat. If nothing else, you could hold it to keep your hands warm. And before you ask, yes, I added lots of mini marshmallows. Just to your specifications." He kissed Amy on the top of her head.

"You get boyfriend points for this. You have to have the right proportion of marshmallows to cocoa," Amy said, snuggling closer to him on the bench.

"Thanks. Any news on the mysterious blogger?" Jade asked, blowing on her steaming drink.

"Nope. And the postings have slowed down. Not sure what's going on. That was my morning read every day. The Mermaid went silent for a couple of days, and that left us all hanging. I was mildly annoyed. Maybe she's getting ready for Christmas," Amy said. "I was waiting for her big reveal that she kept teasing. And so far, nothing."

"She's so mysterious," Jade said.

"You'd think if someone was trying to build a following that they'd be more of a publicity hound. I haven't figured out the motivations behind this one yet," Todd said.

"It is a small town. Maybe she feels freer to speak her mind if no one knows who she is," Amy said.

Before Jade could comment, a "Ho, ho, ho. Happy holidays!" boomed from the pier's sound system and echoed over the water. "Tonight is our final night of the Mermaid Bay Fireworks competition. Don't forget to go to the town's website to vote for your favorite and to enter our contest. We have lots of great Mermaid Bay prizes. Support our local businesses, who make this all possible. And without further ado, may I present Crash Boom Bang!"

The sky over the bay lit up with a series of colorful explosions. The light made it bright enough to see the spectators' awed faces. The show lived up to the company's name with the rapid-fire light bursts that continued for about twenty minutes.

Then the noise stopped suddenly. All was quiet except for some clapping and cheering from the crowd as the smoke blew out to sea.

Then, there was a loud boom, followed by a flash as something moved across the sky. Jade heard faint whirring sounds as a giant white star loomed over the bay. Then, in an instant, it morphed into a Christmas tree and then Rudolph's face, complete with a blinking red nose. The crowd ooohed and ahhhed over the drone light show.

"Well, that cinches it," Todd said. "The other two teams can't compete with this. They've got my vote. This is so cool."

"I am impressed. I can't believe they can do this with drones. Oooh, look. There are dancing candy canes. And now elves," Amy squealed.

The crowd watched as lights flashed and moved in the sky. The reflections in the bay gave it an ethereal look. The mesmerized crowd clapped and cheered as each new image appeared.

"Then 'Thank you, Mermaid Bay. Happy Holidays!' flashed across the sky. 'Love Crash Boom Bang!'"

The crowd went wild. The cheering lasted at least ten minutes.

When the noise level eventually died down to a low roar, Jade yelled, "I don't think Vivian and the town council have to worry about the contest anymore. We have a clear winner. This was fun. Thanks for the hot chocolate. I'll see you guys before you leave for parts up north."

Todd and Amy waved and gathered their things. Jade jogged down the wind-worn steps and hustled against the flow of the crowd to her bungalow. The further she got away from the pier, the darker the night got. The lights from the neighbor's houses and back patios provided some ambient light for her to pick her way to the cut-through to her cottage.

As she rounded the corner, her phone beeped a string of alerts. She paused and fished it out of her coat pocket.

Chapter Thirty

J ade swallowed the lump that felt like it blocked her throat. The store's porch camera showed a short guy jiggling the knob on the front door. Then, in the next clip, he ran away.

She had missed an alert during the excitement and noise of the show. Jade scrolled down and clicked play. She gasped when a tall guy in a hoodie walked up and jigged the knob on the store's back door. He paused and then kicked the back door. She caught her breath as she watched him slam the door with kicks until the wood near the lock splintered. Jade felt like she was watching a TV show, but the realization that it was her store and her back door made her light-headed. The tall guy kicked the door in and stepped over the rubble into her office. *Was this a robbery? What was the guy doing inside 'Tis the Season.*

Taking a deep breath, she ran home and jumped in the Jeep. Driving with one hand, she punched 911 on her phone. She made it to the store in record time and skidded to a stop in the front parking lot. The trees' twinkle lights in the windows gave it a warm glow. No sign of anyone moving around inside. No sign of a burglary. No front porch guy. *Could this be happening?*

When she heard, "Nine-one-one, what's your emergency?" Jade jumped and felt the pricklies crawl up her arms.

She took a deep breath and exhaled deliberately. "This is Jade Hicks at 'Tis the Season. When I left the fireworks show tonight, my store's cameras alerted. I have clips of a guy on my porch trying to get in, and then there is another recording of a taller guy kicking in my back door."

"I'm sending police. They are over at the pier, so it shouldn't take that long.

Is the guy still in your store?"

"I don't know. I'm out front. I don't see anything unusual here, but I didn't have a clip of him exiting. I guess he's still inside." Jade tapped her phone until the live feed of the broken door appeared. Nothing one in sight. The only sound was an occasional cricket and a car passing by on the main road.

"My camera doesn't show any movement," Jade said. "Could you ask the officers to hurry? I don't know what's going on in my store." She took a deep breath to quell the building anxiety.

"They're on their way. You should see them any minute now. Let me know if you see the intruder again," the dispatcher said.

Jade peered out the windshield to see if she could catch a glimpse of any movement. She stared until her eyes started to burn.

"The deputies should be there momentarily. Are you in a safe place?" the dispatcher asked. Her voice seemed to echo inside the Jeep.

"I think so. I'm in my vehicle. I hear sirens. Thanks for your help." Jade strained to see what was going on inside her store. Nothing looked out of place, and she stifled the urge to run around to the back door. Nick's warnings played on a loop in her head. The minutes ticked by and felt like an eternity.

She disconnected the call as two police cruisers zoomed into her lot. The deputies jumped out with guns drawn. One checked the front of the store while the other ran around to the back. Time seemed to drag. She measured the seconds by counting her pounding heartbeat. *What is going on inside? Who are these guys?*

Something moved in one of the lobby windows. Did she see someone, or was it her imagination? She wiped the condensation off the windshield for a better view.

Jade froze when she heard a slam. The door flung open, and a guy leapt off the porch, clearing all three steps. He stumbled in the grassy area, righted himself, and then tore down the street between two of the neighboring cottages. A few beats behind him, a deputy followed.

Easing out of her Jeep, she tiptoed toward the porch. The eerie silence and the darkness seemed to envelop her.

"Stop. What are you doing?" a voice boomed from the side of the porch.

Almost jumping out of her shoes, Jade froze and put her hands in the air. "I'm Jade Hicks. I own this store. I saw a deputy chase whoever was inside my store out the door and down that way. I wanted to see if everything is okay."

"Ma'am, you can't go in there. We need to secure the premises. Another unit will be here shortly. Can you wait in your car for me?"

She didn't recognize the deputy in a Seaport police uniform. He must be helping Nick's team tonight. "Okay. I'll wait there." She pointed over her shoulder.

By the time she settled back in the driver's seat, two other police vehicles pulled in and parked wherever the vehicle stopped near the store's porch. The new arrivals conferred with the Seaport deputy, and then all three disappeared inside the store.

Time continued to crawl. It felt surreal to watch and wait when nothing seemed to be happening. Still no sign of the other police officer who chased the guy out of the store and into the night. *What was taking so long?*

Her phone dinged, and Jade jumped. **You okay? Be there as soon as I can**, Nick texted.

I'm fine. The deputies are still inside. I don't know what's going on. Got a couple of fires to put out here. Be there soon, he replied.

Jade tried some deep breathing and office chair stretching exercises to pass the time in the front seat of her Jeep. Her heartbeat pounded in her ears, distracting her from any coherent thoughts.

The hum of an engine broke the silence as a forensic van pulled into her lot. Two technicians climbed out and hauled gear inside as Jade's pulse skyrocketed. *What was the forensic team doing here? Please let there not be another dead body. I wish Nick would hurry up.*

Chapter Thirty-One

Time dragged like Jade was in some kind of alternate universe. Not wanting to wear down her phone or the Jeep's battery, she sat for what felt like hours in the cold night air. She tried to think of all the things she needed to do before Christmas, but fears of what was happening inside her store kept creeping in and clouding her thoughts. Had all the things that happened at her store this week been related to this? Her anxiety level zoomed through the roof.

A knock on the side window made her jump. *Had I fallen asleep?*

She looked up to see Nick outside. "Hey, how are you?" she asked, opening the door to see him better.

"Okay, for a loony night. What's going on? You okay?"

"I guess. I still don't know what's happening in there. The waiting and not knowing are driving me crazy. The only exciting thing was when a deputy chased a guy out the front door a little while ago. How many people were in my store?"

"So far, there was the one guy who ran, but you told the dispatcher about another person. Can you send me the clips?"

"Yep." Jade tapped her phone and forwarded everything from the camera feed. "Why is the forensic van here?"

"It's a crime scene…a break-in. Let me get the details. Be back as soon as I can. Then we'll get you to tell us if anything's missing. Stay put until I come back." He closed her door and climbed the porch steps two at a time.

Jade's stomach sank to her toes. Would she be able to recover to open the store for the end of the holiday shopping season? How much damage was there inside? *What a nightmare! Maybe Mermaid Bay was becoming like other beach towns. Nothing like this has happened here before. I don't want to lose the charm and the small-town innocence.* Jade wiped a stray tear that escaped from the corner of her eye.

She tried to make a list of the remaining gifts she needed to get, but worries about a damaged store and destroyed inventory kept overtaking her thoughts. She let out a heavy sigh that fogged up the driver's side window.

Using her sleeve to wipe a spot to see out of, Jade noticed movement out of the corner of her eye. Something flashed in the rearview mirror. Turning, she stared out the back into the pitch-black darkness. Definitely something out there moving. She zeroed in on a spot near the fence as something dark came toward the store in the shadows. Was it a person? Jade's heart rate zoomed off the charts again. Trying to calm the jitters, she took a couple of deep breaths and slowly opened the door. Hoping that the figure was too busy to notice her and the Jeep, she slipped out. But the click of the door echoed like a gunshot in the eerie stillness. The figure froze, and so did Jade.

Staring intently into the dark, she waited for any sign of movement. There it was. Footsteps. Creeping closer. Every once in a while, she'd catch a glimpse of the figure in a passing headlight.

Jade ducked around the back of the Jeep and used it as cover. A hunched figure strode across the grass toward the front of her store. Seconds seemed like hours. Should she call Nick? She stared at the store windows. No movement inside. Where were Nick and his guys?

The figure slinked closer to the porch and stopped. He tried to stay in the shadows, but Jade got an occasional glimpse of the person in dark clothes stretching to see in the front windows.

Jade circled the back of the Jeep and inched toward the store behind the shadowy figure. It couldn't hurt for a closer look. She'd call Nick or scream if something happened.

The cold made Jade's legs ache. She fidgeted to ward off the pain. Did he see her? The figure paused and then edged up the steps. Dipping down, he crawled to the first window. He duck-walked to the far window and crouched behind a rocking chair. Jade slipped into the shadows near the porch, where she had a better view of the guy in the dark hoodie as light streamed out from the store. *Who was he, and why was he coming back to the scene of the crime? What is going on here?*

Jade's pulse pounded in her ears. Determined to find out who this was, she shook off the feelings of dread and Nick's warning to stay put. He was busy, and it couldn't hurt for her to find out who the mysterious creeper was. Then she could tell Nick later.

Not sure if her justification sounded plausible even to her, she ignored her conscience and stepped closer. The decking on the porch creaked, and the figure suddenly whirled around.

Chapter Thirty-Two

The shadowy figure paused and then crouched on the porch for what felt like forever. *What was he doing?* Jade tried to count slowly in her head and control her breathing to pass the time. What were the police doing inside that was taking so long? Maybe she should text Nick.

While she was wrestling in her head with a barrage of thoughts, the figure on the porch turned and made his way down the steps. He paused at the base and stared back toward the window. It looked like he was standing on his tiptoes to see better.

Jade took a step or two closer. What was his fascination with her store?

The figure seemed frozen as he stared inside at the twinkling lights.

Jade's phone dinged. The single tone seemed to hang in the air like a foghorn. The figure whipped around, scanning the area behind him. He zeroed in on Jade and then raced off toward the empty lot.

Jade let out a shriek and tore after him. For whatever reason, he zigzagged through the open lot like a gator was chasing him. Jade poured on the speed. He slowed as he approached the fencing, trying to decide which path to take. He stopped and then darted off toward the neighbor's yard that backed up to her lot. Jade matched his speed, and when she could almost reach out and touch him, she launched herself forward.

As Jade landed on the guy's back, he jerked and fell into the sandy soil. They rolled around for a minute with Jade ending up on the top of the heap. He grabbed her wrists and tried to flip her off. Planting her knee in his groin, the man swore quietly and let go of her. He curled into a fetal position as she managed to stay on top of him. He bucked like a bronco, trying to pitch her into the grass.

When he paused for a moment, Jade reared her arm back, ready to punch him, when he shrieked, "Not the face. Not again." He recoiled and flipped, trying to cover his head with his arms, and in the process, he knocked Jade into the grass.

Moaning, he buried his head in his arms and curled up again in a tight ball. "This wasn't supposed to happen. I was trying to fix things. Then it all got worse."

"What are you talking about?" Jade caught her breath and rose gingerly to her feet. She stood over the figure, trying to make herself as tall as possible.

The guy peeked out from under his elbow.

Jade sucked in a breath of cold, night air. "Remo? What are you doing at my store again in the middle of the night? And what's with all the sneaking around?" Jade gritted her teeth and crossed her arms.

"I need to get my stuff back before anyone finds out, especially Grandpop," he whined.

"What—?" A pair of strong arms pulled Jade away from Remo before she could finish her question.

"What is going on?" Nick's voice boomed through the darkness.

"This guy was skulking around the property. I was trying to see what he was up to. I didn't know if he was coming back to the scene of the crime." Jade paused and then added, "And I was trying to figure out why he broke into my store." Jade smoothed her coat and knocked some of the grass and sand off her.

"What crime scene?" Remo whimpered. "I didn't steal anything. It was ours to start with. They stole it from us."

Sebastian trotted down the stairs and stood behind Remo, who raised up one elbow.

"You were returning to my store that you burgled," Jade hissed.

"What? I did not. The only thing I did was check the front door. It was locked. I saw the lights and came back to check it out. You gotta believe me. Listen," he said, pleading with those standing around him. "I had nothing to do with any break-in. I was checking to see if anyone was here. I thought maybe someone lived here and could give me my igniter back. Elio was cheesed that I lost it after getting it back the first time. I didn't steal anything. You gotta believe me." He let out a heavy sigh."

"We've got this," Nick said. He squeezed Jade's shoulders lightly. "Why don't you go wait in your car, and I'll be there in a sec."

Jade nodded and reluctantly trudged toward the Jeep. She slipped inside but didn't close the door in case she could pick up snippets of what they were saying. Straining to hear, she was disappointed that there was no conversation about the break-in. Just a bunch of protests from Remo about his innocence and his desire to get his thing back.

By the time her legs started to ache again from the cold, she closed the door and started the Wrangler for some heat to ward off the creakiness in her joints. With barely enough time to soak up the warmth blasting from the dashboard, a knock on her window made her nearly jump out of her coat.

"Let's go inside, and you can let us know if anything is missing," Nick said.

Jade climbed out, and Nick pointed to the door. She turned and locked the Jeep's door, hoping she didn't roll her eyes. He was always in cop mode.

A loud shout and a scuffle caused their heads to jerk toward the store's porch.

"Stay here," Nick ordered, jogging toward Sebastian, who was wrestling with Remo. The two tussled as Sebastian tried to handcuff Remo who twisted and turned like he was Houdini trying to get out of a straitjacket. Nick waded in to help subdue the guy. Remo's arms flailed, and he swatted at the officers.

"No, you're not listening. It's not my fault," Remo whimpered. "Oww. Not my nose. Be careful. It's already broken. Stop! You've got the wrong guy. I'm the victim here. I'm the one who was robbed and attacked by those goons. You gotta believe me. I changed my mind. I want to press charges." Remo hiccupped. "You've got the wrong person."

Sebastian cuffed him and helped him toward the police vehicles. Remo pulled away, but a quick-thinking Sebastian grabbed him and pulled him off balance.

"Stop," Remo whined. "Those Pefferlys tore up and stole our equipment. They were prototypes that Elio was playing with. Hey, hey, this is really important." Remo paused and looked at Sebastian. "One night, I was at the beach, and I heard some guys talking. There was a big fight. The next thing I remember was the ambulance arriving." He gulped in the night air and stood silently as Sebastian nudged him to move toward the SUV. "That proves I was attacked."

Remo's heels dug into the sandy soil. "Hey. This is crucial. You're not listening. It proves I'm innocent. I heard that the store lady here was looking to find out what the thing was that her dog found. I came here before we left town to see if she'd give it back to me. You've got the wrong person. She can vouch for me. Call her," Remo said. "You gotta let me go. The Pefferlys are coming back. And they're going to try to kill me."

Chapter Thirty-Three

Sebastian wrangled Remo into the backseat of his SUV.

With a burst of adrenaline, Jade trotted after Nick toward her store's porch. The empty rocker moved in the early morning breeze like she had a phantom guest.

He turned and asked, "You doing okay?"

"I'm fine. I don't think he recognized me as the Christmas store lady. And he wants me to alibi him." A slight hiss escaped through Jade's teeth. "I'm curious to see what he did to the inside of my store."

"Remo's not the one Deputy Anderson chased out of your shop. We'll get to the bottom of all of this. Lots of people are interested in your place tonight." Nick held the door for her and then locked it. *I hope I didn't cause all this by asking about that thing Chloe found. I had no idea it was something important.*

Jade blinked as her eyes adjusted to the brightness of the lobby.

"The deputies are out looking for the guy who trashed your back door. That's our best place to start," Nick said, leading her to the office.

"You think Remo's not involved with the break-in?" she asked.

Nick raised a dismissive shoulder. "Who knows? Sometimes suspects tell the truth, or at least part of it."

"Oh, no," Jade wailed as she stepped through the doorway. Contents from the countertops and drawers lay scattered over the floor. Everything on her desk was in her guest chairs or on the floor. It looked like someone had swept everything off of all the flat surfaces. Even Chloe's bed was turned upside down. All the desk drawers had been rifled through and left open. This would take hours to clean and put the place back in order. Jade's shoulders slumped as she looked around her back room.

She fought off a wave of panic. "I need to check the rest of the store." Running to the safe, she opened it. "Okay. Not a total disaster. The bank bag and receipts are where I left them." A wave of relief washed over her. Jade closed and relocked the small safe and headed for the lobby and the display rooms, steeling herself for major damage right before the holidays.

When she returned about twenty minutes later, she felt like a huge weight had been lifted off her shoulders. "Nothing else had been disturbed. It seems the guy's focus was here in the office. All of the valuable ornaments are still locked in their cases."

"Nothing missing?" Nick asked.

"It doesn't look like it. None of the other rooms were disturbed. I'll know more when I get this mess cleaned up. When can I do that?" Jade glanced around at what looked like the aftermath of a tornado. "I have no idea why they were interested in my store files."

"We're almost finished here. I need you to write down everything that happened tonight. By then, we should be wrapping up, and you can have your store back." Nick patted her shoulder.

Jade found a notebook in the pile of stuff on the floor and dashed off a timeline of tonight's events. After a quick read to see if she had left anything out, she tore out the pages and signed the bottom. "Here," she handed Nick the pages. "I think I captured everything."

Nick folded the paper and put them inside his pocket. "Your door needs some work. Do you have any plywood or two-by-fours that I can secure it with?"

"Uh, yeah. I have my hurricane stash in the shed. That will work until I can get Bernie over here to replace it." Jade flipped on her flashlight app and led the way out through the splintered door. Picking her way across the patio, she unlocked the shed and searched in the back for her stash of plywood. Living in a beach community, it always paid to be prepared for the next big storm that might blow through. *I never imagined that it would be a burglar and not Mother Nature.*

"This should do," he said, pulling out two large sheets of plywood. "Where's your toolbox?"

"Inside. I'll get it for you. I can grab the other end of the plywood." Jade said.

The pair wrangled the long sheets of wood outside, and Jade locked up. She grabbed the end closest to her, and they carried it to the back of the store where the door used to be.

"Be back in a second," she said, stepping over splintered wood. "Here," she said when she returned, handing him her hot pink toolbox. "There are some nails and tacks inside. And thanks for doing this. I'll call Bernie as soon as the sun comes up."

"All in a day's work. Meet me at the front door when I holler," Nick said, looking at her girly toolbox.

Jade stepped inside. Nick hammered the wood to cover the frame on the outside. After a series of loud bangs, he yelled, "Okay. See you on the porch."

Jade jogged to the lobby and opened the door.

"All done," he said. "I nailed a board across it to make it harder to pull off. That should hold until Bernie can get you fixed up. Call him. He's always up early. Here's your hammer. I'll talk to you later."

"Thanks. Be careful," Jade said, locking the front door and setting her hammer on the counter next to the cash register.

She turned on her favorite happy music and made a beeline to the coffee maker. "First things first," she said to herself. "Caffeine, and then I tackle this clean up." The thought of someone rifling through her stuff made her seethe inside. The hair on the back of her neck stood up.

By the time the sun popped up over the bay, Jade had righted her office and the workroom area. The only casualties were a coffee mug and a French bulldog statue. The mug was totaled, but she might be able to fix the little figurine later. Dropping the pieces in her desk drawer, she pulled out her laptop and peeked to see what Mermaid Whispers was talking about today. The most recent post was a column about who was dating or not dating whom. That should drive Nosy Nell crazy. She had a lock on the community's gossip for years, and now there was an interloper cutting in on her shtick. Other newish posts were about the excitement building for the premiere of *My Coastal Valentine* in February, with the hint that big news was coming. Could that be from her leaked story? *I only mentioned that to two people. And I'm pretty sure Vivian isn't the blogger.*

Not seeing anything interesting on Facebook or on the *Beach Comber's* site. Jade clicked the link she saved for digitized yearbooks. After multiple searches, she finally found photos of Paolo Zanetti at a prep school in New Jersey. He was Mr. Popularity, no surprise. Remo, always with a sullen look in his photos, was two years older than his brother. After flipping through middle and high school books for the pair, she didn't uncover anything related to the present day. Paolo was popular and involved with everything, while Remo appeared in the chess club and AV Aide photos and with the Dungeons and Dragons crew. Switching her search to Lorenzo, she found him a year behind Paolo. If she didn't know better, they could have been twins instead of cousins. Copying the photos and putting them side by side, the resemblance was uncanny. Lorenzo spent his extracurricular time with the lacrosse team and the science club. *Interesting. Lorenzo and Paolo looked and acted more like brothers than Paolo and Remo.*

Closing the yearbook site, Jade opened her inventory application to track the store's online orders. On the dashboard page, the sales line was off the charts on the first graph. "Whoo hooo," she said to herself with a fist pump. She printed out eight pages and started her ornament search to fill the orders.

Chapter Thirty-Four

Glancing at her smartwatch and deciding that Bernie was probably out and about by now, Jade texted him a request to fix her door. She added a picture of the splintered mess and some tearful emojis for emphasis.

What in tarnation! Eating breakfast right now and hanging out with the guys. Be over later this morning to measure, Bernie replied.

Many thanks. I appreciate it. Plywood's up now, she tapped into her phone.

NP (That's no problem.) I'll have a new one for you today. See you in a bit.

You're the best. Jade added a Santa and some smiley emojis.

With one less thing to worry about, she grabbed her coat and purse and drove home to get Chloe and some breakfast.

After a quick walk on the beach for some fresh air and exercise for the sleepy dog, the pair climbed in the Jeep and headed for the store before Bernie arrived.

Jade unlocked the front door, and once inside, Chloe decided to go on a sniffing tour of the showrooms. The pudgy dog ran from room to room like she was tracking something. Not finding anything interesting, she settled in her bed as Jade grabbed a pad of paper.

Any word on Remo? She texted Nick. Her discovery of the high school pictures probably wasn't big enough news to share.

Not getting a reply, she opened her newsletter file and added a section on ornaments for New Year's and Valentine's Day. She needed to call Amy to see if she wanted to partner on any events or sales. It never hurt to cross-pollinate marketing campaigns, especially since their shoppers shared the same demographics, and there were lots of real and made-up holidays that they could turn into something fun. *I wonder if Amy plans to do something with her sea monsters and dragons idea? Those would be fun ornaments to add to her toy room.*

The bells on the front door tinkled, and she headed for the lobby, expecting Bernie. Shooing a curious Chloe back and shutting the door, Jade was surprised to see Goose Jennings this early in the morning. "Good morning," she said as he stepped inside, followed by a blast of arctic air.

"Hey, I thought I'd stop by before we head out back home. It's been fun. We're looking forward to hearing that we won that fireworks contest." Goose paused and scanned the room like he was looking for someone. "You'll probably see a lot of us this summer," he said with a wink. "Hey, did you ever call Tank? You guys should talk and hang out." He ran his hand through his shaggy hair. "He's a cool guy. You should call him."

Ignoring his question, Jade asked, "What can I do for you on this chilly morning?"

"Sorry to hear about the damage to your door and the problems this morning. Looks like you have it all under control," Goose said, glancing toward the office.

Jade paused and chewed on her bottom lip. Not quite sure how to respond, she went with a casual, "You must have been by earlier." She plastered on a pretend smile and waited to see what he would say next. How did he know about her back door?

"Uh, yeah. We're heading out later this morning, so we had to pack everything." He looked over his shoulder and then took a couple of strides toward the divider door. He poked his head into the back. A tiny growl came from the other side of the door.

"Oh, hey," he said, looking down at Chloe.

"That's my guard dog," Jade said.

A slight smile crossed his face, and Goose shoved his hands in his jean pockets and jingled his change. Before he could reply, the door opened with enough force to hit the jamb. Zeke strode into the store.

Goose froze, and Zeke stared daggers at him.

After a long, uncomfortable pause, Jade opened her mouth and closed it again. She slid behind the front counter, using it to shield her from the two men. Her heartbeat increased, and her glance volleyed from man to man. Jade shifted her weight and planted her feet, trying not to lock her knees. The long silence seemed to last an eternity. The air blowing through the heating ducts sounded like a wind tunnel in the quiet store.

Goose blinked and spoke first after a long, agonizing pause. "Uh, I came in to get our stuff. I saw on Facebook where she had it." He pointed a beefy finger at Jade. "I figured she might want to know what it was since she was so curious, and I wanted to say goodbye. Oh, and to see if she called Tank. He kinda has a crush on her after having drinks at that hotel." A half-smile crossed his face.

Zeke turned his head and zeroed in on Goose. In what looked like a weird dance, Zeke took a step forward, and Goose backed up closer to the door. "What are you now, a dating service? You know what, I'd like to hear you explain what that device was. That should be entertaining, especially since you seem to think you're a pyrotechnics expert," Zeke said.

"Huh, what?" Goose stammered. "I've been in the business as long as you have."

"You wouldn't know technology if it bit you on the…," Zeke snarled.

"Oh, and like you would," Goose interrupted. "I don't see anyone making you the boss. And you certainly aren't coming up with anything new that we can use. At least I found the igniter. Why are you here?" Goose asked, fiddling with the zipper pull on his jacket.

"What? You found it all right with your sticky fingers," Zeke boomed. "You've caused enough trouble. I'm here to clean up your mess as usual."

Goose stared at Zeke, and then he turned toward the door. "See ya around," he said, nodding at Jade. "I guess it's goodbye until we come back for the Fourth of July." He sneered at Zeke and covered the distance to the door in three steps, being careful not to turn his back on his cousin.

Zeke half-lunged at Goose, who scurried through the door.

When Zeke didn't say anything else, Jade filled in with, "May I help you?"

Chapter Thirty-Five

Jade had a tingly sensation in the pit of her stomach. Why were the Pefferlys here at her store again? And how did Goose know about the back door? "Was Goose okay? He seemed kind of jumpy," she said, trying to stall as she slipped her phone out of her pocket.

"He's fine. He's just being Goose. We're used to his weirdness by now." Zeke looked around like he was casing the joint.

Jade's phone dinged. Using a Facebook Messenger alert as an excuse, she clicked on Nick's contact like she was answering the alert. Her shoulders sunk when she heard his voicemail. She hoped Zeke didn't figure out what she was doing. Determined not to miss a chance, when it beeped, she said loudly, "Hey, Zeke. What can I do for you here at the Christmas store so early in the morning? Some last-minute shopping?"

She pushed her phone forward on the counter, hoping that Nick's voicemail would pick up the conversation.

He scowled at her. "Uh, no. We're heading out of town. I'm here for my stuff. You said you had our property. I'm here to fix Goose's stupidity." He shoved a hand in the pocket of his jeans.

"I gave that to the sheriff. I had no idea what it was. I almost threw it away. It kinda looked dangerous," Jade said, opening her eyes wide for effect.

"Only if you hook it up wrong. It's like a big grill lighter. But I kinda need it, so we can get on the road." Zeke's gaze darted around the room. Something caught his eye outside, and he stared out the front window.

When he turned toward her again, Jade said, "I'm sorry. After I messaged you, I gave it to the sheriff. You'll have to talk to him if you want it back."

"The gal at the front desk told Goose that they didn't have it. I'm tired of the runaround. I want my stuff," he said, raising his voice.

"I don't know what to tell you. She must have made a mistake. I could call the sheriff for you if you like." Jade reached for her phone.

Swearing under his breath, Zeke said, "No. Not necessary. I guess we'll have to make one more stop. Goose is the biggest screw-up." Zeke threw both hands up in the air in frustration.

"What happened?" Jade asked, trying to drag information out of him. She hoped her expression looked like she was concerned. Maybe he would keep talking.

"He was bragging about stealing something super-secret from the Zanettis. He also waved it around in a bar and ran his mouth. Paolo's stupid brother saw it, and he followed Goose. You know about the fight. It was guys being guys. But that Zanetti guy was stupid to take on three against one. We got the better of him and his igniter." Zeke's grin looked like an evil sneer. "You'd think they'd leave us alone after multiple encounters that didn't end well for them. They ought to know better by now."

"You all took the other company's equipment?" Jade opened her mouth and batted her lashes to add to the effect. *Of course, he did. I have to stall him as long as I can.*

Zeke's lip curled into a sinister grin. "It's a dog-eat-dog world. Everybody does it. Now, where's the device?"

"I'm sorry. It's not here. I told you the sheriff has it," Jade said a little louder, hoping Nick realized that there was an issue at the store.

Zeke took two strides toward the counter and stared down at Jade. "You're sure you don't want to make sure it's not here? It's kinda valuable. And I'm in a hurry."

Batting her lashes again, she shook her head. "I don't want to waste any more of your time. I told you the sheriff has it. Goose was mistaken. You said he was easily confused." He was close enough for her to feel his hot, stale breath.

After a long pause that caused bats to fly around in Jade's stomach, Zeke rocked back on his heels. "You're probably right. He hasn't gotten one thing right since we've been here. If he wasn't family, I would have canned him a long time ago." The tall man fidgeted and twisted the hem of his T-shirt. "None of the kids in my family are rocket scientists. Brianna's the smart one, and that's not saying much after she ran off with that idiot Paolo." Zeke spit out the name like it was spoiled crabmeat. "I'm the one who cares about this business. They need to go away, too."

"Like Lorenzo?" she asked, egging him on.

Zeke's head whipped around, and he stared daggers. "That was an accident. Paolo was the one mouthing off."

"So, was Lorenzo collateral damage? What happened?" she asked sweetly, still probing for information.

Zeke nodded. "Wrong place, wrong time. Another of Goose's goof-ups. He thought he had taken care of the Paolo/Brianna thing. He was bragging again about getting rid of the problem. And the sick joke was on him. The jerk can't do anything right. He doesn't understand what rough him up means. He's an idiot. He went too far, as usual."

The bells on the doors clanked against the jamb as Goose thrust it open and poked his head inside. "You coming?"

Jade's ringtone stopped all conversation. The voicemail must have disconnected. "Don't answer that," he said, pointing at her. Then to Goose, "I'll be there in a minute. Go wait in the truck," Zeke said, gritting his teeth. "Go back to the freakin' truck."

"I'm not five. Where do you get off ordering me around?" Goose asked. "I don't work for you. And I don't care what you think."

"Shut up. I know what you did. And if you don't check yourself, I'll go to the cops," Zeke said, striding toward his cousin. "I'll be out in a minute. And you better be out there when I'm done here."

"Oh, don't even try to hold that over my head. You were there when we planned it. Your hands are dirty, too. Tank'll back me up." Goose wagged a sausage-like finger at his cousin.

"Don't count on it," Zeke said with clenched teeth. "Tank knows where his bread is buttered. And he knows the truth."

"Then I'll go to the cops and tell them you did it. Don't push me," Goose's laser-focused stare zeroed in on his cousin.

"But I know where the knife is, and my fingerprints aren't on it. So, if you know what's good for you, you'll go wait in the truck." Zeke pointed at the door.

A chill slid down Jade's spine. Taking advantage of their argument, she picked up the hammer and slid it behind her back. She inched closer to Zeke.

"Go now! I'll deal with you later," Zeke yelled. "I said now!"

Goose scrunched his face into a grimace. "It's like when we were kids. You're not the boss of me," Goose snarled, slamming the front door.

Zeke stared at the door. He raised both hands above his head and balled them into fists.

Muttering to himself, he turned around to face Jade with a crazed look in his eyes. "I'm still waiting. Let's go get my property." A sound like a loud engine caused Zeke to spin around toward the door. He jerked it open and stared out at the parking lot. "If he knows what's good for him, he'll be in that truck. Wait. Where's the truck?"

A surge of electricity bounced around Jade's insides, landing in the pit of her stomach. She had to do something to stop Zeke and Goose before they could slip out of town without having to answer for Lorenzo's murder. Jade pushed thoughts of fear and danger out of her head and took a deep breath. She raised the hammer with two hands and heaved it with all her might at the back of Zeke's head.

She heard a crack and then a loud thunk when Zeke crumpled onto the floor, smacking his head against the pine boards.

Slightly surprised that her plan worked, she grabbed her phone and punched in 911. Before the dispatcher could ask any questions, Jade spewed, "This is Jade Hicks at 'Tis the Season on Neptune Road. I had another intruder in the store. I hit him with a hammer, and I need an ambulance. And the police."

"Jade, you hit him with a hammer?" the dispatcher asked.

"Yes. He was threatening me. I hit him, and then his head hit the hardwood floor when he fell."

"Is he still breathing?" the dispatcher asked. "Rescue and police are on their way. They should be there in minutes."

"I think he's breathing." Jade leaned closer for a better look. "His head is bleeding. Please tell them to hurry." Bile welled up in her chest, and she suddenly felt dizzy. Gripping the counter, she tried to steady herself.

The faint sound of sirens grew louder. "I think I hear them."

"They're almost at your store," the dispatcher said.

Jade disconnected as she heard stomping on the porch.

Sebastian strode in, and a slight grin crossed his lips when he got a glimpse of Zeke sprawled out on the floor. "You don't mess around, do you? Where's your baseball bat?"

Jade shook her head and waved her hand with the tool. "Hammer. And I felt threatened. He and Goose were yelling at each other, and he said Goose killed Lorenzo. I kept asking him questions, and he said he knew where the knife was. And he was all blasé about the murder. They were more interested in blaming each other. I had to do something," Jade said sheepishly. "The hammer was all I had handy."

Two EMTs stormed into the lobby and approached the prone body before Sebastian could respond.

"His cousin Goose was waiting in the truck in the parking lot. Is he outside?" Jade asked.

Sebastian shook his head. "Parking lot's empty except for our vehicles." He clicked his shoulder mic and updated the dispatcher. When he was done, he faced Jade. "While we're waiting. I want you to write down everything that happened since the last time I was here today."

"Yep. I know the drill. I'm sorry. I seem to be a magnet lately for trouble." Jade pulled out a legal pad from behind the counter and jotted down what she remembered.

She tore off the pages and stapled them as the EMTs transported Zeke out the front door on a gurney. Sebastian took photos of the floor and the hammer.

Nick strode in, and Sebastian said, "You missed all the fun. Your girlfriend wields a mean pink hammer. When I was at her house, she had a steak knife and a bat. You may want to give her a better weapon for Christmas."

Nick nodded and raised his chin. "She seems to be doing okay." After a pause, he continued, "Seaport stopped Goose speeding out of town in a white truck. They're transporting him to us."

"That makes the rest of my afternoon a little easier. I thought we would have to search for him," Sebastian said. "I'm almost done here."

Jade handed Sebastian her statement.

"You okay?" Nick asked, stopping beside her. "I got your weird voicemail minutes before your call came into dispatch."

"I'm fine. But I think I hit Zeke a little harder than I expected to. Then he smacked his head on the floor."

"He's going to be feeling it for a while," Sebastian said. "You did a number on him. Nick might want to deputize you."

"He said Goose stole the Zanetti's igniter thing, and he was showing it off in some bar, and Remo got wind of it." She paused to catch her breath. "And he said they were after Paolo because of the Brianna thing. Goose was supposed to rough him up, and things got out of hand. Zeke lamented that he was always cleaning up after Goose. But then his cousin hinted that Zeke was in on all of it." Jade took another deep breath.

"I've got to bag your hammer in case it's needed for the trial. Sorry." Sebastian labeled an evidence bag and dropped it inside. He snapped a few photos of the lobby and the blood spot. "That's about it. I've got what I need here. Jade, we'll call you if we have other questions."

She nodded and sank down on the stool behind the register. "It's already been a long day. But I'm relieved that this is finally over. Goose slipped when he mentioned the damage to my back door."

Nick nodded. "We'll be tied up for a while with Goose and Zeke. I'll call you when I can." Nick patted her shoulder and followed Sebastian out the front door.

The store was suddenly silent, and Jade was left with the broken back door and the puddle of blood in the store lobby, her only souvenirs of the Pefferlys' rage. The instrumental Christmas carols playing softly in the background and the twinkling lights made the morning seem surreal. Jade headed for the storage closet for some industrial cleaning supplies before anyone else arrived and noticed the blood on the floor of the lobby.

Chapter Thirty-Six

After scrubbing and disinfecting the floor, Jade returned all her cleaning supplies to the workroom. The bells rang as Jade walked to the front, wiping her hands on a paper towel. Jade let out a sigh of relief that the lobby was back to normal and ready for shoppers.

Patti trotted in with a plate of fudge. "Holy cow. What has been going on around here? I've been sitting in my car watching Nick and Sebastian. Was that one of the Pefferlys with the ambulance crew?" She set the plate down and peeled out of her coat. "Tell me everything, and then try my Peppermint Patti Fudge and Lorelei's Maple Fudge. She sent me her recipe. They both turned out well, if I do say so myself. But details on what's been going on here first. Holy moly, I missed all the action."

"The police have been here since o'dark thirty. Someone was on my porch. And then somebody tore up the back door and broke in. And if that wasn't enough, Zeke and Goose came back for that thing Chloe found, and they had an argument in the lobby. Oh, and did I mention that Remo was here too, skulking around for that same piece of equipment."

A puzzled look crossed Patti's face. "So, Zeke, Goose, and Remo were all looking for that gadget here? Who broke in?"

"I think it was Zeke. When they were arguing, the pair accused each other of all sorts of things." Jade paused and whispered, "Zeke said Goose killed Lorenzo."

Patti's eyebrows shot up under her blond bangs.

"So, was that what they were after?" Patti's eyes widened. "That thing Chloe found didn't look like anything important. Who knew?"

Jade nodded. "Goose stole it from the Zanettis, and somehow Remo found out. That's how he ended up in a fight with them when they dumped him on the porch."

"And then what?" Patti demanded.

"During that fight, Remo lost the igniter, and he came back looking for it. The Pefferlys showed up, too. Goose talked a lot. Their defense attorney will not be happy about all the chatter."

Patti let out a shrill whistle. "It is never dull around here. And you always seem to be smack dab in the middle of things. You got them to squeal on each other. Way to go. Ooooh, this is exciting. You figured out how to tie all this together."

The bells tinkled, and Bernie pushed the door open and stuck his head in. "Safe to come in?" he asked.

"Of course," Patti said. "Jade was telling me about all the excitement. She's at the part where she subdued the killer. Tell us, and don't leave out any details."

Jade felt a flush rush to her cheeks. "I was trying to stall him, so the police could get here. I hit him in the back of the head harder than I had planned. Nick and his guys have a lot to sort out."

"You go, girl. Stopping the bad guy. What did you use?" Patti asked, looking around the store.

"My hammer," Jade said softly. "I left it on the counter after Nick boarded up the door this morning."

Bernie grinned. "A girl after my own heart. Use what you got, I always say. I'm headed to the big box store to pick out a door. I think you should get a steel one this time for extra safety." Bernie popped a piece of fudge in his mouth. "Mmm. This is good. Time to take some measurements. I'll have your back door secured in no time."

"Thanks. A steel door is fine. Save me the receipt. I'll need it for the insurance claim." Jade let out a long puff of air that fluttered her bangs.

"Be back with a new door in a flash," Bernie said, grabbing a couple of pieces of fudge for the road.

Jade picked up her pink toolbox. "Looks like I'll need to get a new hammer, too, since Sebastian took mine as evidence. Who knows how long they'll keep it?"

Patti grinned. "A replacement sounds like a perfect idea for a Christmas gift," she said with a wink.

After finishing the store's January newsletter and scheduling cool ornament posts for her Instagram site, Jade sunk back into her office chair. Her energy level drained, and she pondered closing early and heading home.

Interrupted by her phone, Jade glanced at Nick's text: **Wanna grab dinner tonight?**

Whatcha feel like?

Red Herring at 6? I'm in the mood for clam chowder. Pick you up at home, he replied.

Perfect. See you then.

"Hey, oh, sorry. Didn't mean to make you jump. I've packed up everything. Here's the bank bag and all the receipts. Need anything else?" Patti chirped as she waltzed closer to Jade's desk.

"Big plans tonight?" Jade asked.

"Nope, working on some research for some projects next year. And counting down the days until Christmas."

"Thanks for bringing in the fudge and all the cookies. You outdid yourself. My favorite was the fudge with the cayenne pepper in it. I liked the kick."

Patti smiled, slipping into her red coat. "That's my Ooh-La-La fudge. It's always a hit, and it pairs well on charcuterie boards with wine or cider. I'll send you the recipes for your newsletter. You have plans?"

"Dinner with Nick."

Patti beamed. "Another handsome couple, which means two available singles off the Mermaid Bay market. I hope you have a great Christmas." She flipped her purse strap over her shoulder and strolled out.

Jade's head turned slightly. The doorbells chimed behind Patti, and she reached for her phone. *That comment sounded familiar. Where have I heard that recently?*

She searched *Mermaid Whispers* and let out a gasp. Her pink toolbox and a teaser for tomorrow's article on how a local shopkeeper thwarted a burglary took up most of the site's real estate with the subheadline, "You'll never believe what she used as a weapon!"

Jade's pulse quickened. "Chloe, can you believe it? It's been under our noses this whole time," Jade said as the dog opened one eye. "I think I've solved another mystery, but we still need to figure out the why."

Jade had enough time to walk, feed Chloe, and find an outfit for dinner. Settling on her oversized gray cardigan, she paired it with a sauvignon-colored camisole and a pair of black leggings. Her tall, black boots finished off the outfit.

Her doorbell rang as she was creating a blush storm in the bathroom. After putting on the finishing touches to her makeup, she nudged Chloe away from the front door.

Nick stepped inside, followed by a blast of icy air. He scooped up the bouncing Chloe and kissed Jade. "Hey, you look nice. Hungry?"

"Yep. You put the idea of soup in my head."

"It's a good night for comfort food. The wind blowing off the bay feels like snow's coming."

Jade raised her eyebrows and grabbed her coat. "Behave, Chloe. We'll be back in a bit."

Following Nick to his truck, it took her longer to climb in and fasten the seatbelt than it did for him to drive down the street to the seafood restaurant.

After they settled in a booth in the corner, a waiter with black gauges in both ears dropped menus on the table. "Hi, I'm Kyle. What can I get to start you off tonight?"

"I'll have an unsweetened iced tea," Jade said.

"Coffee's fine," Nick said. "Just regular high test. Nothing fancy."

Kyle smiled. "Any appetizers?"

Nick looked at Jade, and she shook her head. "I know what I want," she said. "I'll have a bowl of your potato soup and a Caesar salad."

"And for you?" Kyle asked.

"I'll have a bowl of your New England clam chowder and a cheddar and mushroom burger with everything. Medium well, please."

"Good choices." Kyle picked up the menus and ambled toward the kitchen.

"So, how was the rest of your day?" she asked, glancing around at the almost empty restaurant. "Especially after it started at oh-dark-thirty at my place."

"I could ask you the same thing. We were busy. It's the holidays, so I'm afraid to ask if yours was quiet after the morning you had."

"Much more normal after you all left, but we did have a lot of questions. On another note, I think I solved the Mermaid Whispers' mystery," she said in a low tone.

Nick raised an eyebrow as Kyle returned with their drinks and a basket of the restaurant's famous cheddar biscuits and hush puppies.

When the waiter left, she continued, "Look at this." She opened the latest post on *Mermaid Whispers*.

"I've seen that toolbox recently. Very recently." Nick steadied her hand, so he could read the teaser about tomorrow's big reveal. "Interesting."

"Sebastian took the hammer. The box was back in the workroom. Besides you and Sebastian, Patti, Lorelei, and Bernie are probably the only people who know that I even have a toolbox. Bernie teases me about it every time he sees it. Look at the background. That's from my back office. That was shot today, and guess who my part-timer was?"

"Lorelei?" Nick's eyes widened.

"Nope, the perky one."

"So, Peppermint Patti has a secret life?" Nick asked, reaching for a hushpuppy.

"Patti said something odd today that I'd heard before. Well, read before. Then I remembered something similar was on that blog. So, I popped over there, and that's when I saw this. And she denied it when I asked her about being the blogger before."

Nick laughed. "It makes sense. She's always in the thick of everything, and everyone talks to her. Good job."

"What about you? Did you ever get Zeke or Goose to admit to Lorenzo's murder in your interviews?" Jade broke open a cheddar biscuit to release the steam.

"Our friends in Seaport stopped Goose for driving erratically. The officer said he rambled and couldn't tell him what was wrong. We have Goose and Zeke in custody. They won't be out anytime soon. There's a long list of charges, and the Commonwealth's Attorney is thinking up a few more. Both of them clammed up and then lawyered up. We'll see which one talks first. And we'll tack on charges for the destruction of your store."

"Neither of them had any problems talking to me this morning," she said, taking a sip of her drink. After a pause, she continued, "You concerned? Will their not talking hurt your case against them?"

Nick shook his head. "We have a plethora of witnesses. After a night or two in jail, one of them will cave. The one who talks first gets the better deal. And both of these clowns will need any help they can get. We'll let them sit overnight and see who wants to talk to us tomorrow. The Commonwealth's Attorney will probably want to talk to you even though he has your statement."

"For the longest time, I couldn't figure out why Lorenzo was murdered. Nothing made sense," she said.

"Except for mistaken identity. Sometimes, something simple turns out to be the reason for the whole thing," Nick said.

"I found yearbook photos of Lorenzo and Paolo, and the resemblance was uncanny. It was probably easy to get the two mixed up."

"Lorenzo was in the wrong place at the wrong time. Goose mistook him for his cousin. Zeke and the family didn't like the Paolo/Brianna thing, and they got the bright idea to take matters into their own hands. Goose kept bragging that he fixed things. The igniter thing was a whole 'nother story, unrelated to Paolo messing around with Brianna," Nick said.

"The firework device belonged to the Zanettis, and the Pefferlys stole it," Jade repeated what Zeke had said at her store as Nick reached for the hushpuppy basket again.

"It's a prototype that Elio was working on for their show. He was testing it with some other equipment at the time it disappeared. If it worked the way he planned, it could have been valuable," Nick said.

Jade's head bobbed slightly. "When I showed it to Bernie, the Crash Boom Bang guy was there. He took a picture of it. He knew right away what it was for."

Before Nick could comment, Kyle dropped off their dinners. "Careful, all the plates and bowls are hot. Can I get you anything else?"

Jade shook her head.

"Then I'll be back to check on you kids later," Kyle said.

Nick stirred his steaming bowl of soup as Jade tucked into her salad.

After a few bites, she said, "What I don't get is who was doing the shooting at my store? It seemed like a dumb thing for Zeke or Goose to do. Why risk it? It was too coincidental to be some random drive-by shooting that early in the morning. It didn't make sense," she said.

"We did get that out of Goose on the ride to the station before he stopped talking to us. There's some bad blood between the cousins. Both think they should lead the company, but the uncles have other plans. Anyway, they are always sniping at each other and trying to top whatever the other was doing. Zeke ratted Goose out for killing Lorenzo and being a failure at just about everything. They fought all the time. On the day that Remo was on your porch, it seems they had another fight after they left here. Things got out of hand, and Goose claimed Zeke shot at him. And, of course, Zeke denies it."

"So, they weren't shooting at you or Sebastian or me?"

Nick shook his head and took a bit of his chowder. After he swallowed, he said, "The cousins were going at it. Goose said Zeke said he had enough of Goose's mouth. And words turned into gunshots. I think the adrenaline and the testosterone flooding through both of them caused pushing and shoving and then into the altercation with Remo. They started sniping at each other, and that situation escalated, too."

Nick picked up his hamburger, and after savoring a couple of bites of the juicy monstrosity, he said, "They each have a string of charges against them. I'm sure one or both of them will have a change of heart about talking to us. Plus, if they think the other is talking, they'll try to make the best deal they can for themselves. They can stew in the tank for a while. Maybe it'll offer them a new perspective." Nick paused to wipe mustard off his chin.

"So, testosterone, competition, and corporate espionage were at the bottom of all this?"

"Yup, and throw in some recklessness and stupidity, and it's a powder keg waiting for a match," Nick said.

"Or an igniter," she added. "Sorry. It seemed to fit. And your burger looks better than my salad."

"Wanna bite?"

"Yum. Thanks," she said, leaning over for a taste. "You can have some of my salad." Jade pointed at her plate.

"Nope. Tonight's chowder and red meat night. No rabbit food." Nick winked at her. "It's been insanely crazy, but we're finally wrapping up this case. You detained Zeke and solved the secret of the Mermaid Whispers. Not too bad for the week before the holidays. Now we can roll into Christmas and New Year's with a little less stress."

"And Vivian and the council can breathe easier that Crash Boom Bang was the clear winner, so no headaches with the competition either. I'm looking forward to the holiday season and a quiet winter," she said.

"You think the debut of that Love Channel show will make for a calm winter?" Nick winked and reached for another hushpuppy.

Chapter Thirty-Seven

"Whew, now that it's finally calmed down, we can talk about your adventures with Zeke and Goose and how you thwarted both of them. I can't believe that those two families caused all that trouble," Patti said as she leaned on the store's front counter. "So, did you ever find out why poor Lorenzo was murdered? All the other stuff seemed like such distractions."

"It may have been as simple as a case of mistaken identity. Zeke and Goose weren't the brightest bulbs on the tree. They got the idea to go after Paolo for seeing Brianna, and it turned deadly. The rest of the stuff was random reactions to things. I don't think they had a plot or a grand plan."

"Amateurs. I knew you'd get to the bottom of all this. I'm glad Nick's guys have both of them in custody after they terrorized the town for so long. And they did so much damage here." She plopped on the stool and let out a long breath. "And I'm soooo glad that neither of them won the fireworks contest. That would have opened a whole 'nother can of worms and sent Vivian into an apoplectic fit."

Jade pulled out her phone and tapped out what sounded like a long staccato beat. "There. Maybe you can use these."

A puzzled look crossed Patti's face as she pulled out her phone from her sweater pocket. Her squeezed her lips together as she scrolled through the pictures Jade sent. Patti fell silent for a rare moment or two. Looking up at Jade, she turned her head like Chloe and stared.

Jade hoped she didn't burst into tears. The normal jovial Patti had a strange look on her face. "I thought maybe you could use them on your blog."

Patti's mouth formed a small "o." "How did you find out? I should have known you'd figure it out."

Jade watched her for a few heartbeats, and then Patti burst out in a fit of giggles. "It was something I did on a lark to see if anyone would notice. And then they did, and I saw all the reactions, so I kept it going, especially when it got under Nell's skin. I was curious to see how long I could keep it going. I never had any idea that it would be the talk of the town. Are you going to out me?"

Jade shook her head.

"I was looking for something new. I heard about Brianna's influencing and Lorelei's social media class. I signed up for the class next semester. I started with the blog, and now, I'm building my own social media. I'd like to try my hand at it. With *My Coastal Valentine* premiering soon, I thought the timing was right. There's so much going on in this town, I'd have content for years."

"What are you planning to do with the Mermaid?" Jade asked.

"Who knows? I may keep her active and pop up every now and then to stir things up. Sometimes, this town gets a little too sleepy for its own good. I gotta keep folks on their toes." Patti's eyes sparkled, and a mischievous grin crossed her lips.

Peppermint Patti Fudge

Ingredients:

- 12 ounces of dark chocolate (chopped)
- 1 can of condensed milk
- 2 tablespoons of unsalted butter
- 2 tablespoons of powdered espresso
- A bit of salt
- ½ cup crushed peppermints or candy canes

Directions:

1. Over low heat, put chocolate, condensed milk, butter, and salt in a medium pan. Stir mixture until melted. Add the espresso powder and stir.
2. Pour the mixture into a 9-inch square tray or pan. Smooth it out with a knife or spatula. Sprinkle the crushed peppermint on top.
3. Cool the fudge in the refrigerator until it is hardened/set. Cut into small pieces. It's now ready to eat or freeze for later.

Lorelei's Award-winning Maple Fudge

Ingredients:

- 1 cup unsalted butter (It works best if it's cubed.)
- 2 cups of packed brown sugar
- 1-5 ounce can of evaporated milk
- Pinch of salt
- 1 tablespoon maple extract
- 1 teaspoon vanilla extract
- 2 cups powdered sugar
- 1 ½ cups chopped walnuts
- ¾ cup toffee bits
- Buttery non-stick spray

Directions:

1. Line an 8-inch square pan with parchment paper or foil. Spray it with butter spray to keep it from sticking. In a large pot, combine the butter, brown sugar, and evaporated milk. Bring to a boil over medium-high heat. Cook for about eight minutes. Make sure you stir the mixture constantly.
2. Remove from heat and add the maple and vanilla extract, salt, and sugar. Transfer the candy to a large mixing bowl and beat for 3 minutes until the mixture is smooth.
3. Add 1 cup of the walnuts and the toffee bits.
4. Spread the mixture into the square pan. Sprinkle the top with the remaining walnuts. Make sure you cool the fudge before eating or

freezing.

Patti's Ooo-La-La Spicy Fudge

Ingredients:

- 3 cups milk chocolate chips
- 14 ounces of condensed milk
- 1 teaspoon vanilla extract
- 1 teaspoon of cinnamon
- 1 teaspoon of cayenne pepper

Directions:

1. Line an 8-inch square pan with parchment paper or foil. Heat the chocolate and condensed milk over medium-low heat until all the chocolate is melted. Make sure that you stir it constantly.
2. Add the vanilla, cinnamon, and cayenne pepper. Ensure that all ingredients are mixed thoroughly. Pour the fudgy mix in the square pan. Cool for 3-4 hours in the refrigerator. It's ready to cut and enjoy or freeze for later.

Patti's Peppermint Snowball Cookies

Ingredients:

- 1 cup of unsalted, softened butter
- 1 teaspoon vanilla extract
- ¼ teaspoon peppermint extract
- ½ teaspoon salt
- 1 cup of powdered sugar
- 1 ¾ cups of flour
- ½ cup crushed peppermint candies or candy canes
- ½ cup white chocolate chips
- ½ cup of additional powdered sugar for the topping
- Parchment paper

Directions:

1. In a large mixing bowl, beat the butter on medium until it's creamy. Add the vanilla, peppermint extract, and salt. Mix in the cup of powdered sugar on low. Gradually add the flour. Mixed in the crushed peppermint candy and the white chocolate chips. Chill the dough mixture in the refrigerator for 20 minutes.
2. Preheat the oven to 350 degrees F. Line two baking sheets with parchment paper.
3. Roll the chilled dough into small balls about an inch wide. Place about two inches apart on the baking sheets. Chill on the baking sheets for 30 minutes.
4. Bake the cookies for 14 minutes until lightly golden. (You may want to

rotate the pans at the halfway point.)

5. Cool the cookies for 10 minutes on the baking sheet and then transfer to wire baking racks.
6. Once the cookies are completely cooled, dust with the remaining powdered sugar.

Jade's Hot Chocolate Cookies

Ingredients:

- ½ cup unsalted butter
- 2 cups semi-sweet chocolate chips
- ¼ cup unsweetened cocoa powder
- 1 ½ cups of all-purpose flour
- 1 ½ teaspoon baking powder
- 1 pinch of salt
- 1 ¼ cups brown sugar
- 3 large eggs
- 2 teaspoons of vanilla
- 12 large marshmallows (cut into quarters)
- Festive sprinkles or crushed peppermint candy (optional)

Directions:

1. In a saucepan, melt the butter and 1 ½ cups of the chocolate chips over medium heat. Once the chocolate is fully melted, set aside.
2. In a medium bowl, mix all of the dry ingredients. Then add the eggs, brown sugar, and vanilla and mix with a hand mixer for about three minutes. Combine this with the melted chocolate. Add flour and mix well.
3. Chill the dough in the refrigerator for about an hour. Preheat the oven to 350 degrees F. Add parchment paper to your baking sheets.
4. Roll the dough into small balls (about an inch and a half in diameter). Press each ball firmly to create a small indent for the marshmallow.

Place the marshmallow on each cookie and gently press down. Bake the cookies for 8-10 minutes. The cookie will be firm, and the middles will be gooey.

5. Cool for 10 minutes. Then, drizzle the remaining chocolate on the top. You can add sprinkles or crushed peppermint candy for decoration.

Sophia's Busy Bean Vanilla Holiday Cookies

Ingredients:

- 2 ½ cups of all-purpose flour
- ½ teaspoon baking soda
- 1 teaspoon baking powder
- 1 teaspoon salt
- 1 ½ cups of sugar
- 2 ounces of cream cheese (cut into cubes and softened)
- 6 tablespoons of melted, unsalted butter
- 1/3 cup canola oil
- 1 large egg
- 2 tablespoons milk
- 2 teaspoons of vanilla bean paste (If you don't have vanilla bean paste, you can substitute 2 teaspoons of vanilla extract.)
- Parchment paper

Decorations:

- Nonpareil sprinkles
- Crystal decorating sugar
- (Note: you can use one or both of the suggested coatings for the cookies.)

Directions:

1. Preheat the oven to 350 degrees F. Line two baking sheets with parchment paper.
2. In a medium bowl, mix flour, baking powder, baking soda, and salt. Set aside.
3. In another large bowl, mix the melted butter, cream cheese, and sugar. Ensure that the mixture is smooth. Then, whisk in the oil. Add the egg, milk, and vanilla bean. Mix until smooth. Add the dry ingredients. Mix completely.
4. The dough mixture should be soft enough to pinch together with your fingers, so that it sticks. If it is too soft, roll it into a ball and chill in the refrigerator for about 15-20 minutes.
5. Pour the sprinkles and crystal sugar into bowls.
6. Using a medium cookie scoop roll the dough into about 1 ½ inch balls. Roll each ball in the sprinkles and/or sugar to coat completely.
7. Place the coated cookie balls on the baking sheets about 2 inches apart.
8. Bake for 12 minutes or until the cookies have a crackled texture. Cool on the baking sheet and then transfer to a wire rack to cool completely.

Sophia's Chai Cheesecake Bars

Ingredients:

- 1 ½ cups of Graham cracker crumbs
- 6 tablespoons of unsalted butter (It's better if it's melted.)
- ¼ teaspoon of kosher salt
- 1 cup of granulated sugar
- 2-8 ounce packages of softened cream cheese
- 2 teaspoons of vanilla extract
- 2 eggs
- 5 teaspoons of chai tea latte powdered mix

Directions:

1. Preheat the oven to 350 degrees F. Mix the graham cracker crumbs, butter, salt, and ½ cup of sugar in a bowl. Lightly grease a 9-inch baking dish. Press the crumb mixture into the greased dish. Bake for 9 minutes. Cool on a wire rack for about 30 minutes.
2. In a bowl, beat the cream cheese, vanilla, and the remaining sugar with an electric mixer on medium. Make sure the mixture is smooth. Add the eggs and beat until they are blended. Save ½ cup of the batter. Pour the rest over the cooled bars.
3. In the ½ cup of batter, stir the chai tea mix. Dollop this on top of the topping. Use a knife to create a swirl design. Be careful not to push the icing into the bars.
4. Bake the iced bars at 350 degrees F for about 20 minutes. Cool completely before serving.

Jade's Crockpot Christmas Candy

Ingredients:

- 2 pounds of white candy coating (white almond bark) (Break into small squares.)
- 1-12 ounce bag of chocolate chips
- 1-4 ounce bar of sweet chocolate (Break into smaller squares.)
- 32 ounces of dry roasted or cocktail peanuts (unshelled)
- Holiday sprinkles for decoration
- Non-stick cooking spray
- Wax Paper

Directions:

1. Spray your crockpot/slow cooker with non-stick spray. Add the white candy coating/almond bark, chocolate chips, and sweet chocolate. Use a clean, dry dish or kitchen towel to prevent condensation from getting into your candy. Put it over the crockpot and then add the lid.
2. Cook mixture on high for one hour. Reduce the heat and cook on low for one hour or until the candy is fully melted. Stir it every 20 minutes. Remove the lid and towel. Don't let the condensation get into the candy mix. Stir in the peanuts. Make sure that all the peanuts are covered.
3. Line several baking sheets with wax paper. Drop the candy mixture by the spoonful onto the wax paper. Add sprinkles to the candy before it hardens.
4. Refrigerate for 30 minutes until the candy is set (firm).

Lorelei's Chocolatey Toffee Bark

Ingredients:

- 1 cup butter (diced or cut into small pieces)
- 1 cup sugar
- 1¼ teaspoons of sea salt (or kosher salt)
- 8 ounces mini dark chocolate chips

Directions:

1. In a medium saucepan, heat the butter and sugar on medium heat. Stir in big swirl motions. Add ¼ teaspoon of sea salt. Whisk the mixture. It should start to look like the consistency of vanilla pudding. Continue to whisk the mixture for about 12 minutes until it is golden brown. Don't burn the mixture. Be careful, the candy is hot.
2. Spread the candy on a foil-lined baking sheet. The candy should be about a quarter-inch thick.
3. Sprinkle the chocolate chips on top and allow them to melt. Spread the melted chocolate until all the toffee is covered. Use the remaining teaspoon of sea salt to sprinkle on the top.
4. Refrigerate for about 10 minutes. Remove and set out to cool and harden for about an hour. Crack the candy into smaller pieces.

Patti's Peppermint Marshmallows

Ingredients:

- 2 teaspoons butter
- 3 envelopes of unflavored gelatin
- 1 cup cold water
- 2 cups sugar
- 1 cup light corn syrup
- ¼ teaspoon salt
- ¾ teaspoon peppermint extract
- Food coloring
- ¼ cup confectioner's sugar
- ¼ cup finely ground peppermint candies
- Candy Thermometer

Directions:

1. Line a 13 x 9-inch pan with foil. Grease the foil with butter.
2. In a large bowl, sprinkle ½ cup water over the gelatin. Set aside.
3. In a large saucepan, mix the sugar, peppermint extract, corn syrup, salt, and remaining water. Bring the mixture to a boil. Make sure you stir it occasionally. Then, cook the mixture until your candy thermometer reads 240 degrees F.
4. Remove the candy mixture from the heat and add it to the gelatin. Beat on high speed for about 15 minutes until the mixture is thick. Spread on the greased foil.
5. Drop food coloring into the candy and swirl it with a knife. Cover the

candy and let it stand for at least six hours to harden.

6. Combine the confectioner's sugar and ground peppermint candies. Lift the marshmallow out of the pan (by the foil). Use a knife or a pizza cutter (coated with cooking spray) to cut the candy into 1-inch squares. Cover the tops with the confectioner's sugar and peppermint candy.

Acknowledgements

I want to thank my family and friends who support me and this crazy writing life: Stan Weidner, thanks for being on this writing journey with me, my parents who instilled in me a lifelong love of reading, Cortney Cain for being my early morning texting buddy and sounding board, Meagan Van Laeken and Jocelyn Cain, my social media subject matter experts, and Bill Cain for always keeping everyone entertained. And I appreciate all the encouragement from my Bethia UMC family.

A huge thank you to Shawn Reilly Simmons and everyone at Level Best Books for letting me share all the fun and craziness that goes on in Mermaid Bay.

I treasure my talented Sisters in Crime, Guppy, Writers Who Kill, and James River Writer friends. Leah Price, Mary Burton, Cynthia Price, K. L. Murphy, your support is invaluable!

To all the readers, podcasters, bloggers, and reviewers. Thank you for making all of this possible and letting me share Jade, Nick, Patti, Bernie, Lorelei, Chloe, and Neville the Devil Cat with you all.

And tearfully, thanks to Dawn Dowdle for all her help, encouragement, and hard work. I miss you.

About the Author

Through the years, Heather Weidner has been a cop's kid, technical writer, editor, college professor, software tester, and IT manager. She writes the Jules Keene Glamping Mysteries, the Mermaid Bay Christmas Shoppe Mysteries, the Delanie Fitzgerald Mysteries, and the Pearly Girls Mysteries.

Her short stories appear in the *Virginia is for Mysteries* series, *50 Shades of Cabernet, Deadly Southern Charm, Murder by the Glass, First Comes Love Then Comes Murder,* and *Crime in the Commonwealth,* and she has nonfiction pieces in *Promophobia* and *The Secret Ingredient: A Mystery Writers' Cookbook.*

She is a member of Sisters in Crime: National, Central Virginia, Chessie, Guppies, and Grand Canyon Writers, International Thriller Writers, and James River Writers, and she blogs regularly with the Writers Who Kill.

Originally from Virginia Beach, Heather has been a mystery fan since Scooby-Doo and Nancy Drew. She lives in Central Virginia with her husband and a pair of Jack Russell terriers.

AUTHOR WEBSITE:
  http://HeatherWeidner.com

SOCIAL MEDIA HANDLES:
  Website and Blog: http://www.heatherweidner.com

BlueSky: https://bsky.app/profile/heatherweidner.bsky.social

Twitter/X: https://twitter.com/HeatherWeidner1

Facebook: https://www.facebook.com/HeatherWeidnerAuthor

Instagram: https://www.instagram.com/heather_mystery_writer/

Goodreads: https://www.goodreads.com/author/show/8121854.Heather_Weidner

Amazon Authors: http://www.amazon.com/-/e/B00HOYR0MQ

Pinterest: https://www.pinterest.com/HeatherBWeidner/

LinkedIn: https://www.linkedin.com/in/heather-weidner-0064b233?trk=hp-identity-name

BookBub: https://www.bookbub.com/authors/heather-weidner-d6430278-c5c9-4b10-b911-340828fc7003

Threads: https://www.threads.net/@heather_mystery_writer

TikTok: https://www.tiktok.com/@heather_weidner_author

YouTube: https://www.youtube.com/channel/UCyBjyB0zz-M1DaM-rU1bXGA?view_as=subscriber

LinkTree: https://linktr.ee/heatherweidner

Also by Heather Weidner

The Jules Keene Glamping Mysteries:
Vintage Trailers and Blackmailers
Film Crews and Rendezvous
Christmas Lights and Cat Fights
Deadlines and Valentines

The Mermaid Bay Christmas Shoppe Mysteries:
Sticks and Stones and a Bag of Bones
Twinkle Twinkle Au Revoir

The Delanie Fitzgerald Mysteries:
Secret Lives and Private Eyes
The Tulip Shirt Murders
Glitter, Glam, and Contraband
Male Revues and Subterfuge

Nonfiction:
Promophobia
The Secret Ingredient

Short Stories:
The *Virginia is for Mysteries* series
50 Shades of Cabernet
Murder by the Glass
Deadly Southern Charm